Beside Your *Heart*

Mary Whitney

OMNIFIC PUBLISHING

DALLAS

Omnific Publishing
10000 North Central Expressway, Dallas, TX 75231
www.omnificpublishing.com

First Omnific eBook edition, June 2013
First Omnific trade paperback edition, June 2013

The characters and events in this book are fictitious.
Any similarity to real persons, living or dead,
is coincidental and not intended by the author.

Library of Congress Cataloguing-in-Publication Data

Whitney, Mary.
  Beside Your Heart / Mary Whitney – 1st ed.
  ISBN: 978-1-623420-41-3
  1. New Adult — Romance. 2. Coming of Age — Fiction.
  3. Family Tragedy — Fiction. 4. First Love — Romance. I. Title

10 9 8 7 6 5 4 3 2 1

Cover Design by Micha Stone and Amy Brokaw
Interior Book Design by Coreen Montagna

Printed in the United States of America

"In the midst of life we are in death; from whom can we seek help?"
The Book of Common Prayer

Prologue

Chicago, Illinois
June 1998

Used recklessly, the Internet could be a cruel invention. I rarely searched Adam's name, but sometimes I couldn't stop myself, and I always regretted it.

It was late one night at the campaign headquarters, and I was one of the few people still there. I needed to create the canvas lists for the following day, so I stared at the computer screen full of names and addresses of potential voters. Clicking on the mouse, I repeated the same actions—cut, paste, cut, paste. I was moving so quickly, I almost didn't notice his name, but there it was—Adam Kincaid.

With seven million registered voters in Illinois, it was bound to happen. There were a lot of Adams in the world and a good many Kincaids as well. Coming across those names separately or attached to another name had no effect on me, but this person was an Adam Kincaid. I stopped and gazed at the screen.

Adam Kincaid in Peoria, Illinois, wasn't my Adam, but seeing his name made me uneasy. My high school friends Rachel and Lisa were backpacking through Europe that summer. I knew they were going to see him. I wondered what they might find.

Making sure no one could see my computer screen, I looked around the room furtively. The few people there were all busy at work or shooting the shit. No one was paying attention to me. With a few strokes on my keyboard and one click, I searched for signs of my Adam Kincaid. I blinked twice at the first few links that popped up for him.

Hello! Magazine?

That's weird. Taking an anxious breath, I scrolled over the link and clicked. The page took forever to load, and when it finally appeared, my heart sank. There was a photo of Adam looking fine as ever but a little worse for the wear as he held hands with a tall, gorgeous redhead. The caption read:

Lady Muff Selbourne and her long-time boyfriend, the Honourable Adam Kincaid, son of Viscount Kincaid, leaving Martin's nightclub with a group of friends.

I cocked my head at the screen. *Muff? He's dating a girl named Muff? And she's a "Lady"? What does that mean? Like Lady Diana?*

I exhaled in disgust with myself, but there was no stopping me at that point. I needed more information. Going back to my search results, I moved on to the next link. This time, the page loaded while I tried not to be insanely jealous of Adam's girlfriend. I reminded myself I had a boyfriend.

If the first photo had wounded me, the next one was a mortal blow. Adam and Muff stood in a large group of friends, obviously at a wedding. The caption read:

Guests at the Mann-Lexington wedding party. From left: The Honourable Adam Kincaid, son of Viscount Kincaid, Lady Mary Selbourne, Lady Penelope Welch, Lord Garrett Welch…

I stopped reading and gaped at the photo. I'd never seen Adam dressed so well. He wore a dark gray morning coat with tails, a vest, tie, and striped trousers. While it would be a little over the top for an American wedding, he still looked achingly handsome. Next to him, Mary or Muff or Twat — whatever her name was — wore a pale pink coat dress with darker pink pumps, making her as tall as Adam. Her hair was pinned up, and she wore a strange vertical hat of feathers and straw that matched her shoes.

What in hell? Is that a hat? The other women were also wearing ridiculous things on their heads. *Must be a British thing.* I grimaced because, despite the goofy hat, she was still beautiful.

Sinking back in my chair, I looked down at my tattered Keds, wrinkled shorts, and old T-shirt. I glanced again at Muff, and then my eyes moved to Adam. At that moment, it seemed impossible that at one point in my life I'd known him so well. He couldn't be the same person.

I looked around the cramped, messy campaign office. Red, white, and blue *Logan for Governor* signs and stickers were strewn everywhere. It seemed more than a world apart from the ancient stone church in the background of Adam's photo.

I shook my head and closed the screen. *Why did I even look? Nothing has changed.*

Two months later, Lisa called to fill me in on the European vacation. She gave me a rundown of the trip, country by country, guy by guy, that she and Rachel had encountered over eight weeks. While I'd been having my own fun working on the campaign, I was a little jealous of their adventures. Rachel seemed to have slept her way through Europe with a new guy in every city, and Lisa had some great stories as well. Yet even as I laughed at my dear friends and their wacky stories, I kept wondering what had happened when they'd met Adam.

As the conversation wound down, Lisa finally brought it up. "So, let me tell you about seeing Adam and David."

My heart jumped, but I kept cool. "How was that?"

"No big surprise. Rachel and David hooked up."

"That's been years in the making." I giggled, thinking of how Rachel had drooled over Adam's cousin when we'd met him in high school.

"We almost missed our train because she spent the night at his place." Lisa snickered. "She was sore for a couple days."

"Poor thing. She was out of commission."

"But not for long."

"What's David up to?"

"Believe it or not, he's an investment banker. He said he's always been a gambler, so it's a good job for him."

"That's hilarious."

Lisa laughed, too, but soon she stopped. "And Adam's doing well also."

"What's he up to these days?" I tried to keep an even tone. Grasping for something to make the conversation casual, I remembered a postcard I'd received from Adam's sister. "Sylvia had mentioned she went to his graduation."

"He's started working at the BBC as an apprentice or something."

"Good for him. It sounds like he's on the right track for what he wanted to do."

"He asked after you, of course—a lot of questions, in fact. He was really interested in your political work. He wanted to know all about it. I think he was disappointed I didn't know more."

The ache I always fought away started to sneak into my heart. It made sense he'd find my work interesting. It was right up his alley. If I'd been there, we would have had a great conversation. I worked with the media all the time now, so I'd be equally interested in what he was doing.

I winced back the sadness and said, "It's fine. You're going to med school. You're into science, not politics."

"I said as much." She took a deep breath. "He specifically asked me to tell you how sorry he was about your grandmother. He said he knew how much you loved her."

I rolled my eyes. *Just kill me now*. I rubbed my forehead, hoping the call would end soon. "Um. Yeah."

"Nicki…why haven't you ever called him or even just sent him an email?"

"It's not like we had cell phones or email five years ago."

"But we do now. He asked me to tell you that he really misses you. The way he said it, I know he meant it. And think about it… he told *me*. He knows I had my issues with him. I think he'd like to hear from you."

Feeling like my heart was being ripped out, I closed my eyes. *This is too much*. I was about to cry when my mind snapped back to reality. Though I knew the answer, I wanted to hear what Adam had told Lisa. "So does he have a girlfriend?"

"Yeah, but…I mean…you have a boyfriend. What's the big deal?"

"Did you meet her?"

"I did."

"Is she pretty?"

"Well, yeah. You think Adam would be with someone ugly?"

"No, he never would."

"She's prissy, though. I didn't like her."

"Whatever. I don't want to know any more."

"Listen. When Adam wasn't around, David joked that he would drop her tomorrow if you walked in the room." Lisa's voice became motherly. "Nicki, shouldn't you reach out to him?"

"For what purpose? We live on opposite ends of the earth, and we're both seeing other people."

"Jeez, you're always dating guys, but it's never serious."

"Jeff was serious."

"No way. Jeff didn't even last a year. He was a rebound, and you know it."

"Regardless, I've moved on. Adam's obviously moved on. Why should I mess things up by contacting him?"

"Because you want to, damn it." Lisa groaned. "Don't you still care for him?"

"Of course." Thank God the conversation wasn't happening in person. I could be stronger on the phone. "But that doesn't change things."

Around midnight, I lay in bed replaying my conversation with Lisa. I hadn't learned very much about Adam, but that's not what I focused on. I kept thinking about when she'd asked me if I still cared for him.

He'd brought me happiness during that awful year — the year of the accident, the year Lauren died, the year Mom mentally checked out. I rolled over and looked out my window. An old memory of Adam climbing through my childhood bedroom window came to mind. I'd forgotten it, but there he was again, late at night smiling at me as brightly as the stars behind him. Remembering that bittersweet year, I broke down in tears, both sad and glad.

Did I still love Adam? Of course. How could I not?

Chapter One

Bellaire, Texas
September 1992

The morning of the first day of school, I started ripping clothes out of my closet. I really hadn't contemplated the clothing problem. Ninety percent of my wardrobe was black. If I wore all black, though, would people think I was in some kind of dramatic mourning? I hoped not—they were the same clothes I'd worn last year.

Just in case, I found a green T-shirt to brighten things up and wore it with a black miniskirt, leggings, and black flats. I looked at myself in the mirror. My clothes were a little baggy. I was never big to begin with, but I had lost some weight over the summer—hospital food sucked, and I'd never gotten my appetite back. The short sleeves showed off one of my many Frankenstein scars. It was a purplish brown railroad track six inches long on my left forearm, though I wasn't even self-conscious enough to cover it up.

School was only a couple of blocks away from my house, but I purposely arrived right as the bell rang. I didn't want to be trapped with downtime in stilted conversations about the accident, my health, and how sorry the other person was for me. I'd already had enough of those.

I slipped into the generic-looking Texas public high school, hoping I looked like every other late student running to my first class. It wasn't like I was dying to go to economics. I'd only signed up for it because it was supposed to be easy and I'd get an hour during the day to do homework. Besides, economics sounded like a substantial course. No college admissions officer would ever know it was actually taught by the soccer coach.

Because the first class of the day was homeroom, Coach Knizki handed out our locker numbers at the end of class. When the bell rang, I walked outside, found my locker, and smiled. *Excellent.* It was a top locker and the first one at the end of the row by a wall — two less people to deal with every day.

Sandra Harold and Trish Keller walked up and pointed to the bottom lockers. "Those are ours," Sandra said.

"Oh, do you want in?" I asked, moving aside to the wall. I didn't know them well. Hopefully, they wouldn't be too chatty every day.

"Nah. We just wanted to let you know," said Trish. She gave Sandra a side-eye glance and nodded down the hall. "We're going to keep our books in our boyfriends' lockers. See you around."

As they walked away, I smiled. They had about as much interest in talking to me every day as I did them. Pleased two more people were out of my life, I put my economics book inside what would be my little home for the year. When I heard the door rattle at my side, I frowned at the end of my privacy. I was no longer alone as I heard, "Hello, Nicki."

I knew that voice. It was distinct among the three thousand students in the school. I took a breath and closed the door.

There he was — Adam Kincaid. Even though I'd been with my old boyfriend, John, when Adam had moved to Bellaire from England last spring, I swooned over the cute British guy just like every other girl. He was tall, played soccer, and had reddish hair and an irresistible accent. It sounded upper-crust to me, and he was always incredibly polite, but he also said "fuck" a lot. He was adorable. His father was some famous geologist, and his sister, Sylvia, was this shy little Goth who had far too cool of a wardrobe for Bellaire, Texas.

Adam had turned out to have some sort of magical personality that allowed him to travel in opposing social circles. He hung both with the popular crowd of jocks and cheerleaders and the ragtag crew I hung out in with my best friends, Rachel and Lisa. Rachel described our group as the Island of Misfit Toys—drama types, radioheads, and assorted geeks. Her boyfriend, Tom, had become good friends with Adam.

The fact that Adam had soon begun dating a cheerleader galled Lisa to no end, so she didn't like him. It was her opinion that because he was English, smart, and sort of hip he rightfully belonged to us. I really couldn't understand why he was dating ditzy Meredith Daniels either, because if he liked her, he must have really been stupid. But Rachel scoffed at my theory; "Please, Nicki," she'd said. "Even smart guys think with their dicks."

Looking at him now, I noticed the econ textbook in his hand and said, "Hi. I didn't know you were in that class."

Adam smiled at me as he put his book in the locker next to mine. "You sat in the front of the room. That's why you didn't see me. I sat in the back."

I nodded. I really had nothing else to say. I'd seen him at a party a few weeks ago and couldn't think of anything to say then either. Normally I was a talker, but not around him.

Yet he seemed to want to keep the conversation going. "It's nice we're neighbors."

"Good fences make good neighbors." I cringed. *Why did I say that?* It sounded like I was a bitch or pretentious or both.

His brow furrowed. "Pardon?"

I realized he had no reference for what I'd said. He probably wasn't familiar with twentieth-century American poetry. "Uh, it's a line from a poem. Not really apropos here, though." I faked a glance at my watch. "I should get to my next class. I'll see you later."

"Yes," he said with a nod. "See you later."

Holding my books tight to my chest, I walked away. What the hell? Couldn't I catch a break? I was going to have to spend nine months watching a never-ending stream of cheerleaders meet Adam Kincaid at his locker. And I felt so awkward. I didn't want to be nervous every time I needed a textbook.

I decided to keep my books with me for the rest of the day. The fewer trips to my locker the better.

Drama was my fourth period class, which was great because Tom and Rachel were in it with me, and we got to eat lunch together. Lisa and I would both admit even to Rachel herself that we were happy to be her friend rather than her enemy. She had the sharpest tongue around, but was also otherworldly beautiful with gray eyes, long dark hair, and legs for days. Adding spiked heels to her five-foot, eight-inch frame made her stand out even more. She was the antithesis of your average Texas high school girl.

Only Tom could tame her. Towering over everyone in the school, he was handsome like a great actor, with a unique face that could somehow be both average and dreamy. The funny thing was, you forgot about his looks because he was so funny and sweet. Anyone with sense at all wanted to be around him.

After we sat down with our trays, Tom stretched in his chair and looked around the giant cafeteria, which was loud with excitement from the first day of school. It seemed like he was surveying the masses.

"Who are you looking for?" I asked.

"Oh, I thought Adam might have lunch now, but he doesn't." He gave me a sly look. "He mentioned you two are locker mates."

My lunch turned in my stomach. I was going to have to get over Adam or it was going to be an even worse school year than I'd already expected. So I replied with fake excitement, "Do I get Meredith, too?"

Rachel burst out laughing and high-fived me while Tom rolled his eyes and said, "Will you give the guy a break?"

"No," Rachel and I said in unison. She wrinkled her nose and added, "Why should we?"

"Because she's his girlfriend," answered Tom.

"She's also an idiot," I said.

"Thank God he doesn't bring her around when he's out with our group. The only thing interesting about her is her balance," Rachel said. "Somehow she keeps standing rather than pitching forward because of her chest."

We all laughed because it was true. And I was always pleased whenever I saw how badly her red hair and light freckles looked with the red of her cheerleader uniform. I'd mentioned it to Rachel once, and she'd snorted and said, "As if. I promise you, no guy is looking at her face. They're staring at her tits."

"Tom, are you going to say he likes her for her mind?" I asked.

He rubbed his neck for a moment in pretend thought before he smiled. "I might not go that far."

"See?" I said.

"He's from a foreign country. Let him have some fun while he's here," Tom said.

"What did you just say? 'Have some fun'? Tom, I love you, but you sound like a frat boy." Rachel placed her hand on her stomach. "Have fun? Like have sex with Skanky Meredith. That's such a gross thought. I think I'm going to hurl."

"Yeah," I said, pushing my cafeteria tray away from me. "At least you're not the one who's going to see them together every day."

My last class was AP English — what should have been my favorite class of the day. Unfortunately, I needed to dump off my other books in my locker beforehand. As I was walking up to it, I saw the nightmare I had envisioned earlier: Meredith Daniels was leaning against my locker, gazing adoringly at Adam while he put his books away. They were laughing, and she had her hand on his arm.

As Rachel had predicted, the scene was nauseating, but I took it head on.

"Hi, Meredith. That's my locker. Can I get in?"

Her eyes widened, and she moved out of my way. "Oh, hi, Nicki. Excuse me."

I nodded. That was enough conversation for me, so I practically threw my books in my locker in order to get out of there. When I turned around, I avoided looking at either one of them. "See you later."

As I walked around them to get to class, I heard Meredith's voice. "Nicki?"

"Yeah?" I said, looking toward her.

"I just wanted to say how sorry I am that I didn't make it to Lauren's funeral. I was at cheerleader camp. My mom said the service was lovely."

She was obviously uncomfortable as she said it. I'd known her since first grade, and though she'd always been silly, she was a nice person. That day she proved it. Only somebody incredibly dumb and earnest would think to try to talk to me about my sister's death the first day of school. But why did she have to say Lauren's name out loud? And why did it have to be in front of Adam?

I thought I might lose it. I breathed in and repositioned my bag on my shoulder. "Thanks. Thanks very much."

Without another look, I strode down the hall, wishing I was actually walking home instead. When I arrived at class, I sat down in the back and stared at the syllabus the teacher had put on the desks. I wasn't really reading it. When Lisa came in and sat at my left, I glanced over to acknowledge her.

"Are you okay?" she asked with a frown.

I shrugged, and Lisa nodded before quietly reading the syllabus herself. Knowing her, she'd probably already read every book that summer. Because she was tall, black, and, more importantly, her father used to play for the Houston Rockets, the world thought she should be an athlete. Lisa was out to prove to the world she'd make a better doctor. I thought it was pretty obvious she was clumsy as all get-out, but wicked smart.

After a moment, I sensed some motion on my right side and peered over to see Adam sitting beside me.

"Hello again," he said.

My nightmare continued. Wonderful. I was completely out of sorts. I couldn't even try to be nonchalant, so I mumbled, "Hi," and went back to looking at the piece of paper.

"What's on the syllabus? Have you read any of the books?" I heard him ask.

Why wasn't Mrs. Anderson starting class? Why was I getting caught in a conversation with Adam? I looked up and saw our teacher going down the rows person by person, checking us in. She was chatting with everyone. *Great.* I was trapped.

Things needed to change now with Adam, so I decided to try a normal conversation. I stole a look at him—he was so easy on the eyes. Normal conversations would be hard. His tousled, rusty hair was longer on top than on the sides, so it fell into his dark brown eyes. The color contrast was beautiful and very distracting.

I went back to my piece of paper. "Yes. Some."

"*To Kill a Mockingbird*?"

"Yeah. Great book. Great movie. Scout is one of my all-time favorite characters."

"What kind of character is he?"

I raised my eyebrows at him. "*She* is a wonderful little kid. Really brave and good-hearted. A better person than most adults." I paused a moment. There was something else I would have said if my world hadn't changed. I took in a breath and decided I could still say it. "Scout has always reminded me of my sister." A warm feeling struck me as I thought of Scout and Lauren, and I realized that it had been right to say it aloud. I half-smiled at Adam.

He nodded slowly, but there was no follow-up question about my sister; maybe his good English manners kept him from being intrusive. Instead, his eyes dropped to the paper before him. "No British literature. Isn't this supposed to be an English class?"

"Uh." My ancestors would've been proud of the jolt of American patriotism that hit me. "There was a revolution two hundred years ago. We write our own books now."

He leaned back in his seat with a smile. "I think I heard about that."

"We still share the same language."

"Sometimes I'm not too sure."

"I bet not." I could imagine what he thought of a Texas accent.

He picked up the list of books again. "What about *Catcher in the Rye?*"

"I read it a long time ago when I was, like, eleven." I laughed a little as I remembered how I'd first come to read it.

"Is there something funny about that?"

"Yeah. My father had suggested I read it then. The book is the classic coming-of-age story. Clearly, he wasn't really thinking about whether or not it was appropriate for an eleven-year-old."

"Really? Why?"

"Well, for one thing, the main character is a guy who swears a lot."

"I suppose I swear a lot." He cracked a sly smile. "At least compared to you Yankees."

"Yankees? You're in the South." I laughed.

"What else is inappropriate about the book? Now I'm interested. It can't only be a few swear words."

"No, it's not just that. It's…" I hesitated for a moment as I realized I was about to bring up the topic of sex with Adam Kincaid. *What the hell,* I thought. I should be matter-of-fact about it. He had a girlfriend and would never want anything with me. I could hide that I thought he was hot, so I shrugged. "Holden, the main character… he's a little sexually frustrated."

His eyes twinkled, and it felt as if my words hung in the air. I wanted to squirm in my seat. *"Sexually frustrated"—like me checking out Adam Kincaid.*

His proper upbringing showed again as he sidestepped the issue, yet he smirked. "That sounds like an adventurous book to be on an American high school syllabus."

"Like I said—it's considered an American classic." I laughed. "I guess some things are sacred."

"But of course." The gleam appeared in his eye again, and he turned toward me in his seat. "Teenage sexual frustration is sort of a rite of passage, if you will."

There went the good-English-boy manners out the window. His tone, the look in his eye, his body language—was he flirting with or taunting me? I decided the former was impossible, and if the latter, I wasn't going to back down. With two parents who were lawyers, debate was a family routine.

"A rite of passage? More like a biological fact, isn't it?" I asked, casually clicking my pen. I raised a brow. "Especially for guys."

"You're right about that," he said with a grin.

His eyes shifted downward, and I could feel him give me a once-over. I wondered what he thought. I was no Meredith, but I had enough self-confidence to know I wasn't butt-ugly either—even with my scars. I couldn't tell, but he'd distracted me so much, I jumped when I heard Mrs. Anderson ask, "Your name, dear?"

"Nicki Johnson."

A look of recognition came across her face. She stopped writing my name and placed her hand on my shoulder. "Oh, Nicki. I'm glad to meet you. I heard about your family's loss. I am so sorry."

Gone went any distraction Adam had provided. I knew Mrs. Anderson meant well, but I hated it when people talked about our "loss" or how we "lost" Lauren. When you lose things, they might come back—like a dog that finds his way home. Or, you might find them — like a key left in the wrong spot. I also hated it when people said she had "departed" — like she was on a plane with a destination or a return flight. Lauren wasn't coming back — on her own or if I looked for her. That was my problem.

I faked a smile. "Thanks, Mrs. Anderson."

Then she kneeled down to look me in the eye. "Please just remember, dear, this is God's will. He has a plan, and she is in a better place. Okay?"

Ugh. It was the double whammy. Lauren could arguably be in a better place — if heaven exists, shouldn't it be better than Bellaire? But the idea that God had willed the death of my sister was bullshit. What kind of God would do that? It made me so mad, I knew my eyes were popping out. But I only nodded and said, "Thank you."

She smiled, patted my shoulder again, and moved on to the next person. I said in a low voice, but still to myself, "I'll keep that in mind."

Adam cleared his throat. "I thought that predestination was no longer a commonly held belief."

I knew he was trying to be nice, but I couldn't look at him. I simply said, "You're in Texas now."

Lisa leaned toward me and whispered, "If you want, you should go home. Who would stop you?"

I nodded and, as quickly as I could, got my things together. I walked over to Mrs. Anderson, who'd moved on to the next row of desks.

"Mrs. Anderson, can I be excused? I'm not feeling well." I could feel my eyes beginning to burn with tears. She had to have been able to see it herself.

"Of course, dear. Just go. If a teacher stops you, just tell them to talk to me."

I choked out a "Thanks" and left the room, doing everything to look straight ahead and not cry. Wiping my eyes, I walked toward the school doors. When I was outside, I announced to the empty sidewalk, "So much for the first day of my junior year."

Chapter Two

The driver had died a few days after the accident; he'd been drunk. I had been pretty out of it afterward, but I remembered hearing my Grandmother Stuart say something about "the Lord dealing with it." That was probably good, because my dad had kept saying he wanted to kill him.

When Mom, Lauren, and I had walked out to the car that night in June, it was a typical Texas scorcher. After I'd called "shotgun," Lauren demanded the car air conditioner be set on high and said, "If I have to sit in the back, I'm going to be comfortable." Unfortunately, we weren't talking about something important or having a wonderful family moment at the end. Instead, we were bickering over where to eat. She wanted a burger, and I wanted Mexican. I think the last words I heard Lauren say were "C'mon, Nicki." And then I heard a screech of breaks coming from our left side. My mom had been making a left turn — supposedly a protected left. When I turned my head to the noise, I saw the truck coming toward us. Seconds later, the crash and crunch of metal were deafening.

Unlike Mom and Lauren, I'd been wide awake for everything — the crash, the pain. First the noise slammed my ears, and then the pain slammed my body. Life started moving at double-time after that. There was a searing, constant pain, which was so bad that I at first couldn't pinpoint it in my body until I realized it was pounding in my middle more than anywhere else. When the car finally settled slightly on its side, it was shaped sort of like an L.

I was in a little pocket toward the top of it. I immediately called out, "Mom? Lauren?"

Neither of them answered, but I saw Mom crammed close to me. Her hand moved, so I knew she was alive. I couldn't see Lauren, though. I panicked and started calling for them repeatedly, but no one answered. I only stopped because the center of my body felt like it was imploding.

I could hear the chaos around the car. It turned out that no one else had crashed. Instead, people from the other cars at the intersection were mingling around us. Eventually, they found me and asked if we were okay. I answered with a question: "Can you get my mom and sister?"

A big man craned his head over the windshield to look at me. He wasn't in uniform or anything. He just seemed to be the "every-man" of disasters — one of those men who takes charge in tragedies. There always seems to be one in the movies, and at that moment, my life was no longer my life. It felt like a movie I didn't want to watch.

"Honey, I think we can get you pretty easily through this angle. Your mom and your sister are going to need the Jaws of Life. I'm real sorry."

That was when I knew Lauren was dead. I just knew it. I had never heard of the Jaws of Life, but I knew whatever it was it couldn't have been good. I began to cry hysterically, and I would have started convulsing but couldn't move. *Lauren, don't leave me*, was all I thought.

Very soon after that there were sirens and a roar of something. I later learned it was an air compressor for the Jaws of Life — Jaws of Death, in this case. They got me out with little difficulty and put me on a stretcher. I saw them put Mom on a stretcher, too, but she'd passed out. I knew that she was alive, though somewhere in the craziness I overheard someone say the words "one fatality." Later, I imagined what Lauren would have thought about her death being in the paper one day as a "fatality." She would have said something like, "At least it would make the news!"

I'd passed out on the way to the hospital. When I finally woke up after my first surgery, Grandma Stuart and Dad stood above me, both crying and smiling. They looked so relieved that I instantly remembered Lauren was dead.

They'd seemed too happy to see me.

Chapter Three

I woke up to my blaring alarm. The second day of school — it could only get better, I thought. That morning I frowned at my closet again, wishing I hadn't loaned my gray shirt to Rachel.

Screw it. I'm wearing black.

I grabbed a red, fringed scarf to throw some color over a black dress, but it was so hot outside, I went with bare legs. People could just deal with the scar on my leg — just like the one on my arm.

As I walked up to my locker, I was taken aback when I saw Adam and Meredith kissing just a little too passionately for a school hallway. His hands were around her waist too near her breasts, and hers were too low on his hips. I gulped. Did I have to have it thrown in my face they were having sex?

I felt like I had been knocked in the gut. I hated to admit it, but I was jealous. Crushed. How did this happen? How had he gotten under my skin in just a day?

I was about to turn around and go straight into class without my economics book when Adam looked up and saw me. He froze for a moment before pulling away from Meredith. She turned around and smiled shyly. "Hi, Nicki."

All I could think was that this situation really, really sucked. I breathed in deeply and forced a smile. "Hey. Can I get in there?"

"Sure," Adam said, shuffling aside. "Um. Good morning."

As I exchanged my books, again as quickly as I possibly could, I heard Meredith say, "I love that scarf, Nicki."

Great. After seeing her in a compromising position, she was trying to make conversation with me. "Thanks," I said.

"Where did you get it?"

I smiled behind my locker door. She deserved this one. I grabbed my economics, physics, and Spanish books and closed the door. Then I gave her a fake, sweet smile. "Goodwill."

Meredith was probably scared of even dropping off donations to Goodwill, let alone shopping there. She looked horrified, while Adam just looked blankly at me.

Pleased with my zinger, I continued smiling as I walked away. "Have a good day!"

My smile faded as I pretended to thumb through my book as the other students sat down. I didn't notice if Adam had walked by me, but I knew he must have since my desk was in the front. I tried to parse out what I was feeling. Sad. Mad. Irritated. Humiliated. The first few things could be explained, I thought, but why was I feeling *humiliated?* No one knew I'd begun to have a crush on Adam. I'd barely even known, and I hadn't said a word to anyone.

Oh, God. He must know. That would be the only reason to feel ashamed. I played out the few interactions I'd had with him since that one party before school had started. I'd said so little, but he'd caught me looking at him—more than once. Plus there was the whole sexual frustration conversation from yesterday. That was it. He knew I had a thing for him. I wanted to puke. For the rest of class, I pretended to write notes from the lecture.

The bell rang, ending first period, and I darted out of the room. Thank God I'd taken my books for the whole day. I wasn't going to have to go back to my locker until after school. The thought of having to see them again nauseated me.

As the day wore on, the weight of my books made me think twice. It wasn't like Adam and Meredith would be stopping what they were doing, and playing this locker game every day would really suck. Besides, avoiding my locker altogether because of him was ridiculous. I was still trapped every day for an hour sitting next to him in English. I had to get over my stupid crush.

When I walked into English, I decided there was no time like the present to get over Adam Kincaid. He was already in his seat reading the textbook. Wanting to prove my strength to myself, I decided to talk first and say hi.

Adam looked at me, smiled, and said, "Hello."

Did he have to be so damn cute? I thought to myself that I needed to move on — I would be normal around him. So, normally when I missed a class, I would ask a classmate what we'd done.

"What are you reading? Did I miss an assignment yesterday?"

"We had to read a chapter about American Puritanism as background for *The Scarlet Letter*."

"Okay. Thanks." I turned to my textbook and thumbed through the first chapter.

"Let me show you. It begins with a bit about the theologian Jonathan Edwards," Adam said, and before I knew it, he was leaning over me and flipping pages. I took a deep breath to steady myself, but it did the opposite. He smelled great — just soap. No cologne like so many American guys trying too hard. His arms touched mine, and I could feel the warmth of his body. It was almost like he was hugging me. I looked at the muscles in his arms and his golden arm hair, and my stomach tightened. He said something about *The Scarlet Letter* being set in the year Oliver Cromwell had ruled England. I think it was a reference point for him, but I really wasn't listening. Instead, I was thinking that I'd been sent directly to hell — without passing Go, without collecting my two hundred dollars.

When he finished talking and moved away, I tried not to look too dazed. "Thanks. I think I got it. Jonathan Edwards. 'Sinners in the Hands of an Angry God.' He sounds like a great guy."

His eyes danced a little. "Yes, I'm rather chuffed that all of these prudes left England before I was born."

"Right." I smiled at his charm. "Thanks for sending us all the Puritans. You know by now that they're alive and well in America."

Mrs. Anderson called the class to order, so we both had to turn our attention to her. Still, I glanced over at Lisa, who gave me a very suspicious look. *Shit.* Now she knew, too.

After school, I walked home, trying to clear my brain of Adam by studying the houses along the way that I already knew far too well. My house was smaller and more modest than most in Bellaire. My parents had bought it while my father still worked at the district attorney's office. Then, three years ago, my father had taken a job with a big firm and made considerably more money, but we'd decided to stay in the house. Well, three of us had wanted to stay. My father had decided to have an affair with a younger attorney at his firm and move to Chicago.

It only took a few minutes before the expected call from Lisa arrived. She knew I was home alone, so she wasted no time. "Okay. Now tell me what is going on."

"Well, hello to you, too, Lisa. I have no idea what you're talking about."

"Yes, you do. Are you crushing on Adam? Because if you are, that is a really, really bad idea."

"I think I know that."

"You didn't answer my question."

"Okay." I sighed. "Yes. A little bit."

"Nicki…"

Rapid-fire, I blurted out my excuses and pleas. "He's so nice to me. It catches me off-guard. I know that he's just taking pity on me, but I can't help it. Please don't make a big deal of it. I'll get over it quick." Even as I said it, I knew it was a lie.

"Well, I don't think he's paying attention to you out of pity, but I'm not sure what his story is. He has a girlfriend. He's so hot, though, maybe he's used to dating multiple girls. Anyway, my personal opinion is that he's bad news. I don't want you getting hurt."

"Thanks, Lisa. I would prefer not to get hurt, too." I sat straighter in my chair as if that would strengthen my resolve. "That's why I'll be over him tomorrow."

Chapter Four

did everything I could to get Adam out of my head. It was easiest first thing in the morning when I had to witness him and Meredith draped all over each other. The irritation I felt seeing them together so early kept my mind off him most of the day.

Every day she had her arm on him, staking her claim. The sight annoyed me, but we'd exchange hellos, and I'd get out of there quickly. I had to admit I took a little comfort in the fact I'd never walked up to them making out again. It was stupid of me, though, because I knew they were up to that and more elsewhere.

English was the problem. Adam always seemed happy to see me and wanted to talk. He was funny and interesting. Then his hair would fall into his eyes, and I would just get sucked in. The worst part was that occasionally I found myself mentioning Lauren. Then I just wanted to talk more because he usually responded when no one else would talk with me about her.

I was under Lisa's watchful eye, though. I could feel her eyes boring into me if I talked more than five minutes with him. I would turn to look at her, only to get a disapproving scowl. I hated it because she was right. I didn't need to be talking to that boy. I'd frown in acknowledgment that I was violating her rules, and then I'd go back to my book.

Other than that, I might bump into him at the lockers between classes, but there wasn't really any time to talk, and I left quickly after school. Except for the moments I looked at him and wanted to sigh, all in all, I thought I was doing okay.

I also didn't see Adam at all the first weekend of school. On Fridays, if there wasn't a party, Tom would usually host a movie night at his house. His parents were professors at Rice, and they were cool with us invading their home as long as we weren't too rowdy. The movies were usually old or very arty. And afterward, Tom would lead the crew to the twenty-four-hour diner. My theory was that he had seen the movie *Diner* one too many times and was trying to recreate it. It was an easy place to hang out, though. Parents didn't care because there wasn't any alcohol, and we liked it because it was open all night. As for Adam, he had a girlfriend who was a cheerleader. There was football and all of that crap, so he wouldn't be hanging out with the misfits on Fridays. I assumed that would be the norm.

When Tom called out Adam's name from across the diner the following Friday, however, I was surprised. As he walked over to us, I checked my watch and saw it was late enough for the football game to be over. Where was Meredith, though?

There were five of us at a giant booth: Tom, Rachel, Lisa, Ben, and me. Ben was a quiet math geek who had been mooning over Lisa since seventh grade. I liked him a lot because he was thoughtful and occasionally let out a really funny zinger. Lisa was sweet to him, but I think she was a little embarrassed because he really was a huge nerd. So, she had her own secret crush, but at least hers was interested in her.

Lisa and I sat at either end of the booth. If Adam was going to sit down, it would be by one of us. I swallowed hard when it was clear he was veering toward me.

"May I?" he asked with a smile.

"Sure." I looked over to see a very disapproving Lisa.

"So, Adam, how was the game?" Tom asked.

"Tedious. American football is not my sport." He grimaced as he said it, so I believed him. We had something in common. I thought football was boring as hell, too.

"Well, it's not like you're there for the game anyway." Rachel smirked. "Where's Meredith?"

"At home. She was knackered."

I focused on my cup of cold coffee, which had become the most fascinating object in the world to me. Meredith as a subject of conversation was not one I wanted to engage in. I felt incredibly awkward, especially with Lisa's eyes on me.

The waitress came by to see if Adam wanted anything, and he immediately asked me. I sputtered out a "No, thank you," and thought to myself that I should really leave. It was too soon after he'd arrived, though. It would look rude and weird.

While Ben and Tom started a debate over which one of them had a crappier car, Adam turned to me. "How was the movie?"

"Awesome. We watched *Heathers*."

"Maybe I'll join everyone next time."

That was interesting. I had to ask, "Have you given up on football?" Oops. That sounded terrible. He might think I meant he had given up on Meredith.

"I'd like to." He took a breath. "Meredith and I just had a row about Homecoming. I really don't want to go."

"That one is kind of important to her crowd. You might want to reconsider." I couldn't believe I had just helped Meredith out. She owed me for life now. If her boyfriend didn't take her to Homecoming, she might drown herself in the Gulf of Mexico. I looked over at Lisa, who actually looked pleased.

I glanced back at Adam, who was smiling at me. "I'll think about it."

His smile was warm, but his eyes were calculating. I decided to go back to staring at my coffee cup. Tom then asked Adam something about English driving, which created a lengthy discussion about traffic rules, and I was officially off the hook.

I put up with the conversation for an hour, but I really wanted to go home. I'd gone far beyond my limit of being casual and normal around Adam, and my mind had started to wander into all the wrong places. I hadn't been that close to a guy I liked for months. When I caught myself glancing down at the crotch of his jeans, I knew I had to leave. I looked pleadingly at Lisa and raised my eyebrows toward the door.

She nodded, saying, "I think it's time to head out."

Everyone agreed, and we started to get up. Ben turned to Lisa. "Can I give you a ride home?"

"Oh, Nicki and I came with Tom and Rachel."

"It's okay, Lisa," I said. "Go with him. Y'all live close to one another." It was a geographic exaggeration, but I didn't want her to lose out on a good make-out session just to make sure I wasn't a third wheel.

"Are you sure?" she asked.

"Of course."

As I got out of the booth, Adam asked me, "Where do you live?"

"Close to school."

"I do as well. Can I give you a lift?"

Lisa had to be watching me, and I knew what the right answer was. Instead of giving the right answer, though, I said, "Sure." I didn't look at Lisa, but I saw Tom smile.

We said our goodbyes, and Adam guided me to his black Honda. My stomach did flip-flops. This had been a very bad idea. Lisa was right. This was not good for me.

Adam opened up my door, and I grasped for a way out. "You don't even know where I live. It could be really out of your way in BFE."

"BFE? Where is that?"

"It's just a more polite way of saying Bum Fuck Egypt."

"Of saying what?" He laughed.

"Oh, uh, Bum Fuck Egypt. It's kind of an American saying for the middle of nowhere."

Closing his eyes for a moment, he shook his head and grinned. "Bum. Fuck. Egypt. So you fuck someone in the bum in Egypt and that means the middle of nowhere?"

"In the bum?"

"Bum. It's another word for *arse*."

"I never really thought of it as being someone's ass before." I giggled. "You might be right, though. I thought it was more like you were a bum and *fuck* was short for *fucking*, as in 'fucking Egypt.' Does that make sense?"

"The whole thing doesn't make sense, but it's funny." He leaned against the car door with the same look in his eye as when we'd talked about sexual frustration in class that other day. "You know, I don't believe I've ever heard an American girl say fuck."

I was in an eye-lock with him, biting my tongue. I bet Meredith liked to have sex all the time, but she'd never say fuck. "It's not very ladylike," I said.

"But you're not bothered."

"Well, I *try* not to say it."

"Of course, but you don't seem to bother much about what people think of you."

I looked down, wondering if that was true, and the scar on my arm caught my eye. It was a perfect example. With all that I'd gone through, I didn't *fucking* care. I shrugged. "Unless they're my friends or family, it doesn't really matter, does it?"

"No, it doesn't." He rested his chin on the door as he studied my face. I felt like I was being appraised again. With him being British and all, I wondered if he thought I should be more proper. Maybe that's why he liked Meredith. A moment passed, and his voice brightened again. "You just said you lived by the school. So do I. Your home can't be that far away."

"Probably not." Giving in, I got into the car. "I live on Pine."

"And I live on Pocahontas. Not far at all."

"I don't believe I've ever heard Pocahontas said with a British accent before," I said with a giggle.

"I believe my father chose the house because of the street. It's sort of a joke in our family." He smiled and shut my door.

After he got in the car, I gave him the driving directions. I quickly looked at the clock on the dashboard and figured that I only had to deal with ten minutes of this self-inflicted torture. *Why did I agree to this?*

Thankfully, it had only taken nine minutes when we arrived at my house. Adam had kept the conversation going the whole ride, asking me about growing up in Bellaire. With my hand on the door handle for a quick escape, I said, "Thanks very much for the ride. I'll see you on Monday."

"Oh. I'll walk you to your door."

Please not that. "Thanks, but I'm okay." I tried to make it light. "I'm a big girl."

He laughed as he opened his door. "No, you're not. You're rather petite, actually. I'm walking you up."

I had opened my door, but he was there to shut it right behind me. "This is much better service than I get from Tom."

"It sounds like he has several passengers to deal with."

"He usually does."

Silence prevailed until we arrived at my porch, when I turned to him. "Thanks, Adam. I'll see you on Monday." I gave half a smile. Awkwardness killed the other half.

He then took a step backward. "Yes. Monday. Have a good weekend."

As he walked away, I let myself in, closed the door, and shook my head. Letting him drive me home had been a very, very bad idea.

Even though it was close to one o'clock when I walked inside, Mom was awake and reading on the cushy old sofa. Still recovering from the accident, she kept odd hours. She patted the couch. "Hi, darling, did you have a good time? Come sit by me."

Just a few months ago, I would have grunted at her and gone straight to bed. Now I found it comforting just to be around her, but I still didn't have much to say. After kicking my shoes off, I curled my legs underneath me as I sat near her.

"Yeah, Mom. It was good to be out."

"It was nice to see Rachel and Lisa again when they came to pick you up. Did they have a fun summer?"

"I guess so. We haven't really been comparing notes about our summers, if you know what I mean."

In a low voice, she said my name like it was a command. "Nicki."

Sometimes my sarcasm about the accident worked with Mom, and sometimes it didn't. Usually, it didn't. I never joked about Lauren's actual death, just about all the crap around it. Lauren would have laughed, too, because so much of it was worth at least a little ridicule.

"Sorry, Mom. I should go to bed, and so should you. I love you." I gave her a hug, and she grabbed me. Her hugs had changed. Sometimes now I wasn't sure if she was going to let go.

After saying our goodnights, I headed upstairs to my room. My walls were completely covered in posters, newspapers, random photos, drawings—pretty much anything that caught my eye. You couldn't see any paint except for the ceiling, which was purple. Mom only tolerated it because I kept such a neat room. The good grades let me get away with a lot, too.

A bathroom connected my room and Lauren's. Mom called it a Jack and Jill bathroom. Lauren had always corrected her, "No, Mom. Jill and Jill."

Even with as much time as I could spend in a bathroom, I hadn't opened the door to Lauren's room since she'd died. But I should have been able to open it and go in because nothing was in there. It was no longer the room of a thirteen-year-old girl; it was just an empty, freshly painted room now. Grandma Stuart, Mom's mom, had seen to it that things were cleared out right after the accident.

I also should have been able to go in because it was *still* Lauren's room. I might have felt closer to her there. Yet it wasn't like I'd decided that I wouldn't go in there. I just ignored the door like it was a wall.

Trying to get my mind off Adam kept me occupied as I waited to hear Mom's crying. She wouldn't talk about Lauren except when forced to, and she kept those conversations short. When I heard her cry, it reminded me that someone else missed my sister, too. I couldn't talk with her, but at least I knew someone else shared what I felt.

Both Mom and Dad had wanted Lauren buried in a cemetery even though she'd been cremated. At the time, I'd objected, but as usual, I was overruled. I knew that Lauren absolutely would not have wanted that. She would have wanted her ashes to be scattered in the Gulf, not a fancy headstone in a cemetery full of creepy strangers.

It was stupid of me, but it was only the first time when Mom had asked me to go to the grave with her that I'd realized why she'd wanted her buried. Standing on a beach wouldn't have made her feel close to Lauren; sitting at a graveside with Lauren's name on a tombstone would. After that one visit to her grave, I said no every time she asked me to go again. It was too much watching her sit and stare at the stone.

Chapter Five

spent the rest of the weekend at home and tried my best not to think of Adam. Lisa called to check on me and also give a mild lecture on how he was sure to be trouble. I could do nothing but agree with her; I knew I was just going to get hurt.

Monday morning confirmed it. There was Meredith once again at Adam's locker, talking with him while holding onto his front belt loop. We did our same exchange of "Excuse me" and "Hello," and the week continued. Every day in English, Adam and I would talk to each other a bit—usually about the reading, but often we strayed onto other topics like movies or music. Lisa watched me the whole time. Wasn't he noticing that?

Occasionally, I would surreptitiously look over to Adam writing or doodling. He had very fine handwriting, masculine but crisp. He also doodled a lot, usually cartoons with such realistic-looking people, I could identify some of the politicians—his drawings of Bill Clinton were hilarious. They were so different than the average high schooler's doodles that I asked him about it once.

I pointed to the sketch of a man in a suit with goofy eyeglasses. "That's John Major, right?"

His head snapped up. "You know who John Major is?"

"He's like the British prime minister, right?" I shrugged.

"Yes, but it's just…" He shook his head. "I'm sorry. If I'm being honest, Americans seem quite ethnocentric. Most don't seem to know much about the UK, especially our politics. It's just a surprise." He glanced down at his drawing and muttered, "And you're a gir—"

"Excuse me?" I leaned back in disgust. "Are you saying because I'm a girl I'm not smart enough to know anything?"

"No. Not at all," he said, his eyes widening. He had that look like he'd made a huge social faux pas. "It's just that the only person I've been able to talk to at all here about home is Tom. He has an interest in it. One day he wants to try his hand at theater in London. The girls I've met here, though, don't seem that keen on things outside America."

A snippy remark was on the tip of my tongue. There were so many great responses to that—like, "*Consider the company you keep*" or "*You probably don't spend too much time talking to Meredith anyway.*" Dropping a golden opportunity, I decided to be nice, though it came out a little curt. "I keep up with the news. My parents are both into politics."

"Really? What do they do?"

"My dad's a lawyer, and my mom is a law librarian."

"What's a law librarian?"

"She's a librarian in a law library." When he frowned at me for making fun of him, I smiled. "Sorry. That was mean. If she wasn't one, I wouldn't know what they were either—they're very specialized. She has a law degree plus a master's in library science and works at the county law library."

"Do you want to study law, then?"

"I feel like it's inevitable. I want to major in English, but my dad says no one is going to pay me to read books unless they're law books." I nodded at his drawings. "What about you? You must like politics."

"I do." He nodded but then hardened his expression. "Not because of my parents, though. They don't talk about politics much because they don't really agree. My father is a Tory, and my mother is for Labor."

"That sounds like it would make for some great family debates."

"There's not a lot of that in my family. Like most Brits, we avoid conflict." He looked down at his drawings. "I like political cartoons, but these are just doodles."

"They look great to me." I smiled and shook my head. "I certainly couldn't draw John Major."

Turning in his seat fully toward me, his eyes brightened. "I bet you could with some practice."

There was a hint of flirt in his voice, and I held his stare, basking in it. I was experiencing physical and intellectual lust. I shook my head. "I have no skills other than reading and writing. It's very limiting."

"I doubt that. Your cartoons would be funny. You're very clever."

The way he said "clever" with his accent was so charming. I swore that my brain and body were melting as we held each other's eyes. What was I going to say to that? If I were so clever, I would be staying away from him. I bit my tongue and took note of that thought.

"Thanks," I said in a soft voice before I turned away.

My eyes darted to Lisa. She lowered her head so Adam wouldn't see and in silent accusation mouthed to me, *You are blushing.*

I gulped hard, guilty as charged.

Placing her hand on her heart, she smiled like I was a hopeless case. She was right.

That Friday, everyone went to Tom's again to watch a movie — *Blood Simple*, which was sure to put me asleep. I was prone to taking a nap in the middle of a film anyway, but one with *blood* in the title made it a sure thing. I was just curling up on the sofa when I heard Tom in the kitchen welcoming Adam.

Of course, Rachel asked the same question that was on my mind. "Why aren't you at the game, Adam?"

"Meredith and I have come to an agreement about American football." He sounded uncomfortable.

As he walked into the room, I watched him spy the empty recliner. When he saw me, though, he walked straight toward the sofa. "Do you mind if I watch the film with you?"

"Uh. Of course not," I said scooting over. "I'm very bad company, though. I'm guaranteed to fall asleep."

"I don't mind," he said and took a seat next to me.

As Tom put on the video, Adam stretched out, resting his feet on the coffee table just as casual as could be. I, on the other hand, was freaking out. I was very aware of what was his space, what was mine, and, most importantly, the very little space in between.

Normally, my eyes would be droopy fifteen minutes into a movie. Not this time. I was so nervous with him next to me that I was hyper-alert in my purgatory. I barely moved, but I couldn't have told anyone the plot of the movie because I concentrated so hard on not fidgeting.

Soon I heard him whisper in my ear, "When do you fall asleep?"

Adam whispering in my ear? This was hell again—not just purgatory. I realized that I needed to escape the situation. "I need some water."

At once, I got up and went into the kitchen. As I found a glass and then filled it with water, I heard a whimpering outside the door. Tom's St. Bernard, Helga, sat on the deck outside the kitchen, looking for attention. I loved dogs, so I decided to join her.

Relaxing on the back stairs with Helga was a good idea. It was a beautiful night, and Helga was stress-free company. When the door creaked, I turned around to see who was disturbing my peace just as Adam said, "Oh, I see you're with a friend out here."

I smiled at his playful expression. "Have you and Helga met?"

"Yes, Helga and I are mates." He sat on the steps with Helga between us. *Thank God.* "So, you like dogs?"

"Yeah, a lot." I scratched Helga's ears. "Our dog, Mario, died two years ago. We had him since he was a puppy. He was a beautiful, big mutt."

"Why didn't you get another?"

"Well, Mario was really Lauren's dog. After we had to put him down, my dad offered to get her another, but she said…" I looked aside just for a second to center myself. It was tough, but I could finish it. "Lauren said she couldn't just replace Mario. He was a member of the family. She needed some time, and she would let us know when she was ready." *Ugh.* Why was I talking with him about Lauren again?

Adam nodded, waiting a few seconds before saying, "I would feel the same way."

"Do you have pets?" I asked in an effort to move the focus away from me.

"Sadly, no. My sister, Sylvia, is allergic to dogs."

"I haven't really met her. She's a year younger, right?"

"She's very shy as well. The move has been hard on her. She's having a difficult time making friends."

"You should bring her along. She seems cool." I then thought aloud, "You both must miss the rest of your family and friends at home."

"I do, although we keep in touch. Actually, I have a cousin traveling in the States at the moment. He's coming to visit soon."

"That will be nice."

"Yes, but I miss my mates and my old girlfriend a bit."

"But you've moved on." Leave it to me to rudely state the obvious. It sounded catty. Then I remembered the display he and Meredith put on every day in front of my locker, and I didn't feel badly at all.

"Ah, yes." He laughed but with a curious look at me. "But my friends here…they're nothing alike, though…Kate…Kate is more like you."

He might as well have punched me in the gut. That's why he wanted to be around me. I reminded him of his old girlfriend — that was it. I looked straight at him and was taken aback to see him smiling at me. His dark eyes looked happy.

Raising his right hand toward me, he continued, "But you're more…you're more…" Abruptly, he pulled his hand back like he had accidentally touched something hot. "You're still quite different."

I looked away. What a ringing endorsement. I faked a laugh. "The same, but different."

He was smiling again. "Different in a good way."

Not different enough, I thought as an image of Meredith sashaying around in her cheerleader skirt passed through my mind. I'd had enough of him, so I got up. "I should go see the rest of the movie so I know how it ends."

He nodded and followed me back into the living room. Sitting next to him this time was a little easier. Now I knew where I stood in his world: I was fine company in private, away from his other crowd, but in public he wanted Meredith. Except that he wanted Meredith in private, too, just in a very different way from me. I felt like shit.

Of course, Adam didn't know I had figured things out, so he seemed flummoxed at my reply when he offered again to take me home.

"Thanks, but Lisa can take me."

"I really don't live far from you." His brow knitted together.

Oh, God. I was such a sucker for this guy. I looked down. "Okay, then." As soon as I said it, I kicked myself.

When I went over and told Lisa that I didn't need a ride, she pursed her lips in concern. "Fine," she said. "I'll call you tomorrow."

As we got in his car, he kept the conversation going by asking me questions about what kinds of movies I liked. I absentmindedly rattled off some answers in the five minutes it took to get home. I wanted to flee and had my hand on the car door handle again. "Thanks very much for the ride. Have a good night."

He smiled. "I'll walk you up."

The words flew out of my mouth without my thinking of just how badly they sounded. "C'mon. It's not like this is a date."

At once, he stopped smiling. He looked away, took a breath, and quickly said, "No. No, it's not. But, I'll still see you to the door."

I was already closing my passenger door as he came to my side of his car. We walked in silence all the way to my porch, where I at last spoke up to say, "Thanks again for the door-to-door service."

I couldn't tell if he was looking at me or at the ivy growing up the porch column. When he did make eye contact, it was brief. "Er. My pleasure. Have a good night."

As he turned around and started back to his car, I felt the punch in my stomach again.

The next day, I already had plans with Rachel and Lisa for dinner at Juanita's, a Mexican restaurant that never carded anyone. The margaritas were so strong that we called them the Truth Serum. Lisa drove because she wanted to get information out of Rachel, too.

Lisa was also being a designated driver for me, though. All my friends were being really cool about my new prohibition on driving with anyone who had touched alcohol. That was why I walked so much. Whenever we drank, I couldn't get home otherwise. Admittedly, I did it more out of respect for Mom than my own safety. Two dead daughters would send her over the edge.

Lisa actually waited until both Rachel and I already had one drink before she began the inquisition. She interrogated Rachel first, probably because she wanted corroborating evidence.

"So what's the deal? What does Tom say about Adam?"

Rachel was finishing a sip of her margarita. "Not much. Adam is dating Meredith. She is *really* into him, and he sort of likes her. God knows why. Well, I take that back. We know why."

"I think I could have told you all of that," Lisa said with a slight sneer. "What else do you know?"

"I don't think Tom knows more, or at least he's not telling me anything else." Seeming a little pained, Rachel looked at me. "Nicki, I think Adam actually does like you." I silently shrugged her revelation off, and she continued, "In fact, I think he really likes you, but frankly, I think he likes screwing Meredith, too."

A nauseating image came to mind, and my words were bitter. "*More.* You mean he likes screwing Meredith more."

"Oh, Nicki, I don't want you anywhere near him," Lisa pled.

"Don't say that," said Rachel. "He's Tom's best friend. Adam *is* a good guy. He's just a stupid guy, too." She turned to me with some hope in her voice. "Tell me what happened last night when you talked outside and when he took you home."

"Nothing," I sighed. "Absolutely nothing that would change the situation you just described. Everything that did happen just reinforces it. Apparently, I remind him of his old girlfriend in England."

Rachel's mouth twisted like she'd tasted something sour. "Eww. He said that? What a dunce."

"I don't think he's stupid at all," Lisa said, crossing her arms. "I think he sees you as some sort of emotional and intellectual replacement for an ex while he fucks Meredith."

My voice got really tight. "I think it's even worse than that. I think I'm the emotional replacement that he doesn't want to be seen with — at least not when he can be seen with Meredith."

"Noooo," moaned Rachel. "That's not true. What guy wouldn't want to be seen with you? You're a babe. And I really don't think that Adam would ever do that to anyone. But forget about him. You deserve more, especially right now."

"Nicki, he does not deserve you." Lisa said it like she was issuing a verdict, and turning to Rachel, she issued another. "And I don't agree with you. If he really cared about Nicki at all, he wouldn't be acting like this. That's a terrible thing to do to anyone, but with what she's been through this year, she especially shouldn't be put in that position."

I focused on my margarita glass in silence as I traced the stem of it with my finger. After a moment, I said in a choked voice, "But really, I shouldn't be dating anyone right now. I'm messed up." The alcohol had gotten to me, and I wiped a tear coming out of my eye.

"It's okay." Lisa gave me a hug. "Like Rachel said, forget about him. There are plenty of others out there."

As always, Rachel knew the best thing to do was make me laugh, which she did. "Maybe you're right. You shouldn't be dating right now, but I totally think you should be getting laid. Let's find *that* guy!"

Chapter Six

Walking up to my locker on Monday morning, I found that nothing had changed. There was Meredith giggling away while Adam tugged on her cheerleader sweater.

Screw it, I thought. *I'm not coming back here today until I have to.* I took the books that I absolutely needed for the day and left the rest. If a teacher called on me, I would lie and just say I'd forgotten the book at home.

Despite my lack of books, I was the perfect student during the day. If I wasn't taking notes for a class, I was working on homework assignments. And Rachel must have said something to Tom, because he was making more of an effort than usual to make me laugh at lunch, and Adam's name never came up.

I timed it so that I walked into English late—that way I wouldn't talk with him. But when Mrs. Anderson gave me a peeved look, I realized I was a little too tardy. She snipped at me. "Thank you for joining us, Nicki."

I skulked to my desk and pulled out my copy of *The Scarlet Letter*. We were reading it in class, so I kept my eyes on my book. When Mrs. Anderson had asked for volunteers to read to the class their favorite quotes, Lisa's hand went up immediately.

I noticed she shot a quick look over my way before saying, "I really like this one regarding Reverend Dimmesdale: 'No man, for any considerable period, can wear one face to himself, and another to the multitude, without finally getting bewildered as to which may be the true.' I think it can be applied to so many situations."

Mrs. Anderson thanked her, but Lisa wasn't looking at her. I thought she was staring at me until I realized she was looking past me. I looked to my right and saw she was actually glaring at Adam. He met her gaze, and his brow crumpled.

Oh, God. I looked down. Lisa meant well, but did I have to be around for it?

Unfortunately, after school I had to get my physics book out of my locker for a test. I was pretty sure I could do it without having to talk with Adam. But after I shut my locker door and turned around to leave, I heard him say, "Have you started writing your paper yet?"

"I'll do it tomorrow night." I shrugged, hoping that would be the end of it.

"Procrastinator?"

"Probably," I said as I glanced at him, trying not to return his smile but ultimately failing. "It works for me." It was true. I needed pressure to write.

"Do you know what you're going to write on?"

I wanted to say, *Dimmesdale as a pathetic piece of shit.* Instead, I said the truth: "Pearl as a sign of feminist hope."

"That's much more cerebral than my theme of Puritanism as a form of government."

I felt myself slipping into the downward spiral of crushing on the cute, smart boy. Time to leave. "Better get to work. Bye."

"Oh. Okay." He took a step backward like he should get out of my way. "Have a good evening."

The rest of the week I gave myself no opportunity to talk with Adam. I barely went to my locker, and I came into class as late as I could to avoid any conversation. But out of sight didn't mean out of mind; it just made me mopey.

At a party at Ben's on Friday night, I was feeling so low that I ended up drinking too much. Adam showed up, but I made sure I was never in the same room with him. Knowing he was there, though, made me nervous, and that only added to my alcohol consumption. I hadn't been that drunk since long before the accident.

By midnight, I knew I should get to bed. I'd ended up in a long conversation with Ben about Lisa, and I was tired. I politely extricated myself from him to find Rachel and tell her I was walking home. Unfortunately, she was with Tom, who was talking with Adam.

I gave a quick smile to the guys while tugging on Rachel's shirt. "I'm out of here," I whispered.

Rachel took one look at me and raised her eyebrows. "I think Tom and I should walk you home, Nicki."

Rolling my eyes, I couldn't get an answer out before Adam offered to take me home.

"Thanks, but I don't think I can handle being in a car," I said.

"I shouldn't be driving either," he said.

Rachel stole a look at me and said, "Tom and I will do it. We could use a walk, too."

"It's okay. I live closer to her," said Adam.

I knew that I should say no, that a walk under the stars with Adam was a really, really unhealthy thing to do, especially without all of my wits. But I was just too drunk to *not* do something that I really wanted to. With no willpower at all, I nodded at Adam. "Okay. I'll go with you."

As I kept my balance heading out of the kitchen, I realized it wasn't going to be a romantic stroll. By the time we started walking, I already felt really sick—sick from alcohol and sick from risking my heart. We didn't talk much, which was good because I needed to concentrate on not puking in front of him. We were only a couple of blocks away from my house when I had to stop.

"Uh, I need to sit down." Without hearing an answer from him, I plopped down on the curb. I put my head between my legs and concentrated on breathing in and out.

He snickered and sat down beside me. "It's okay. It happens to all of us."

Seconds later, I felt his hand gently stroking my hair. It felt amazing. No one had touched me in so long, and I so badly wanted him to. But what was he doing, and why was he doing it? It was pure torture. I wanted to turn to face him, but I didn't know what would happen if I did.

Instead, I breathed in deeply, lifted my head, and turned away from him. Maybe if I was drunk and didn't look at him, I could ask the question I had wanted to ask for weeks. Maybe I could get an answer. "Adam, why are you always so nice to me?"

He stopped touching my hair for a moment but left his hand on my back. "Well, I want to be your friend. I like you, and…I wish you were happier."

I still couldn't look at him. What he'd just said would be confusing even if I weren't wasted. But because I was drunk, I could at least say the truth. "You're being too nice."

"Really? How so?" he asked with his hand still on my back.

Why was he dragging this out of me? I swiveled around. "You have a girlfriend. So stop it. Stop being like this with me."

He took his hand away and looked down. "I know. I should… Wait." He looked back up at me. "What do you mean 'stop it'?"

I shook my head at him, my eyes burning with tears. He was fucking clueless.

My raised voice wavered a little. "I can't. I can't do it anymore." Standing up, I looked him in the eye. "Please just leave me alone." I started to turn around, and my voice broke altogether. "I'll walk myself the rest of the way."

"Please, Nicki. Don't go. I'm so sorry—"

I jerked my arm away in a huff, but he placed a hand on my shoulder, which forced me to look at him.

"Nicki, please," he said, exhaling as he spoke. "I've wanted to be your friend since I moved here. I like being with you…so much. And you…you seem happier when we talk. You actually smile, and when you smile, you're even more beau—"

I shrugged his hand off my shoulder, irate. "So I'm a pity project for you? The Make Nicki Happy project?"

"No! Not at all. Please believe me. I care for you, but I haven't known if you're—"

"Care for me?" Thank God I was drunk, because I could say what I wanted. "Right. I'm sure you think about how you care for me when you're fucking Meredith."

Stunned by that one, his face went blank and then saddened. I was proud of myself. "Now leave me alone," I said with finality as I walked away.

This time, he didn't try again to catch up and talk with me. That was good, because I wasn't sure if I could deliver lines that well again. When I crawled under the covers, my bed was spinning. I tried to focus on something, but that just brought back all the bad parts of my conversation with Adam and its final result: no more Adam in my life.

My heart actually ached, and I began to cry like a whimpering baby. He didn't want me to be sad? How could I possibly not be? I felt destroyed. Mercifully, the alcohol took over, and I passed out.

I spent the rest of the weekend in my room. I told my mom I wasn't feeling well. That was partly true, after all, since I did have a hangover. But mostly, I wanted to avoid talking with people because I was full of regret for going psycho on Adam. I meant what I'd said, but I couldn't believe I'd actually said those things to *him*. What would he think of me now? What would he say to Tom? When Rachel and Lisa called and asked about my walk home with Adam, I played it down, saying I'd been wasted and didn't remember much. That was a lie. Much to my dismay, I remembered every minute of it.

By Monday morning, I'd convinced myself that I could chalk up my behavior to alcohol in case anyone asked. I also had resolved that I wasn't going to let Adam rule my life. I was going to use my locker and sit in class like he was any other classmate—any other classmate with whom I never talked.

When I got to my locker and saw no one there, I thought maybe my little tirade had forced him and Meredith to her locker for their morning rendezvous. But when he hadn't shown up by lunch, I wondered if he'd left his locker for good.

In English, I averted my eyes from him the whole time, although I knew he was beside me. After class, I assumed I wouldn't see him at the lockers, so I was startled when I heard him say my name. I looked up, and he pointed off to the side.

Ann Webster stood a few feet away, hovering around like she wanted to talk. Ann was a very plain girl who kept to herself mostly.

We didn't really know each other that well but were often in classes together. What did she want from me?

"Nicki, can I talk with you for a minute?"

"Sure." I was hoping Adam would leave, but it seemed like he was moving in slow motion.

"Well, you may know that I'm in Students Against Drunk Driving."

Possibly the least popular club at school. Then I realized the conversation was about to go nowhere good. "Yes," I said warily.

"Well, we were wondering…only if you were up to it, if you would come to our next meeting. Maybe talk about your experience. I mean, we understand if you can't, but your story is really important."

I stared at her, thinking I must remember that Ann Webster—of all people—meant well, but I still couldn't believe anyone would ask that of me. I didn't even want to think about it, let alone talk about it. I did everything not to rehash the accident. Of all the pain and loss I had over Lauren, nothing brought it on more acutely than recalling that night.

I shook my head. "No, Ann, I can't do that. I'm sorry."

She looked disappointed. "Oh, I totally understand. I just wanted to let you know that we're here for you."

"Um. Thanks."

Ann nodded a goodbye and walked away. I took a deep breath and turned around. I had to get out of there fast, but then I heard Adam's voice say, "You all right, Nicki?"

When I turned to face him, he was leaning against his locker. His expression was full of concern for me, but there was no way I was going to talk with him about Lauren ever again. That had been my worst mistake. "Don't worry about it," I said.

"Do you want to talk?"

Shaking my head, I started to turn around. Why was he doing this to me again?

"Are you sure?"

Why, oh why, was this happening? I took a deep breath and faced him. "I'm sure that I don't want to talk to you."

"You don't want to talk to me right now? Or you don't want to talk to me at all?"

I knew what I was supposed to say, and somehow I found the resolve to say it. "Does it really matter?"

"It matters to me."

"The answer is both."

He seemed to flinch after I spoke, so I sped away for both our sakes.

I made it home without crying — probably because I was too agitated. When I got inside my room, I sighed; things were really over and done with. I doubted he would speak to me again.

I curled up on my bed, clutching a pillow to my chest as reality set in. The fact was, I desperately wanted to speak with someone — about the accident, about missing Lauren, or how Mom was doing and Dad was reacting. As I thought back on the recent weeks, those couple of sentences I'd exchanged with Adam about Lauren had been the most I'd said to anyone about her since she'd died.

And when I thought of my friends and family, I knew there was no one there for me. Lisa and Rachel felt it was their job to shield me from all things painful. Mom — well, she just wouldn't talk at all. And Dad had been so withdrawn to begin with that he was useless. So although I spent time with some people and kept relatively busy, I was lonely. Adam had been a nice distraction in a way. Now, I had no one.

Chapter Seven

My totally dorky biology teacher placed random sayings on poster boards around the classroom. Some of them were typical teacher BS, like, "Luck is the meeting of preparation and opportunity." One saying was different, though, or at least I thought about it differently. Because I watched the clock for most of class, every day I saw the words he had placed underneath it: "Time is passing. Are you?"

The simple answer was yes. Of course I was passing. My life would never be normal again, but I wasn't failing in school, for God's sake. If anything, my grades were better than usual. Staying at home most of the time had that effect.

But I read another meaning in the question. Time passed, but I really wasn't doing anything to pass the time. I was never much of a joiner at school anyway, but this year it was easier for me to simply not interact with people. The whole Adam fiasco had taught me that. So I didn't do any extracurricular stuff. Instead, I stayed in my room, listening to music or talking with Rachel or Lisa, and I slept—a lot. Thankfully, Mom let me be. I overheard her once talking with Grandma Stuart about me. She just said something like, "It's her way, Mother. You understand."

Even on my seventeenth birthday, I made sure it received as little attention as possible, with the exception of margaritas with Lisa and Rachel. Until the accident, I'd been dying for a car when I turned seventeen. Yet after almost dying *in* a car, it was the last thing I wanted. At my request, Mom gave me a couple of books and a cupcake, and Dad sent me a gift certificate to a local bookstore. I was sure his assistant had arranged it, but in this case, the thought really did count.

Homecoming came and went. It wasn't an event for me at all, and I thought Meredith should really thank me she had a date. Speaking of said date, except for English class, I rarely saw Adam at the lockers. I guessed he kept most of his books in Meredith's locker. He also never showed up with our crew on Friday nights anymore. Either it was a self-imposed exile or Rachel had guessed correctly and told him he was unwelcome.

In English, I did my best to ignore him, avoiding looking to my right as much as I could. We never talked, which was fine by me. He had become almost a stranger in my world, except for few times where we accidentally looked at one another. Once or twice I thought he might say something to me, but he never did.

The week after Homecoming, we were finally finishing up *The Scarlet Letter* in English. One day that week, Mrs. Anderson began passing out *To Kill a Mockingbird* to get us started on it. Out of the corner of my eye, I could see Adam thumbing through the book, and I heard him clear his throat a little before saying, "Nicki, you had said—"

I looked up at him, stunned, but I then heard Mrs. Anderson say, "Mr. Kincaid, please join the class discussion." He didn't talk to me again that day, and the next couple days he wasn't in school.

When I saw him on Friday standing at his locker, there was a tall blond guy next to him whom I didn't know, and his sister Sylvia was standing off to the side, looking a little bored. She was still adorable, though, like a Goth Audrey Hepburn, in a French sailorman's shirt with black leggings and Doc Martens. Then I saw Meredith was back for the first time in weeks. *Great…*

Adam and the blond guy were talking and laughing with Meredith and another cheerleader, Jennifer Mitchell, both decked out in their tiny little uniforms. Rachel had deemed Jennifer "mentally incompetent" a few years ago. She was cute in a way, but I always thought she resembled a pug.

Another English accent—it wasn't Adam's voice—chimed over the noise of the hallway. "Brilliant. We'll see each other tomorrow, then."

That must be the cousin he had mentioned before, I thought. Maybe he was why Adam had been gone. Luckily for me, Meredith and

Jennifer walked away seconds before I was going to have to say, "Excuse me," and draw attention to myself.

Instead, I was able to walk around the cousin straight to my locker. I heard Adam say, "Hello, Nicki."

Still working my combination, I glanced at him. "Hi." I sort of acknowledged the cousin with a nod. Of course, he also would be hot—sandy blond hair, light blue eyes, and a very angular face. He looked a little older than Adam.

"Nicki, this is my cousin, David. He's visiting for the day. And I'm not sure if you've ever met my sister, Sylvia."

Act normal. I smiled at David and Sylvia. "Hi. Nice to meet you both."

Sylvia squeaked out a "Hello," and her eyes darted to David. He had a sexy grin, which felt like it was directed at me. Considering how chatty he'd been with Jennifer, I could only guess he was an even bigger player than his cousin.

I felt his eyes on me as he spoke. "It's good to meet another friend in Texas. I hope they don't kick me out of your school today."

His accent was different than Adam and Sylvia's—less refined-sounding. Cockney maybe? It was still a nice voice to match the nice face. I decided that it wasn't David's fault his cousin was a jerk, so I thought I would be hospitable.

"Be careful what you wish for," I said with a smile. "You know, there are a million better places around here to spend a day than at Bellaire High School."

David's eyes twinkled. "I don't doubt that, but you know, I thought I'd hang with these two and see what a typical day is like for them. Maybe you can fill me in?"

Damn. He really was cute. His hair was longer and a little scraggly, and his clothes were more rumpled than Adam's. If he didn't have an English accent, he would have looked like a surfer boy. Plus he was nice. I wondered if Adam had said anything to him about me. Regardless, I thought I'd be nice back.

"Well, Adam and I have two classes together. You're about to be taught economics by the soccer coach. If you're lucky, you might learn how to balance a checkbook. English is at the end of the day. You'll hear about Puritans there."

"The Puritans? Weren't they Englishmen who came to America? They were oppressed in England because of their religion."

"That's right." I held his gaze. He was definitely older and confident, and I was pretty sure that if Rachel saw me talking to him, she would be pissed if I didn't flirt a little. I leaned against my locker and said, "Religious oppression. Sexual repression. That pretty much sums up the pilgrims."

"Sexual repression?" Raising his eyebrows, David smirked. "The last class sounds interesting. Why were the pilgrims repressed when it came to shagging?"

"A strict moral code leading to scandalous affairs."

"Really? I like the last part."

I tried to keep my eyes from bugging out. *I bet you do*, I thought. Time to tone things down, so I said, "The affairs just lead to self-mutilation. Reverend Dimmesdale deals with his by burning a big letter A for *adultery* into his chest." I looked over at Adam, who gave a nervous laugh. I guess he didn't like hearing about Dimmesdale again.

David turned his body so it was toward me, and he crossed his arms, settling into our conversation. His voice got a little lower and kind of sexy. "That part doesn't sound like much fun to me. What do you think?"

Was he flirting with me? I wanted it to continue. "Hmm. I'm not good with pain." And I knew something about pain.

"Well, that class sounds sorta painful to me. What do you say we skip it?"

There was no doubt Adam's cousin was flirting with me, and my heart began beating at 4/4 time. No one had flirted with me in forever—since my old boyfriend, since my old life had ended. All of a sudden, I felt normal again. I laughed up into David's gorgeous blue eyes. "Don't tempt me."

Right before David asked me about my other classes, I saw Sylvia tug on Adam's shirt, leading him a few feet from us. David was talking to me, but I distinctly heard Sylvia's prim accent both reprimand and beg her brother. "Adam, why are you letting this happen? Do something."

I couldn't hear his reply. I guess Sylvia didn't think it was appropriate for their visiting older cousin to be hitting on random girls at their school. I couldn't have cared less. I was engaged in a heavy flirt session with a hot, nice guy who liked me and didn't mind showing it to the world. When the bell finally rang, I said goodbye to the three of them and quickly skedaddled, knowing I would see them again right after class.

As I walked away, I clearly heard David ask Adam, "Mate, why ain't we hanging out with *her* tomorrow night?" I was on cloud nine.

Curiously, Adam went to his locker more than usual that day. David and I bantered back and forth in between every class. Adam would laugh a bit at our jokes, but sometimes when I glanced at him, I thought he looked uncomfortable. Meredith made an appearance twice. By the second time, I swore she eyed me suspiciously as I talked to David. I even heard her say something to Adam like, "Well, when the four of us go out tomorrow, blah, blah, blah…" I didn't care, though, since David just continued talking to me.

Over the course of the day, I learned that David was nineteen and taking some time off from school. He had just spent six months traveling in Central and South America with a friend. They were headed home, but they each had friends in the United States they wanted to see first. David had spent the last couple days touring Texas with Adam and his family. He was in town only until Sunday, when he would fly to meet his friend in New York before heading back home.

At lunchtime, Tom announced, "I met Adam's cousin earlier, and I believe Nicki has a new admirer."

Rachel turned to me. "Why didn't you tell me?"

I'd wanted to tell her about David, but I didn't want to do it in front of Tom. Now I was embarrassed. "I wouldn't call him an admirer."

"Tom, how do you know this?" Rachel said, her lips easing into a grin.

"Adam and I have French together." Tom leaned back in his seat and smiled. "David was asking Adam questions about Nicki."

"And what did Adam say?" Rachel's voice was coy.

"Not much. David ended up getting information from me."

"Adam's cousin crushing on Nicki? Oh, that's beautiful." She nodded her approval. "And David is beautiful, too. This is good, Nicki."

Rachel's reaction made Tom's smile disappear, and he gave me a parental look. "Nicki, this little flirtation with David doesn't have anything to do with Adam, does it? You're not trying to make him jealous or something, are you?"

Wanting to nip that thought in the bud, my tone was firm. "Um. No."

Rachel placed her hand on Tom's arm and shook her head. "Babe, no woman would need a motivation other than David himself to want to be with him. He's hot, and he's got that accent. I'm sure Adam is the last thing on Nicki's mind."

I tried to shrug it off with a joke. "She's right. Adam who?"

After English, Adam, David, and I were at the lockers again when David asked, "So do we get to see you tonight?"

His saucy grin made me feel like he wanted to do more than just *see* me tonight. Somehow I kept my voice even as I answered, "Well, I think that depends on whether Adam is going to Lance's party." I didn't look at Adam when I said it.

David turned to Adam and laughed. "We're going to Lance's party, all right."

Adam gave a half-smile. "Happy to oblige."

Lance's house was often the site of parties because his parents traveled a lot, plus it was really cool. His family was very wealthy, and his house was a giant art museum. When we arrived around nine-thirty, New Order blasted through the house, and with the décor, it felt like a club.

It was an unseasonably warm night, so we found Adam, David, and Tom by the keg on the deck. We all said hello to one another, and I immediately knew something was different with David. Adam seemed to be acting the same as he had at school—a little quieter than usual. David was still very nice to me, but he seemed more reserved.

The guys were talking about the perennial topic of whether alternative music was really alternative if it was played on top-forty radio. Rachel and I plopped down on a sofa in one of the many sitting areas on the big deck. Lisa had left us as soon as we walked in because she spied an old crush of hers, Peter, who was now in college in Austin.

I was pleased that it took only two minutes before David walked over to us. The sexy smirk was back as he asked, "Fancy some company?"

"Of course," Rachel said with a grin. She eyed me and stood up. "I'll be back, though. I need to get some water."

She lied so fluidly that I think David actually believed her. He smiled. "No worries. I'll save your place."

When he sat down beside me, he sat much closer than Rachel had been. I smiled at the close proximity and asked, "How was the rest of your afternoon?"

"Good. We went back to Adam's place. When I walked in, Adam's mum, my Aunt Judith, was on the phone to me mum. They're sisters."

"Was she checking up on you?"

"Probably." He laughed. "I didn't think of that, but you're right. She hasn't been able to keep tabs on me for the last six months."

We talked for a while about his travels, and I could tell something had changed from the afternoon. He wasn't really flirting anymore. *Maybe flakiness runs in their family.*

When our conversation lulled, I started to feel awkward. I was about to grab at any sentence I could find in my brain, but David startled me by putting his hand on my left arm. My dress was just a simple shift, so my arm was bare, and when I looked down, I saw his tanned fingers were very gently touching the mauve scar on my pale skin. What was he doing? It wasn't like I wanted to hide my scars, but the only other person who had touched one was my doctor. I was embarrassed and nervous, so I tried to make light of it. "It's kind of scary, I know."

He kept tracing the railroad track up and down. It felt exquisite. And to have someone touch one of my damaged parts was especially sweet. I was shocked when he softly said, "Aunt Judith told me about it."

"What?"

"We were talking, and I mentioned that I met you. Apparently, she knows your mum from church. She said she was impressed by how well your mum was doing."

A fleeting memory came back to me of seeing Adam in the packed congregation on Easter Sunday last spring. It made sense that they would go to an Episcopal church if they were English and in the States. But I hadn't gone to church since Lauren's funeral and had no plans on going back until Mom made me.

"I don't think that I've met your aunt," I said, shaking my head.

"Yeah, Aunt Judith said that. She said that she really didn't know your mum either but that she went to the funeral."

Adam's mom was at Lauren's funeral? That's weird. Even if I'd known what she looked like, I probably wouldn't have recognized her. I had kept to myself that day as much as I could.

"I'm sorry I didn't get to meet her," I said.

He continued feeling my scar. It felt so nice. Actually, a little more than nice; it felt sexual. All of a sudden, I realized that I was getting a little aroused. Had my mind left my body? I was getting turned on while talking about my sister's death.

"I'm sure she understands," he said as his finger crossed my skin. "It's not exactly the place to meet people. Anyway, she said your mum seemed like a wonderful woman, raising a level-headed daughter by herself."

"Ha!" I snorted. "Your aunt really doesn't know my mom, or she would have heard her opinions on my hair and wardrobe. I don't think she would say I'm levelheaded."

David chuckled, but he then removed his hand from my arm and looked at me intently. "After hearing your story, I'm gobsmacked Adam hadn't mentioned it earlier."

"Why didn't he? It's not a secret." I tried to joke. "It's been in the paper, for God's sake."

"I asked. He said he didn't know if you'd want people talking about it. He also said you seemed to have good days and bad days."

"Well, that's true." I looked over at Adam. He was about twenty feet away talking with Tom. He didn't appear to be paying any attention to us. I really wanted to change the subject.

"Yes, that makes sense to me, but I didn't think it was the whole story."

"What do you mean?"

"Well, I thought it was strange that Adam hadn't told me anything about you before we met. You're in his circle of friends." He touched one of my stray curls. "And you're quite something."

I could feel the heat of a deep blush on my cheeks. "My scars are something, at least."

"No, I'm serious. This afternoon, I asked him if he ever fancied you, and he didn't really answer."

"He has a girlfriend," I said nonchalantly, hoping the topic would close.

"That don't mean anything," David said, shaking his head. "Sylvia told me that he liked talking with *you*."

"Yeah. He likes talking with me because I remind him of his old girlfriend." Boy, did I sound bitter…

"Did he say that to you? Kate? You remind him of Kate? What a prat! I can't believe he said that. Though I s'pose you're more like Kate than Meredith. You two are both clever and pretty, but Kate is very conventional."

The conversation had become so bizarre that I went silent. And I really didn't like having to hear about Kate and Meredith in the same sentence.

While I was quiet, David kept talking. "Have you ever fancied Adam?"

He was staring at me with those blue eyes, and there was something about his Cockney accent that was so humble and genuine. I had to be honest. "I'm not sure if I've *fancied* him, but I did start to think about him when he was so nice to me all the time. But I knew he wasn't into me. I mean, he and Meredith make out in front of my locker every morning."

Nodding, David looked down at my arm and started tracing the scar once more. "Well, I have to ask if you were only flirting with me because you're actually keen on Adam."

I frowned at being asked that again. "That question doesn't speak very highly of me, and it's silly."

"I'm sorry. I know it ain't nice to think that, but I'm curious."

His blue eyes were locked on mine. It felt like he was pulling information out of me. I stumbled as I said, "There are a lot of reasons why I like being with you, but honestly…none of them have anything to do with making Adam jealous."

"Is that right?" The smile from earlier that day came across his face again.

Absolutely, I thought. I wanted to be with *this* guy. I bit my lip before replying in almost a whisper, "That's right."

I was expecting him to turn and give me a kiss — like most guys would do. Instead, he turned, gazed at me for a moment, and asked, "Don't be offended, but can I see your other scars?"

I smiled at the sudden change in mood. "You didn't see the one on my ankle?"

He bent down and swept his fingers around the ugly mark. His touch felt so erotic, slightly uncomfortable. I had to readjust my sitting position.

After a minute he said, "With that bad of an accident, I'd think there were more."

"Well, there's one on my thigh that I would show you right now, but it might cause some stares if I were to raise my dress."

"I'd certainly stare."

His grin was so devilish that I swatted him on the shoulder. Shaking my head, I covered my stomach with my arms. "There's no reason to stare anyway. I have a pretty gruesome scar on my stomach. It's really ugly and big. No more bikinis for me."

"Now that's really disappointing."

"The rest are small and scattered around here and there. Only my face came out okay."

"I'd say it came out more than okay." He raised his hand up to my hair and tousled it. "You're so lovely."

I wanted to kiss him badly, but there were too many people around, including Adam. Despite everything, I really didn't want to rub it in Adam's face. I looked down at our empty beers and asked, "Should we get another drink?"

"Sure." He got up and gave me his hand. But when I stood, he let it go. I immediately thought that was a bad sign until he put his arm around me, guiding me into the house. As we walked by Adam and Tom, he asked, "Do you two want another drink?"

Adam answered David but looked at me. "In a bit," he said.

When we got in the kitchen, I excused myself and went to the bathroom. I tipped my head over and fluffed up my hair; otherwise, I decided that the rest of me still looked okay. When I returned to the kitchen, David was gone. I wandered around looking for him, and we ended up walking into one another in a tight hallway off the kitchen. Right as we exchanged hellos, a loud group of guys started barreling down the hallway just as another couple came from the other side. I had no idea what was behind me, but David moved his arm around me. He must have opened a door, because he said, "Let's get out of their way."

We ended up in a large pantry, and he closed the door as the noisy crew walked by. Not knowing what to do, I flicked the switch, but the light had a dead bulb. Being alone in a small, dark room with David made me nervous, so I joked, "Even Lance's pantry is nicely done."

"True," he said.

With only a one-word reply, he obviously wasn't interested in conversation. I could sense this was it. We were already very close, but we stepped toward each other. He leaned down and moved his right hand behind my neck and into my hair and put his left hand on my hip. And then we kissed. Even the first simple peck was tantalizing. I couldn't remember the last time I had felt that alive.

At first it was a series of long kisses with our mouths closed. I wove my fingers into his hair and had my other hand on his chest. Soon our tongues met, and everything became very soulful. Since I had already been aroused just sitting by him before, I was losing my mind now. I pressed my body to his. We both started to breathe a little heavily.

He pulled away and looked to a stepladder at our side. He grinned. "This might be fun. How 'bout we move you?" All of a sudden, he sat me down on the top step of the ladder, evening out our height, and he was kissing me again.

I parted my legs, which hiked up my dress, and he moved in between my thighs. Repositioning me, he pulled me closer to him. *Oh my God.* He was hard against me, and the fact there was almost nothing between us didn't seem lost on him. He began kissing my neck and pressing himself against my panties. His hands traveled down my side, grazing my breasts before settling on my hips, giving him some leverage to rub his dick against me in earnest. I was pretty sure my crotch would explode. In my mind, though, I knew there was only so much that could be done in a pantry.

"I think…I think we should go outside." I tried to cover up the gasp that I'd let out by enunciating a little more clearly. "Maybe by the pool?"

"That sounds nice," he said and kissed my neck. "But I never knew how much I liked ladders."

Giving him a giddy peck on the lips, I jumped down from the ladder and straightened myself up. He kissed me again before he took my hand. To my joy, this time he didn't let go. I led the way out of the pantry only to see Lance heading down the hallway with Adam and Tom behind him.

Oh shit. Lance had a big smile on his face. I knew something snarky would come out of him. "Nicki, it is so nice of you to give such a thorough tour of my home to our international guest. I would have never thought to show David our pantry."

There was no good way out of this. Adam stared at me with that curious look. Tom laughed heartily. I forced a smile and turned away, but I heard David say, "It's just as nice as the rest of the house."

"Oh, I think you probably liked it more than the other rooms," said Lance.

Before it got any worse for me, I ignored them and dragged David out of the most uncomfortable of uncomfortable situations. Leading him outside, I walked us down the steps to the pool. I remembered that it had some intricate gardens with hedges in a modern pattern around it. There was pool furniture everywhere, and it was easy to find a secluded chaise lounge.

When we sat down, we didn't immediately pick up where we left off. Instead, we talked for at least an hour about school and books and the places he had traveled. I was jealous of his journeys. I sat there thinking, *This is what I need. Someone who is kind and adventurous and who genuinely likes me.* Then at one point when the conversation waned, David smiled and tousled my hair. That's when things picked up again.

The kisses began sweetly, but they soon became incredibly passionate — all playful tongues searching out the other person. He was holding me very gently, running his fingers all over my arms and neck. I was so happy. This wonderful man — and he was a man, not a boy — was loving me.

The kissing continued as we lay down on the lounge. I was off in some la la land and didn't realize that I had immediately opened up my legs to him. He groaned while positioning himself between them again. If I had any presence of mind, I should have been embarrassed being so forward. After all, I was flat on my back spread-eagle for a stranger, but I was off the charts aroused now. I even had a brief thought that this really wouldn't be a bad way to lose my virginity. But that was kind of stupid — I'd said no to my old boyfriend because he was leaving for college, yet here I was, ready to go with a tourist.

My dress had shimmied up to my waist so that I was really only half-clad. He looked down at me, brought his hand to my face. "Nicki, you are so gorgeous. Incredibly so."

"Oh, David," was all I managed to get out of my mouth. My body said the rest as I rubbed myself into his rock-hard erection. Kissing me again, he began thrusting gently against me — the latter starting to send me over the edge. He was wearing khakis, not jeans, so I felt him distinctly through my panties — so distinctly that I thought he might have gone commando.

When he moved his body away and began tickling me over my panties, I went nuts. And I was only climbing to another plateau when his fingers found the right spot, making my brain blur. My whimpers spurred his fingers on while his other hand went under my panties and grabbed my ass.

I faintly heard him ask, "What do you want me to do, Nicki? I'll do whatever you want."

I was so far gone at that point, though. I gasped, and my body shuddered into his from an intense orgasm.

Holding me close to him, he gave me tiny kisses everywhere. As soon as my mind registered what had just happened, I was really embarrassed. Nothing like that had ever happened to me before. John had only gotten me there once, and it had taken a long time. All I could say was, "That was embarrassing."

He chuckled and stroked my hair. "Embarrassing? Jesus, not at all. That was bloody fantastic. And you…you are lovelier than ever."

I froze when I heard my name called from over the hedge. "Nicki? Nicki?"

Thank God, it was Rachel's voice. If there was one person I could handle talking to right now, it would be Rachel. "Yeah?"

"I just wanted to let you know that I'm going home with Tom now. Lisa left with Peter a few minutes ago. Do you want to go? We can wait for you."

I really didn't want to go, but I knew that I should. I needed to be doing things that made sense, not crazy things like losing my virginity to a Cockney Brit in Lance's backyard. Of course, I also didn't want to face any aftermath with Adam.

I whispered to David, "I really should get going."

He furrowed his brow. "Hmm. Shame. I don't like that idea at all."

I thought for a moment and had an idea. "Everybody has been drinking, so I'm going to walk home. You can walk with me if you want."

"I guess that shall have to do, won't it?" he said with a kiss on my nose.

Rachel called again to me, "Nicki? Are you coming with us?"

"It's okay. I'll walk myself."

"Are you sure?"

I could tell that actually meant, *Are you sure you want to be with David?* So I assured her, "Not a problem. I'll talk to you tomorrow."

"Okay." Then she laughed. "Bye, David. Nice meeting you."

David laughed with her. "You as well, Rachel."

And then we heard it—Adam's voice from up on the steps. "Where are they?" he asked.

"By the pool." Rachel was curt.

"What are they doing?" he asked. I thought he sounded almost worried.

In true Rachel form, she retorted, "What do you think?" I could hear her walking up the steps as she added, "It took a little bit because I was trying not to interrupt."

There was no response from Adam.

I looked at David, who also seemed to process their exchange. I couldn't tell what he was thinking, so I offered, "You don't have to walk me home, you know. I mean you don't even know your way around here. How will you get back?"

Focusing again on me, he smiled. "I've spent the last six months working my way round tiny streets in South America, and I don't speak Spanish. I can handle this place, easy. I'll go tell Adam."

David left me, and I sat there thinking about what had just happened while I got myself back together. I felt fantastic. I was on a physical and emotional high from being with a great guy. Then I thought about never seeing him again, because that's exactly what was going to happen. Just my luck.

When he came back, David smiled. "I'm meeting him afterward at the house."

I nodded and wondered what he'd said to Adam, but I didn't ask.

David must have known what I was thinking, though, because he put his arm around me. "Adam didn't say anything."

His smile didn't look trustworthy, but I ignored it. I motioned toward the gate. "Let's get going."

David held my hand as we walked home, and we talked more about his trip and what he would do when he got back to England. About halfway to my house, I looked up at him at one point as we were talking. He looked down at me and kissed me. Afterward, he shook his head and frowned, saying, "It's really unfair that I only met you today."

"I know." Then I told him what I'd been telling myself. "But it's not like we're really geographically compatible."

He laughed and replied, "That's true." We continued walking—this time not talking until he said, "I want to see you tomorrow, but I can't. I have to spend the day with the family, and Adam has this date set for tomorrow night."

Of course I already knew the answer, but I had to play dumb and ask, "A double date with Meredith and Jennifer? Is that why she was at the lockers?"

"I'm afraid so."

"You'll have fun," I said, trying not to snort.

When we got to my porch, I felt it immediately: finally, I was standing at my door with a guy and it wasn't weird or awkward. Instead, David bent down and gave me an amazingly long kiss. *Here we go again*, I thought. The kisses were getting a little too passionate for a front porch, and my body was glued to his in a way that my mom would not have liked the neighbors to see. I needed to stop it.

"This is a nice goodbye," I said. "But now I really do need to go."

"Damn. I hate this." He groaned as he placed his forehead to mine.

I wanted to stay there, but that confidence that had been building somewhere inside me came out. I could do this. I could be the one to end it.

I whispered, "Enjoy the rest of your time here, travel safe, and take care of yourself."

Taking my face in his hands, he kissed me before saying, "You look after yourself, princess."

If any other guy had called me princess, I'd have laughed in his face, but coming from David, it made me want to pounce on him again. Good thing I was on my front doorstep. I kissed him again and stepped inside.

The following morning, my mom was out running errands when Lisa called to tell me she and Rachel were dropping by. They wanted details on David. When they came over, we hung out in the living room, but Rachel was literally bouncing in her seat. I could tell this was going to be girl talk in the raw.

"So, tell us everything," she said, grinning away.

"There's not much to tell." I giggled at the end, which totally betrayed my words.

"I *heard* you last night. And it sounded good. So what happened?"

I realized I needed to set something straight. "Well, I'm still a virgin if that's what you want to know."

"But you had an orgasm. I heard it." Her tone was definitive like she was a detective, and after a moment her eyes widened. "Oh my God! Did he go down on you? Is that how you came?"

An image of David—down there—went through my mind. *I wish.* Shaking my head, I smiled. "That would've been nice, but no. You won't believe this, but we both had all of our clothes on. Mostly it was just a lot of bumping and grinding."

Rachel cackled. "*A lot* of bumping and grinding, I'd say, if you had an orgasm!"

"I don't believe it," Lisa blurted out with a guffaw.

"Believe it," I said.

Rachel was spazzing. "Ah! That's so damn hot. Not quite as hot as oral sex, but wicked hot. And with your clothes on? How? I mean, really. What does he have, a magic dick?"

I held up my hands. "I told you. I don't even know!"

After we stopped laughing, Lisa asked, "So what about tonight? Do you two have plans?"

"No. None at all. He's with family right now, and tonight he's stuck on a date with Jennifer, Meredith, and Adam."

"Yuck," Lisa said with the sneer she usually saved for school cafeteria food. "Why is he doing that if he was messing around with you last night?"

"Adam and Meredith set it up. I didn't tell him what he was in for," I said with a snort. "Regardless, I think it's fine to end things where they are with him."

"That sucks." Rachel crossed her arms. "He would have been the perfect guy for you to have sex with for the first time."

"You have got to be kidding me," I said, looking at her like she was insane. "The last thing I need to be doing is mooning over someone I'm never going to see again."

"That's the beauty of it, though. There wouldn't be any awkwardness for you. You'd just get it out of the way with this amazing guy."

"Rachel, you're crazy," said Lisa. "Most women don't work that way. I mean, I don't, and I'm not even a virgin anymore."

"Well, that's all well and good," Rachel said. "But hot guys with an accent like Sir David I-Can-Make-You-Come-With-Your-Clothes-On don't come around that often. That's a once in a lifetime opportunity."

We made plans to go to Juanita's that night. I offered to be the designated driver because, after last night, I thought I needed to have my wits about me. Dinner was fun but uneventful. Rachel took it as an opportunity to grill Lisa about Peter.

Lisa played everything down and smiled. "We just kissed. He's doing the college thing. I'm stuck in high school with y'all and my special friend Ben waiting in the wings for me."

We left early since Rachel said she needed to meet up with Tom later that night. As we exited the restaurant, walking along the sidewalk were David, Adam, Meredith, and Jennifer. I turned to Rachel immediately and said, "Did you know about this?"

Rachel smirked. "I have my ways."

Thank God, I'd actually gotten a little done up for tonight even though it was just with the girls.

Adam spied us first. "Hello, ladies."

David smiled straight at me. "Evening, Nicki."

After the seven of us met on the sidewalk and exchanged some polite hellos, David came over and grabbed my waist from the side. "It's good to see you again."

Jennifer let out an obviously nervous laugh. "You two know each other?"

"For the last thirty-six hours," I said. I was pretty sure she hated me.

Dimwitted Meredith was smart enough to know she needed to get her friend out of an awkward situation. She tugged on Adam's shirt. "I'm hungry. Let's go eat."

"Right," he said. He turned to David. "Shall we?"

"You three go inside," David said, pointing to the door. "I want to talk to Nicki for a moment."

"Okay. See you in there," Adam said. He glanced at me, and I swear his lips were curling into a smirk as he guided Meredith and Jennifer into Juanita's.

"Nicki," Rachel said, "Lisa and I will meet you at the car."

As everyone walked away, David leaned down and gave me a kiss like we were about to go at it right there and then in the parking lot.

I pulled away and laughed. "I'm happy to see you, too, but I think you should go inside. Your date is waiting."

"Don't remind me." He let his hands rest in the small of my back and smiled. "I think Adam owes me one for setting me up with that dull bird. She's nice, but I'd rather be with you."

Hearing he preferred me to Jennifer the Pug tickled me pink. I gave him a kiss on the cheek. "I'd rather be with you, too."

"Then it's fate that we've met again. How do I get to see you later?"

I wanted to, but I knew it was a bad idea. What good was going to come of it? I just saw emotional messiness all around. I shook my head. "That would be nice, but I don't think it's a good idea in the end. I mean, let's leave what was great—great, okay?"

"You are far too mature for me," he said, stroking my hair.

I stood on my toes and gave him another a peck. "Goodbye. Take care of yourself."

"You do the same, princess," he said before planting another one on me. This time, he rubbed his dick against me.

"Are you trying to show me what I'll be missing?" I giggled.

"Maybe."

"You're incorrigible."

"I'll take that as a compliment." He lowered his lips to mine again. Damn, he could kiss. When he pulled away, he studied me for a moment and said, "I've been thinking. Since I'll never be here again, I don't think you should give up on my numb-nuts cousin just yet. All right?"

"Right," I said with a little huff. I patted his arm. "Now get back in there with your date."

When I got to the car, Rachel said, "You can start thanking me now."

"Thanks, Rachel. That was nice."

"So what are the late-night plans?" Lisa asked.

"No plans," I said.

"You have got to be fucking kidding me, Nicki," Rachel said, trying to sit up straight in a bucket seat. "You said no to the guy?"

"Listen, thanks for setting this up for me. That was really sweet, but like I said, I don't think it's a good idea for me to get caught up in a guy I'll never see again starting tomorrow."

"Fine," Rachel grumbled. "Anyway, it wasn't hard to figure it out. Tom told me where they were going."

"Well, thanks for thinking of me," I said.

Rachel shook her head. "I'm just telling you, Nicki. David and his magic dick are an opportunity of a lifetime. Not to be missed."

"I know, I know." I sighed. "You'll be able to say I told you so if I ever regret it."

Chapter Eight

On Monday morning, Adam was at the lockers again with Meredith at his side. They weren't talking, and I swore she gave me an irritated look. Maybe I had ruined their double date on Saturday night because of my fling with David. *Excellent.* I felt a little smug about it.

Adam just gave me a flat hello, and that was it. *Fine by me.* I would never feel the need to discuss the weekend's events with him.

So he startled the shit out of me in English when he said, "You know, you broke David's heart on Saturday night." I looked up from my book but wished I hadn't. I was sure I was all wide-eyed and red-cheeked. Why was I so embarrassed?

He had said it sort of matter-of-factly, but he was grinning — like he knew something I didn't. And of course that was true. He'd talked with David. Who knew what David had told him about me? David seemed like a wonderful guy, so I didn't think it would have been anything bad, but it was enough to make Adam grin like the stupid Cheshire Cat. I knew there was a reason I hated *Alice in Wonderland.*

Then I remembered something else: Adam never had a crush on me the way I had on him, so he wouldn't be uncomfortable talking about how I'd hooked up with his cousin — unlike me.

Regardless, I thought I did a pretty good job at answering in a normal voice. "Yeah. I really doubt that."

"Then you would be wrong."

His eyes told me he was enjoying teasing me, and there was his charming smile again, tugging at my heart. I needed to stop the conversation; it was too unnerving.

I gave him half a smile before saying, "We'll disagree, then," as I turned toward the front of the class.

He stopped me mid-turn, though. "So, are you going to read the book again?"

"Excuse me?"

"*To Kill a Mockingbird*? You said you knew it well. Are you going to read it again?" He had stopped grinning. No longer teasing me, he seemed to really want to talk.

The thought hadn't even crossed my mind. I had stuck the book in my locker once we'd gotten it, and I hadn't thought of it again. *Great.* I must have been unconsciously avoiding it because reading about Scout would only remind me of Lauren.

I sighed. "I remember enough of the story to get by in class, but I guess I've got to read it again when we write a paper on it. I mean, I don't exactly have quotes memorized by heart. I'm going away this weekend. Maybe I'll read it then."

"Oh. You're not going to be here? Where are you going?"

"Just to see my dad. He lives in Chicago." Why was Adam talking to me so much? We hadn't spoken like this in weeks.

"Do you miss your father?" he asked.

That was it; time to end the chat. He'd looked so sincere when he asked me, but I wasn't going there. I wasn't going to let him in my head again. Lisa was right: he was trouble.

I looked at Adam warily and gave him an answer that was suspiciously vague but the God-honest truth at the same time: "Some." Hopefully, he'd get the hint that I was ending the conversation. I turned to the front just in case he didn't.

The rest of the week was uneventful, except that Meredith was at the lockers all the damn time. Though she hovered over him, she and Adam didn't talk much, or at least he didn't talk to her. The vibe was so awkward, it was almost as uncomfortable for me as when they used to paw each other.

Sylvia also would periodically show up, which seemed to shoo Meredith away. I liked that, but I also liked talking with Sylvia, who was always chatty and a little quirky. She didn't seem shy anymore. But the problem with Sylvia was she would just run off, leaving me alone with Adam. He would try to keep the conversation going, but I'd fend him off. I thought about my time with David last weekend, and in the end, it really didn't change anything with Adam. I still needed to keep my distance from the guy.

Adam must have thought otherwise. I guess in his mind, my messing around with his cousin meant that we were friends. That's why he was trying to speak with me again.

I knew it couldn't work that way for me. I couldn't be friends with him. I would just end up wanting to be more than that, and then I'd be right back in the same place. This time, though, there would be no one to blame but myself.

Before English on Friday, Adam asked, "So when are you leaving for Chicago?"

"Soon after school. My mom's picking me up and taking me to the airport."

"You're missing a great film at Tom's tonight—*Naked Lunch*."

"Believe me. I would rather be at Tom's than at my dad's." I'd frowned as I said it, so I shrugged to make light of it. There was nothing light about it, though. This would be my first trip to see him without Lauren.

"Why don't you want to see your dad?" Adam asked. Not waiting for an answer, he added, "Don't you two get along?"

I couldn't help but flash him a look. I knew I had asked for it with my comment, but his question was out of bounds. Even if I weren't trying to avoid him, I wouldn't answer that question. It was pretty personal, and we weren't friends.

Adam backed away from me in his seat. "I'm sorry. That was terribly rude of me."

"Don't worry about it." I glanced at him and saw that he really did look sorry. Feeling badly, I added, "It's not a big deal."

Adam nodded. You could tell that he knew not to press it, because he went back to his reading.

As much as I could complain about Dad, he was smart and nothing got by him. When he picked me up at O'Hare in Chicago, he saw the book in my hands and said, "I thought you read that a few years ago."

"Yeah, but I'm going to have to write a paper, so I need to reread it."

He kissed my forehead. "We'll see that you get some downtime."

That sounded good to me. By the time we got to his house in Lincoln Park, I was worried because I was sure that I had exhausted all the small talk I could think of about my life. What in the hell were we supposed to talk about for the next two days? I'd never spent so much time alone with my dad.

His house was gigantic considering only he lived there. Dad might have left Mom for another woman, but apparently he didn't to want to live with her either. He told us he wanted a house with a lot of bedrooms so that Lauren and I had our own rooms, just like we had in Texas. He had even let us do whatever we wanted with them. I'd gotten the idea to paint each wall with a different shade of the same color. Mine was four hues of purple, and Lauren had four different blues.

Mom had explained the divorce very simply to Lauren and me: "Your dad and I just got married too young." I wanted to believe her, but it's not like they were eighteen when they married. They were twenty-three. Twenty-three still sounded too young for me person-ally—marriage wasn't on my farthest horizon—but for back then it was reasonable. Mom never lied to us, so I knew her statement was just a generalization of something more specific that she didn't want to go into.

As I went up the stairs to my room, I stopped midway. I realized I was about to see Lauren's room—right across the hallway from mine. Had Dad changed it?

When I got to the top of the stairs, Lauren's door was closed, so I couldn't tell, but I had to know. I didn't even look at my room before I started opening her door. It opened an inch, and I saw the blue walls.

It's the same, I thought.

I was going to close the door, but I had an urge to see more. I was curious. Had anything changed? As I opened the door wide open, I saw that nothing was different: the same sheets, the same posters, and the same stuffed animals. Dad hadn't touched a thing.

Even the brush that she'd accidentally left here in May was still sitting on the desk. I went over and picked it up. It still had some of her light brown hair in it. I touched the strands with my thumb. *Lauren's hair.* Lauren's hair was here. And like everything else about her death, there was no one for me to share it with, so I said aloud to myself, "But *she's* not here anymore."

More than anything in the world, I wanted her with me right in this room. I wanted to tell her everything that had happened in the last few months. I wanted to hear about her. I simply wanted to be with her again. The tears began.

When I heard someone walking down the hall, I turned around and saw Dad standing in the doorway. His face was composed, but his voice broke. "I'm really sorry, Nicki." He took a moment, and his voice become clearer. "I should have warned you that the room was like this."

Still crying, I whispered, "It's okay. I didn't even think about it until now."

Dad walked over to me and put his hands on my shoulders. He looked around the room, saying, "Michelle suggested I not do anything without talking with you first. I know that your grandmother took things upon herself to redo Lauren's room in the other house. I'm happy to do whatever with this room as you like, and I mean that. You can leave everything like it is, or I can make it into a room for you, or we can pack everything up and turn it into another guestroom."

I had no idea what to say. Michelle had thought about this? Dad's annoying mistress/girlfriend/whatever she was? I tried to talk, but my tight throat wouldn't allow it. So I whispered, "I don't know. We can talk about it later." With the back of my hand, I wiped the tears off my face.

Dad squeezed my shoulders two times and left. I felt trapped. Should I stay in her room for a while, or should I skulk away? I decided I couldn't deal with anything right then. So after I laid the brush back down on the desk, I wanted to leave, but when I got to the doorway I was stuck. What was I supposed to do now? It felt mean to shut the door but strange to have it open. I decided shutting it would be easier.

The next morning, I dragged myself out of bed when I couldn't tolerate the sun in my eyes any longer. Dad had been clomping around the house for the last two hours, so it wasn't like I was getting any sleep. I was just avoiding getting up. I'd thought this trip might suck, but not this much. When I made it downstairs after a shower, it was nine.

Dad smiled at me. "Don't feel bad for sleeping late. I'm just a little jealous."

Late? It was nine on a Saturday—that was early. I mumbled, "Sorry," and got a glass of water.

"So, I don't have any plans for the day, but Michelle wanted to see you again. She's coming over for dinner."

Great. Michelle—Dad's gorgeous girlfriend who may or may not have been the one he'd had an affair with. I tried not to think about it because my parents' sex lives were not something I wanted to concentrate on. From the way Mom always bristled at Michelle's name, though, I thought it was safe to say Michelle was the other woman.

Dad deserved a typical teenage response for springing this one on me, so I said, "Okay," while I searched for some cereal.

We spent the morning at the grocery store and Home Depot because that's where Dad spent every Saturday morning. His house was old, and he liked tinkering with it. Only in the afternoon did I find some time to myself. Rather than reading like I should have been doing, though, I decided to venture into Lauren's room again.

Closing the door behind me, I admired the different colors of blue, which looked pretty with the afternoon light. It looked like there were thirty blues rather than just four. I sat down on the bed and sighed. *So far so good,* I thought. I moved toward the top of the bed and leaned against the pillows and headboard. My eyes studied the room as I tried to remember Lauren as I'd always seen her in there, hanging something up in the closet, shoving the bottom dresser drawer closed, talking on the phone, or writing at her desk.

I'd always had too good of an imagination. Even the everyday memories of her were too vivid. I closed my eyes in pain. *I wish you were here, Lauren. Oh, how I wish you were here.*

In July, some unthinking neighbor at home had given Mom a book on the stages of grief. She'd accepted it with a smile and a "Thank you," but closed the door and immediately threw it on the bottom shelf of a rarely used bookcase. I was curious, so I'd dug it out and skimmed the book. I didn't understand some of the stages at all.

The first one was supposed to be denial, but I had never been in denial about Lauren's death. All of my medical problems, plus Mom's, made denial pretty impossible. There was no refuting there had been an accident.

I had also never been in the angry stage. I must have skipped it. With Dad always saying he wanted to kill the driver, even though he was already dead, Dad was angry enough for the entire family.

As for bargaining with God for Lauren to live again, well, I never did that. I mean, she was great, but she wasn't the Second Coming. I wasn't banking on miracles.

The other two stages were depression and acceptance, and I was stuck somewhere between the two of those. I'd accepted Lauren had died, but I wasn't over being sad. Was there even a way out of despair when missing someone was so painful? Where was the stage of simply missing someone so much that it hurt to breathe? And how long would that stage take?

Because right then, it seemed like it would never end. I had no memory of a life without Lauren, so a future without Lauren seemed bleak. My heart crumpled again, and I began to cry, but not my usual controlled tears. I was sobbing. When I realized I must be loud, I didn't care; I just put Lauren's pillow over my head.

I woke up when someone sat on the bed. After I saw it was Michelle, I was totally out of sorts. She was the last person I'd expected to wake up to. Why was she here? Why did I fall asleep?

I got up on my elbows. "Hi. I'm sorry. I didn't mean to fall asleep."

She smiled kindly, which only made her prettier as her white teeth contrasted with her black hair. "It's okay. I just wanted to say hi."

"Okay. How are you?"

"Good. Did your father tell you about the room?"

"Yeah, that's really nice of you to think of me like that."

"Not at all." She waited a moment and then asked, "Did you know my mom died when I was in high school? I was an only child, and she'd meant the world to me."

Not expecting a conversation like this with Michelle, I just shook my head and fumbled for something to say. "Um. I'm sorry. That must have sucked." Ouch. That sounded terrible.

"Yeah, I would say it sucked," she said with a snicker. "It still sucks."

"Sorry, Michelle. That came out wrong."

"No. It's not a problem. I just wanted you to know, and not because I think I know what you're going through, because I don't. I don't know what it's like to be sixteen and to almost die and to lose your sister—not to mention have your mom almost die, too. I just wanted to tell you that in my experience it does get easier, but it takes a long, long time. So that's why I told your father to let you keep the room however you like."

I nodded, but I could feel my face contort again. I couldn't believe I was going to cry in front of Michelle, but I was. I couldn't control it. I was such a mess. She was talking to me in a way that no one else had. She reached over and gave me a big hug.

I looked up over her shoulder and thought that Lauren would find the scene very funny—me bawling on her bed while hugging Michelle, of all people. The thought made me smile, which let me compose myself enough so I could get out of the situation.

Pulling away, I dried my tears with my shirt. "Thanks, Michelle. That means a lot to me." That was about all the emotion I could handle for the day, so I followed it up quickly with "What are we having for dinner?"

Chapter Nine

On Monday morning, Adam was at his locker alone. He gave me a pretty cheery greeting, asking about my trip.

I kept it short and light, wanting to get into class before Meredith descended upon us, but he asked, "So what are you doing for Halloween? It's this Saturday, yes?"

And then Meredith walked up and said, "Hi," before giving us both a suspicious glare. Adam stiffened immediately.

I'm outta here, I thought, but I answered Adam before I left. "I'm laying low. See you later."

Halloween was Lauren's birthday, and she'd loved the fact that her birthday was a holiday where the only goal was to have a good time. Ever since I could remember, we'd always had a big open house that was an event for Lauren in addition to being a Halloween party. Our friends and their parents would come and hang out and use our house as a pit stop for trick-or-treating.

But this year, I had spent the last month doing my best to ignore everything Halloween-related around me. It was hard. A few weeks ago, Mom had announced that we should go to a movie together. I knew she'd want to do it on the thirty-first, and I was right. We didn't need to have a conversation about it. We both knew the holiday should be avoided.

When I sat down in English late in the day, Adam spoke to me as if there hadn't been a five-hour gap in our conversation. "So what does 'laying low' mean for Halloween? Remember, I don't know much about what you Yanks do, but it sounds like a good time."

"I'm going to a movie with my mom," I said with a shrug.

"Really?" His looked at me with disbelief. "You're joking, right?"

I raised my eyebrows and smiled a little smugly. "Nope."

"I thought you might be going to Lance's party."

My stomach twisted. "No. Not this time."

"Do you and your mum go out often?"

I took a breath. I was tired of the continual questions that led nowhere with this guy.

"No, we don't," I snapped. "I'm going because Halloween is my sister's birthday, and I can't stand the idea of celebrating it this year. Does that answer your question?"

Shock spread over his face. *Got him.* He was silent for a moment before saying, "Nicki, I had no idea. I'm sorry for prying. It was very rude."

I was so irritated, but I also didn't want to make a bigger deal out of it than I already had. "Apology accepted," I said and turned away from him. I looked at Lisa because she must have been listening. She was more than listening, though; she was glaring at Adam. My eyes flicked over to the side for a second to see what he was doing. He never looked up from his book. After class, he skipped going to his locker, so I didn't see him again.

Whenever he *was* at the lockers the rest of the week, any conversation was very superficial. I also noticed about mid-week that Meredith was never around anymore. When I mentioned it to Lisa, she gave me a disapproving look and said, "Not your business, Nicki."

I smirked and rolled my eyes at her. "It was just an observation."

"Okay. I'll play," she said with a giggle. "Maybe the stress of the football season is getting to her."

For all the dread that I'd felt about Halloween, the actual night wasn't that bad. Probably because I had been preparing for the worst for so long, I was okay. Mom wanted to eat dinner early before we went to the movie, which meant that we were gone for hours from the house. By the time we came home, Halloween was over in the neighborhood.

Late that night, though, I was in my bathroom when the door to Lauren's room caught my eye. After having been in her room at Dad's, surely I could walk in there now. Would it have the same effect on me? Mom was already in her room, so I could go in there without freaking her out. I didn't think she'd like seeing me in there. She certainly never went in.

When I turned the doorknob, the door was stuck from the new paint job; no one had visited the room since it had been redone. There was a loud crack when I opened it, and the room was dark with the shades down. The shades were all that was left in the room because Grandma had even gotten rid of Lauren's old curtains. The walls were all stark white, and the carpet had been cleaned. Nothing distinguished the room anymore. There wasn't even a hanger in the closet. I felt more of a connection with Lauren when I opened the fridge and saw her favorite mustard still sitting in the door.

Shaking my head, I wondered what Grandma had done with all of Lauren's stuff. I could have called and asked her directly, but I wanted to talk with Mom. I felt like this weekend might be the one when I could.

There was another question, though, that I wanted to ask but knew I shouldn't: *why* had they taken all the things from Lauren's room? Dad hadn't done it. Why had Grandma, and why had Mom agreed?

About midway through our breakfast the following morning, I found the courage to ask. "I was looking for a notebook from last year. I think I had left it in Lauren's room. Where are those boxes?" It was a lie, but a very white one.

Mom took a sip of coffee as if to prepare herself for the discussion. "Grandma thought it best that we put everything away for a while. Lauren's personal items are all boxed up in the attic. It would be pretty difficult to get them down."

I knew I was looking at her like she was nuts, but I kind of felt that way. I couldn't believe what she was saying to me. Mom usually talked straight with us; now she was feeding me total bullshit.

Difficult for whom, you or me? And in what way? Are the boxes heavy, or will they make you cry if you open them? How could it possibly be that Dad had thought more about how I'd deal with Lauren's death than Grandma and my mother? What alternate reality was I living in?

I got a huge lump in my throat. I knew I shouldn't pick a fight with Mom over Lauren, but I was so angry and hurt. I looked down at my cereal, focusing on the milk bubbles, and said, "Why didn't anyone ask me?"

"Oh, Nicki. I'm sorry." She put her hand on my arm. "Grandma was just doing what she thought was best."

Best for whom? Not for me. Probably not for Mom. Sure, she was fully functional to the outside world, but if you saw her insides like I did every day, that was another story.

I kept staring at my food, but the tears welled up. I had to say it. "I don't see how that could possibly be best."

Mom continued to stroke my hand, saying, "Nicki, it would be hard however we did things."

She was right about that. I wiped the tears from my eyes, but I wasn't going to let this go. "I really do need that notebook. Can I go up in the attic and get it? Not right now, but maybe some afternoon." I added the second part so that she knew she didn't have to be here for it.

She gave me a wary look. She was right to be suspicious—I would never go up there normally, especially for schoolwork. She also must have decided to let it go, because she shrugged. "Sure."

"Thanks." That was all I said. But what I thought was, *This is so fucked up.*

"Nicki, do you know what today is?" she said after clearing her throat.

"Uh, Sunday?"

"Yes. Sunday." She gave me her don't-be-a-smartass look. "It's All Saints' Day. I think you should go to church with me."

Two things had occurred since the accident: Mom went to church more and I went to church less. That was a feat on my part because I hadn't had great attendance to begin with. But she hadn't pushed me much since the accident, and church was one of those things she'd relinquished on.

I'd had enough Sunday school, though, to know the significance of the day. She wanted me to go this Sunday because of Lauren. It wasn't the time to try to weasel my way out of going, so I simply said, "Sure."

She nodded and rose from the table. On her way out of the room, she called back, "And can you make sure that you look presentable?"

The deadly wardrobe and hair discussion. It always was a bad one, but it was particularly nasty when it came to church. Given the reason Mom wanted me to go, I knew I should stay away from this fight, too. I sighed. "Yes, Mom."

And I did as I said. I wore the navy boat-neck dress that Mom actually liked even though I'd gotten it at a thrift store. I even pulled my hair back. She said I looked like Jackie O until I put on my choker necklace with big white beads. She wrinkled her nose. "Now you look a little like Barbara Bush, but I'll take it."

The church service was actually fine. We sat in the back, and I could totally zone out. I wasn't interested in listening to a single word about dead people and saints.

When coffee hour arrived afterward, though, I was itching to leave. My few friends had left quickly after church, so I was waiting around for Mom to stop gabbing with her gossip partners. As I stood off to the side, I read the little mini-history of the church someone had assembled in photos on the wall. I'd seen it a hundred times before. I turned around in boredom, and my eyes widened when Adam and his family walked in. I hadn't seen him in church, but there were a lot of people that Sunday.

Adam's father was distinguished and tweedy, and his mother was in a sharp suit, but she had a cheery smile. Sylvia looked even more adorable than usual, having ditched her Doc Martens for a pair of pointy-toed flats.

Adam must have seen me in church, because he strode toward me. He looked achingly handsome all dressed up — so fine that I *should* have noticed him in church. Somehow I mustered up an anxious smile when our eyes met. I was all shifty and nervous when he got to my side, but he seemed perfectly normal and at ease.

"Morning. I didn't expect to see you here," he said, his eyes shining.

He touched his tie as if remembering what he was wearing. It wasn't like I needed reminding how good he looked.

I clenched the side of my dress for support. "Hi. Yeah, well, it happens…occasionally."

"Same here. I usually watch football on satellite TV on Sunday mornings."

For a moment, I thought he meant American football, but then I clued in. "Oh. Soccer. Right. It would be on early here with the time difference, wouldn't it?"

"It is, but my mum thinks I should spend my Sundays differently."

"So does mine." Then I was at a loss for words, grabbing at my dress again. Somehow being with him outside the safe confines of school left me unable to make small talk with him.

My shyness must have amused him, because he gave me a huge grin. Out of nowhere, he declared, "You look lovely. You know, I've never seen eyes like yours before. They're so brown that they're almost black. They're amazing."

My mouth fell open. I eventually got a "Thank you" out, but I wasn't sure how audible it was. *Why did he say that?* I could feel flames take over my cheeks. *Great.* As if he needed more proof of how I really felt about him. I tried to make a joke out of it by grumbling, "You made me blush."

"I know." He had a cocky smile as he spoke, but his face softened and his voice lowered. "You look even prettier now."

And then I was speechless. For all my trying, I was right back where I'd started with Adam Kincaid: in the middle of a hopeless crush. I just stared at him, but I noticed something was different. He held my gaze, too. After a few seconds, my breath caught as I realized that wherever I was, he was right there with me.

"Nicki, I'm so sorry," he said, the words tumbling out of him. "Truly, I am."

I was confused for a minute because I didn't know what he was apologizing for. Then I remembered the Halloween discussion. With a quick shake of my head, I brushed it off. "Don't worry about it. Halloween was fine." But remembering the disastrous talk with Mom about Lauren's stuff, I let something escape. "And what wasn't fine isn't changing, so it doesn't matter."

"But it does matter, doesn't it?" His eyes seemed so earnest. "Maybe you could tell me about it sometime?"

Shrugging my shoulders at the thought, I choked out, "I don't know." How on earth would that possibly work? He had a girlfriend. I couldn't bare my soul to him; I'd be crushed by my crush.

"Nicki, really, I'm sorry for everything. I've made a mess of it all." He winced as he said it.

His apology was so heartfelt, I looked down and shifted my weight. When I looked up again, his grimace slowly morphed into a smile. "I just wish we could start all over again."

My heart stopped. Every possible fidget occurred one after the other. I touched my necklace, crossed my legs, and looked to the side before finding the right sentiment. When I looked into his eyes, they were shining at me. I grinned, but I stopped when I saw a hand on his shoulder.

The hand was older, and I looked up to see his mother. She smiled and said in an English accent that seemed a little closer to David's than Adam's, "Hello, I'm Judith Kincaid. You must be Nicki, Gloria Stuart's daughter."

I knew that I needed to stop being embarrassed and instead muster all of my manners to impress her. I smiled. "Yes. Hello, Mrs. Kincaid. It's a pleasure to meet you."

"The pleasure's all mine. I've heard a lot about you."

From who? I thought. She was still smiling warmly at me. Then I remembered David. She may have heard something from David. *Yikes. Don't want to go there.*

Luckily, I didn't have to respond before she said, "Maybe now that Adam's seen you here, he'll come to church more often."

My usual negative reaction to everything related to Adam came out. "I really doubt that," I said and immediately wanted to take it back.

Adam looked at me in disbelief. He must have thought I was being snarky to his mom.

Oh, God. There goes my first impression.

She looked at me quizzically. "Really, why's that, then?"

Uh oh. I had to dig myself out. I conjured up a little laugh. "I mean, I don't come to church that often either."

She smiled. "Well, it sounds like your mother and I have something in common."

"I think you do." She laughed with me as I said it. For some reason, I got the feeling she knew she was helping me out. Still, I decided that I needed to flee before I said something else inappropriate, irrational, or just plain rude. "I should probably find my mom. It was nice meeting you, Mrs. Kincaid. I'll see you at school tomorrow, Adam."

After we exchanged goodbyes, I spotted Mom and headed toward her. It was a miracle I was walking while my mind couldn't get over what Adam had said to me. I tried to make sense of it, but I couldn't.

I knew that how he treated me the next day at school would be the deciding factor if things had changed. I didn't want to tell Rachel and Lisa, though; it would be too humiliating if things ended up just like they'd always been.

When I got home, I watched endless reruns of *21 Jump Street* for the rest of the day to keep my mind off him. Like it worked — not.

Chapter Ten

On Monday morning, my stomach did flips as I made my way to the lockers. Adam was there alone with the same smile that he'd had for me the day before. I was so happy, until I spied Meredith coming from behind. I quickly started tackling my combination. Out of the corner of my eye, I noticed her hand him a note without saying anything.

Adam addressed her bluntly, "I called you yesterday."

It was obvious that whatever was going on was not good. Of course, I wanted to know details, but I didn't want to witness them firsthand like this. It was way too awkward.

I grabbed my books and heard Meredith snap at him, "And I called you back."

Wow. Iciness. Time to get out of here. I closed my door and muttered, "Have a good day."

Adam didn't show up at his locker the rest of the morning. Something was up, but what? As much as I didn't want to actually see the events unfold, I also didn't like the idea of having to fish for information from Rachel or Lisa. It turned out I didn't have to.

As usual, I went to the bathroom at the end of lunch. No one was ever in there then, but I always went to the farthest stall. I was readjusting my tights when I heard the door open and an incredulous voice ask, "No way. They broke up for good?"

Another voice replied, "I swear. Meredith told me this morning. It's finally a done deal, and she's a wreck."

It was totally creepy for me to hang out in a bathroom stall eavesdropping on gossip, especially gossip that mattered to me. I knew I should walk out, but I couldn't. I had to hear it. Desperate for an alibi, I pulled my tights back down and sat on the toilet.

The first girl's voice asked, "Well, what happened? I thought they were a great couple. They were so cute together. I mean, I even heard she lost her virginity to him this summer."

My eyes bugged hearing that. Meredith had been a virgin before Adam? *Wow.* We had all been wrong about her.

Then the voice with all the information answered, "Yeah, that's all true, but things weren't perfect, you know. Meredith said he always would run hot and cold with her, and things started to go downhill when school started."

There was no reason for me to take credit for it, but that last part made me smile. My smile got bigger when she added, "They haven't gone out since that hot cousin of his was in town."

"Gosh. I had no idea what was going on," the other girl said.

"She was so into him that I don't think she wanted people to know that things weren't good. She was crying before class. I told her she could do so much better."

I scrunched up my face because that was doubtful. Meredith's last boyfriend, Stacy, was a dumb football player who had no neck.

"You think so?" the other voice asked in doubt. "He's way cuter than Stacy."

"Adam seems weird to me. He's got some friends that are freaks. And Meredith says he's uncircumcised, which is totally disgusting if you ask me."

My hands flew to my mouth to stop myself from giggling. Rachel would laugh hysterically when she heard it. When I started to wonder what Adam's uncircumcised penis might look like, I got a little distracted.

"Uncircumcised? Eww. That is gross." That seemed to turn her opinion against him. "And you know what? You're right. He's hot and all, but there's something weird about him. That drama guy Tom he hangs with has got to be gay, and that girl Rachel is a total bitch."

I couldn't let that one go. I flushed the toilet again, tugged my tights up my legs, and stepped out to the sinks. Well, there they were — Brittany Taylor and Cici Arnold, two very popular airheads. I barely knew them, and I was pretty sure they knew little or nothing of me.

I smiled as I started to wash my hands.

Brittany scowled at me. "You were eavesdropping."

Drying my hands, I was a polite bitch. "It was hard not to. I was here first. You should've made sure that you were alone."

I turned, and as I opened the door, I heard Cici say, "She's friends with Rachel."

"Well, she's a bitch, too," said Brittany.

Grinning, I left the bathroom. None of it really changed anything for me, but the details were fascinating. I couldn't wait to tell Lisa and Rachel.

Adam wasn't at the lockers before English, and then he walked into class late. He gave me a half-smile and a "Hello," but he didn't look happy at all. The day must have sucked for him. I wondered what he would think about me eavesdropping on two of the silliest girls at Bellaire High School discussing his uncircumcised penis. I had to stop myself from laughing.

Lisa smiled at me and whispered, "What's so funny?"

I shook my head. "I'll tell you later." Pressing my lips together to keep from smiling, I saw out of the corner of my eye that Adam was staring into his book. He was obviously not reading a word of it, and he didn't look up the entire period.

After class, I went to my locker to get my economics book for the test the next day. A few hours of rote memorization were all it was going to take to study for it, so I'd have plenty of time for a gossip session with Lisa and Rachel. Just as I was about to leave, Adam walked up. He looked grim.

"Bye, Adam," I said with a small wave. "Have a good night." *What do you say in a situation like this?*

"You, too." He looked like he might say more, but instead he just started to work his locker combination.

When I got home, it didn't take long for my phone to ring with Rachel saying, "So I'm guessing you know."

"Yes, but only because I overheard a gossip session between Brittany Taylor and Cici Arnold while I was in the bathroom."

Rachel squealed, "Oh my God. I'm coming over. If Lisa is free, I'll get her, too."

By five, Lisa and Rachel were in my living room. Lisa had only begrudgingly tagged along. "I still don't trust the guy, Nicki."

Ignoring her last comment, I urged them on. "Whatever. This is good gossip."

"Is that why you were laughing to yourself in English?" Lisa asked.

"Sort of. I saw that Adam was having a bad day, which isn't funny." I snickered. "But then I started laughing because he would feel ten times worse if he knew that Meredith had told half the cheerleading squad that he was uncircumcised."

Rachel, God love her, started bouncing up and down and screamed, "Oh my God!"

Lisa burst out laughing, but then cocked her head to the side. "Hmm. I guess they really don't do that as much over there."

Still giddy, Rachel said, "That's the gossip jackpot—like, I can't even tell Tom. He would be pissed at me for repeating it."

"Adam's not my favorite person," said Lisa, pursing her lips, "but that really is shitty of Meredith. How fucking stupid and naïve is she that she would tell Brittany that? She has diarrhea of the mouth."

"C'mon, Lisa. We are so not above talking graphically about guys' penises," I said. I also couldn't believe that she had defended Adam.

"I guess so, but it feels like she violated a confidence."

"My problem is how I can ever talk to him again without thinking about what his dick looks like." Rachel giggled.

"So, what else did you hear?" said Lisa, turning to me.

"I heard that she lost her virginity to him."

"Lucky bitch." Rachel scowled. "And here I thought she was a slut all this time, but instead she gets to lose it to a guy like him."

"And I heard that he was hot and cold with her—like sometimes he was into her and then sometimes not."

"That would be his M.O.," Lisa said.

"Anyway," I said, dismissing her comment, "apparently for the last few weeks he's been all cold. And today they broke up. I saw them at the lockers this morning, and something was definitely weird. I guess they broke up after that."

"That's what I heard." Rachel nodded. "Adam caught up with Tom as we were walking to drama. I went on ahead so I didn't listen firsthand, but later Tom told me a little. I think Adam and Meredith both cut a class to talk. The conversation went poorly because Meredith didn't really see it coming."

Then Rachel shook her head and squinted. "And it's stupid that she didn't expect it because apparently he's wanted to break up with her for weeks. I got pissed at Tom when he told me that today. He wouldn't admit that he'd known it. Anyway, that's all I got from him — and all I probably will get. He thinks I would just go tell you whatever I heard."

"Well, wouldn't you?" Lisa questioned as though testing her loyalty.

"Of course!" Rachel snickered. "He's right not to trust me."

"Okay," Lisa said. "Then the discussion is over. They broke up. And we now know something about Adam's anatomy that we could have come up with ourselves had we thought about it."

Rachel smiled smugly. "Well, we can test that theory. Nicki, had you already thought about Adam's dick? Had you already figured out he was uncircumcised?"

"No!" I threw a sofa pillow at her. I wasn't about to tell her the truth.

"Touchy…I was just asking. Anyway, Lisa is right. There's not much else to say at this point."

"There's one other thing," I said to Rachel and raised my eyebrows. "Just so you know, Brittany and Cici called you and me bitches."

"Excellent!" she chortled.

When I was lying in bed after studying for my economics test, I finally let myself think about the fact that Adam was single. *Is that what he meant when he said he wished we could start over? He isn't dating Meredith anymore?* Maybe. An image leapt into my mind of the line of girls — all much better looking than me — who would die to go out with him. Then I remembered when he'd said I was lovely. I sighed and rolled over, trying to find some sleep.

Chapter Eleven

In my seemingly constant state of anxiety, I walked up to the lockers the next day. What was it going to be like talking to Adam, the single guy? We exchanged hellos, but he wasn't smiling. *Fine.* I didn't want to smile either.

I had my head in my locker when I heard him say, "I suppose you know about Meredith and me."

My hand stopped as it touched my folder. I couldn't believe he'd brought it up. I had to say something in return, so I looked from behind the door and nodded. "Um. Yeah."

"It's been…difficult." He shuffled his feet with unease.

What was I supposed to say? *I'm sorry? Ha!* The idea that they were broken up made me want to smile. And truth be told, I was a terrible person. I wasn't sorry that he was having a hard time with it. I felt badly for him, but not that much considering he'd brought it on himself and dragged me through part of it. Then I wondered why he was telling me about all this. I did *not* want to be his confidant about Meredith.

After a moment too long of silence, I simply stated a fact. "It's always hard, right?"

He nodded slowly. "I guess you're right."

"I hope things get better."

"They will," he said, his charming smile slowly forming. "I'll see you later."

For the rest of the week, Adam and I saw each other during school and when out with the gang, but we didn't really talk much. Occasionally, I'd steal a look at him and catch him looking at me. He'd always stop at once and turn away. In the back of my heart, I hoped he was simply waiting for an acceptable period of mourning before flirting with me again. I hated to think that day at church would be the last of it.

The following Monday, Mrs. Anderson started class by saying, "I have good news and bad news for you today. First, the bad news: your essay on *To Kill a Mockingbird* is due next Monday. It should be an analysis of the relationship between two characters of your choosing. The good news is that next week we'll watch the movie version of the book."

Everyone began laughing and chatting. Lisa turned to me and said, "That's cool, don't you think? I can do my trig homework in here. What do you think you're going to write on?"

I didn't say anything. I was panicking. I knew my tolerance for things that reminded me of Lauren. I wasn't going to be able to sit in class and watch that film without breaking down. How was I going to get out of this? Not to mention that I still hadn't picked up the book again. How was I supposed to write anything? But writing a paper in my room wasn't half as bad as watching Scout on the screen in a classroom full of people and thinking about Lauren the whole time.

"Nicki, hello? You didn't answer me."

Snapping out of it, I replied, "Sorry. I spaced out." An idea popped into my mind. "I think I'm going to write about Mayella and her dad."

"You're kidding me, right?"

"No." I had my reasons. I just didn't want to get into them with Lisa. I'd never told her about Scout and Lauren, and I didn't want to start the conversation now.

"You want to write about incest? About child molestation? Why? It's disgusting. Not to mention that it's one of the most depressing parts of the book."

I looked down for a moment. *No, the most depressing parts are anything to do with Scout.* I made light of it with a shrug. "Well, I bet no one else will write about them. And, besides, I think the topic will creep out Mrs. Anderson. She might give me an A just so she doesn't have to read it."

"Well, it creeps me out. I'm not sure what I'm writing about, but it definitely won't be about those two."

At the lockers after class, I heard Adam ask, "Why, Nicki?"

"Why what?" Adam had talked to me so little lately that I was startled simply by his voice. A vague question like that made me even more flustered.

As he leaned against his locker, I noticed how his green shirt contrasted with his eyes, and my heart sped ahead of my mind. He looked at me thoughtfully and asked, "Why would you write about those two characters? That's a grim topic."

Closing my locker door, I stared straight into his brown eyes that always seemed to melt away my walls. I sighed, as they'd done it again. "Remember when I told you that Scout reminded me of my sister? Well, I…I don't want to have to write about Scout. And she's interwoven with all the other characters. I can write about Bob and Mayella and avoid everything about her."

Adam nodded. "That makes sense." Not breaking his gaze, he asked, "How are things? We haven't talked for a while. I'm sorry I've not been myself." Afterward, he swallowed hard enough that I could see his Adam's apple move.

Whenever he was so direct and honest with me, I always bumbled through my thoughts out loud. This time was no exception. "What? How am I?" It came out sounding like I was also asking why he cared.

"Yes, how are you, Nicki?" he asked again with a small laugh.

Nobody had asked me that in a while. A pang of sadness hit my heart. What should I say? I didn't understand why he was asking now or why I was reacting the way I was. Instinctively, I went with the safe answer. "I'm fine."

But his eyes seemed so intent on me. Looking straight into them, I felt my throat close as I tried to answer. Thinking of the pain that hadn't changed, I cringed.

"Everything is the same. It's all the same." I looked down and whispered, "I wish it wasn't, but it is."

Even as I bit my tongue, I couldn't stop myself from saying something more—something I wouldn't have said if he were still dating

Meredith. I wanted to see if he really meant what he'd said about wanting us to start over. Raising my head to look into his eyes again, I confessed, "I do want to talk to you, but I can't…not yet."

Even though I had just put myself out there, I felt more at ease after I'd said it—probably because I felt every word of it.

I watched Adam's expression transform from one of intense sincerity to the same flirty smile that he'd had at church Sunday. He leaned in closer to me and placed his hand on my shoulder. "It's okay. I'll wait for you."

He'll wait for me? What does that mean? I thought about how mentally nutso I was. He might be waiting for a very long time. That made me giggle, which was good because I was tense. My entire body was fully aware that Adam Kincaid's hand was on it.

Still smiling, he squeezed my shoulder. "Why are you laughing?"

I shook my head. "No, no reason. It's…it's nothing." I gripped my books for some psychological leverage, as at that moment I personified a stammering idiot.

"I like it when you laugh." With that, he gently squeezed my shoulder again. His hand then followed the length of my arm all the way to my wrist before dropping at his side. The movement was so quick and light that most people wouldn't have noticed it, but to me it was slow and strong. Then he gave his locker a tap and said, "I'll see you tomorrow, Nicki."

"Sure…Have a good night."

Autopilot took over for my brain as I turned and walked home, and I remained that way for the rest of the night. I ate dinner, talked with Mom, watched TV, and even did homework, but the entire time I was totally engrossed in replaying the few sentences I had exchanged with Adam and remembering how he'd touched my arm. What it all meant, I wasn't sure. I could have called Lisa or Rachel and analyzed every last word and movement, but I was afraid to. While I wanted it to all mean something, I didn't want to get my hopes up.

My hopes only got higher and higher, though. The next morning after we got our books, he asked, "Shall we go into class now?"

I was stunned. He wanted to walk into class with me?

For the rest of the week, Adam and I chatted whenever we had a moment together. It was obvious now that both of us were going out of our way to be together. We met up at our lockers between every class and arrived earlier and stayed later at school than we used to. Things were different between us, with very little awkwardness, and we easily talked. He was charming and interesting, and even though we were from such different places, we seemed to have a lot to discuss. Most of all, he made me laugh, more than I had in months.

And as the week progressed, we had more fun together. I played stupid tricks on him, like whenever he was working at opening his locker, I would whisper random numbers to him. It never failed to elicit this silly, adorable giggle of his while he screwed up the combination. To get me back, he was constantly looking over my shoulder and teasing me about something I had written or something in my locker or bag.

Occasionally, he could make me blush, which he took a lot of pride in, always pointing it out to me. After one especially intense teasing session on Thursday afternoon that left me flaming red, I said, "You know, teasing can be a form of torture."

"Then I'd say we're equal." He leaned against his locker.

"How so?"

"Because you've been bloody torturing me for weeks and weeks now."

"What do you mean?" It might have seemed I was playing coy, but I honestly had no idea what he was talking about.

My lungs forgot to breathe as my entire focus went to his face inching toward mine. He was close enough to kiss me, but he didn't. Instead, he whispered, "You are far too clever and beautiful a girl not to understand."

I sucked in some air, and I swore I could taste his breath on mine. Being that close to him ignited something inside me. "If it's what I think it is, then the feeling is mutual."

"Good." The flirty, crooked smile appeared again on his face. "That makes me happy."

After that incident, I spent Thursday night wondering if he was going to ask me out. I knew Tom was going to be out of town, so there wasn't a convenient movie or party for us to see each other at.

On Friday morning, we were chatting before economics when he asked, "So what are you doing this weekend?"

Finally, I thought. *He's going to ask me out.* "Not much. Nothing is going on, and I've got a paper to write. How about you?"

"I had to write mine this week because we're going to Austin this weekend. My dad needs to meet a colleague at the University of Texas, so we're making a family trip out of it. We're leaving after lunch today."

I was bummed there would be no date, but I smiled at how he'd said "University of Texas." Anybody from Texas just called it UT, but with his accent it sounded regal. "Your father is a geologist, right?"

"Yes, at Cambridge. He's here consulting for some oil companies."

"Finding the right spots to drill?"

"Yes, so that they don't cock up the earth any more than they do already."

"That's a noble goal." I grinned. "So he's a professor? Has he stopped teaching?"

"He's on sabbatical." He inhaled like he was fixing to make an announcement. "We're only here for a year. We'll be going back home after the end of term."

At once, I did the math — basically, six months. Adam was leaving in six months. I would never see him again in six months. That wasn't a long time at all. Lauren had died almost six months before, but it felt like yesterday.

My eyes widened. *What in the world am I doing with him?* I was only going to get hurt. But who was I kidding? I was already hurt. And I couldn't hide it.

"Oh," I said flatly.

His forehead wrinkled. "Nicki, I'm sorry. I thought you knew." Then he shook his head. "No. That's not true. I *hoped* you already knew and that it didn't matter."

"It's okay. It's not a big deal." I bit my lip, which I soon realized was pretty much an international sign of not being okay. He got the signal immediately.

"No, it isn't okay." He cleared his throat and continued, "After everything you've been through this year, I'll understand if you don't want…" He grimaced and stopped. I waited for him to say something else, but he remained quiet.

If there was one thing I had learned from Lauren's death, it was how to be nonchalant — how to give a blank stare as if I didn't care when in reality I really, really did. So I did just that. I shrugged my shoulders, too, as if it was water rolling off my back. "I don't know."

Neither of us said a word, but our silence broke as the bell rang. I felt like it was tolling the end of the conversation and whatever burgeoning relationship we might have had. "We should go in," I said reluctantly.

Adam nodded toward the door, but he was uneasy. He looked like he still wanted to talk. I didn't, though. I skipped going to my locker for the rest of the morning until I knew he had left for the day. I had told him that I didn't know what I wanted, but I did.

There was no way I was getting close to someone I liked as much as him when he was just going to leave. Lauren was gone forever. I wasn't going to be abandoned again — at least not knowingly.

I was depressed. For the rest of the day, I did everything to hide it from Lisa and Rachel, but they could tell something was up. Lisa even commented I seemed glum. I told her that I had hit a rough patch with Mom about Lauren. That kept her from asking any more. It was easy to blame Lauren's death for being down because I wasn't lying. That sadness was a constant.

I thought about what Lauren might say to my using her death as an excuse for moping over a guy. I could just hear her grumble, "Don't blame me for something stupid you did." It made me smile — the only thing that did all weekend.

Chapter Twelve

On Monday morning, Adam was waiting for me at the locker, even though I was breezing in with only a minute to spare. He was really chipper, and I was friendly, but nothing like I'd been the week before. Over the last couple months, I'd learned my lesson with that guy. I had played with fire more than once, and I got burned each time. No more playing with matches.

At first he seemed a little hurt when I wouldn't respond to his teasing. That afternoon before English began, he asked, "So how was the book the second time around?"

"Honestly, I have never been able to read the book again. I…"

"You, okay, Nicki?" he asked hesitantly.

His face was full of concern. It was another kind invitation to talk. *Fuck it again*, I thought as I gave in. "I'm a little worried about having to watch the movie in here today."

"I think you should just bunk off. You won't miss anything."

Huh? What did "bunk off" mean? It sounded like a circle jerk at a boys' camp, but that couldn't be it. What if it did mean something sexual, though? I wasn't up for a conversation like that with Adam. But his expression didn't change, so I think sex wasn't really the context he'd meant.

I shrugged. "I should watch the movie and get it over with."

All those things about Scout that reminded me of Lauren really don't come out in the beginning of the movie, so I was doing just fine. Then there was the scene where Scout talks with Jem about their mother, who had died a few years earlier. I felt the tears coming, but I didn't want to give in and leave class. I didn't want to be like Mom and just put it all away in a box to be looked at maybe someday, maybe never. Yet, I also didn't want to display all of my emotions for my whole fucking class. I decided the easiest thing to do was put my head down and close my eyes.

I didn't want to look at Adam, so I faced Lisa. She was watching the movie, so she didn't see me. I still had to listen to the words, but having my eyes closed helped a lot. I ended up falling asleep.

I woke up to the lights and to Lisa's grin. "I can't believe you even fell asleep watching a movie in class. You're ridiculous. What do you do on a date?"

My eyes blinked at the light as I stretched and smiled. "I try not to fall asleep on dates."

At the lockers after class, Adam chuckled. "So are you going to catch up on your sleep over the next few days?"

"Well, it worked, didn't it? I don't think it's such a bad idea."

Adam looked at me quizzically for a moment. "Do you want—"

"I don't think so." It came out curt and sharp. I had no idea what he might have been asking me, but the outcome could only be bad. I almost added, *because I don't want to get destroyed in the process*, but he gave a nod as if he understood. I couldn't tell if he really did, so I wanted to acknowledge that he'd tried to be nice. "Thanks, though. See you tomorrow."

The rest of the week, Adam was withdrawn again. He must have gotten the picture.

Despite the fact that I knew Adam would be there, I went to Tom's on Friday because he was doing it up that night for *The Godfather.* He was cooking spaghetti and had been talking about it for weeks.

As soon as I entered Tom's living room, I found a single recliner where Adam couldn't sit by me; I didn't want to be awkward and uncomfortable for the whole night. When Adam walked in the room, he looked at me and then walked over to an empty space on the sofa and settled in. *Good.* Everyone was in the right place.

But after our spaghetti intermission, I went back to the recliner and found Lance there.

"Sorry, Nicki. Finders keepers."

"I'll remember this." I looked for another spot, and there was Adam moving over for me.

"Come and sit by me. You can have the arm end."

With no other option, I acquiesced. "Sure." *Must act calm, cool, and collected.* I sat down next to him as Tom started the movie again. I was once again incredibly aware of the precise property lines between Adam's and my personal space.

Luckily, I had a pillow to my right on the armrest that I could lean into and away from him. The pasta was sitting in my stomach like dead weight, bringing my eyelids down with it. As I was about to close my eyes and lean my head to my right, I caught Adam's eye. He wore a little smirk.

The theme music eventually filled the room, but I clung to my sleep. I was warm and cozy, yet after a while, I forced my eyes open. They widened even more as they registered that only millimeters away was the plaid fabric of Adam's shirt. My heart felt like it stopped, and it stayed stopped as I realized that my head was on his shoulder while my body was curled beside him with my hand on his chest. I felt his right arm around my back and his hand resting on my side. *Oh my God.* What had I done? I jerked up.

"Oh, God. I'm so sorry. How embarrassing." That was the understatement of all understatements.

"Why? It was nice," he said with a grin as he started slightly rubbing my back.

Nice? Horrifying! I'd literally thrown myself at him. My subconscious had taken over my physical being. I could feel my cheeks become fiery hot. I had to know what happened. "How did I get over here?"

"You were restless in your sleep and curled into me, so I put my arm around you. After that, you slept soundly."

What could I say to that? I then remembered there were about ten other people in the room who'd seen me sleeping on him. I was mortified. I couldn't think of a response that wouldn't make me an even bigger idiot than I already was. "Thanks. I promise I'll stick to my side next time."

In front of everyone, Adam moved his right hand up to my hair and smoothed it off of my face. He wore a small smile as he said quietly, "Please don't."

God, I wanted to kiss him, but I thought better of it. I looked over at Lisa who was smiling at me, albeit a little suspiciously. What world had I woken up to? Adam didn't mind me sleeping on him? Lisa was smiling at me being close to him?

When I looked back at Adam, he asked, "Can I give you a lift you home?"

"Sure. Thanks." For a split second, I wondered if I was dreaming, because I was not acting rationally.

As we got ready to leave, thankfully no one made any snarky comments. Rachel simply said her usual, "I'll call you tomorrow." Lisa nodded. And Tom was busy feeding Helga her dinner. He said to Adam, "See you after the break. Have a good trip." I wondered what that meant.

I was beyond nervous as Adam let me in his car. I needed to break the ice, so I asked him about the movie. He did some talking, which, if ever asked what he said, I would have never been able to repeat. I was too overwhelmed with the situation. I'm sure I sat there with my mouth open looking like a total dork.

When we got to my house, Adam cut the engine and smiled. "So are you going to tell me again that I can't walk you to your door?"

"Maybe," I said, returning his smile.

"Because this isn't a date?" He moved his hand to my hair.

"It's not a date because I try not to fall asleep on dates, especially literally on my date."

He laughed and continued to stroke with my hair. "I believe I overheard you saying something like that at the start of the week."

The conversation was light, but his fingers in my hair felt emotionally heavy. "I did," I whispered.

"Nicki," he said, his voice more serious, "about me leaving…I know it's complete shit, but please realize I'm taking a risk here, too."

I looked down. Guilt only added to the awkwardness of the situation. "I guess you are."

When I raised my head, he was moving toward me, and I instinctively leaned into him to meet his lips. The kiss began so softly, but sweet and nice didn't seem to be what I really wanted. I opened up my mouth to his, and our tongues met for the first time. After a moment, he murmured, "You don't know how long I've wanted this."

"If you told me, I wouldn't believe you anyway."

"God, I wish you would," he said before kissing me again.

It felt like we were both making up for lost time—not long into it, I was stroking his chest and arms, while he cradled my head with his other hand wandering to the lowest part of my back. I never knew that part of my body was an erogenous zone until I felt Adam's hand softly stroking it. The kisses were hard then soft and then hard and then soft, and my heart was in every one of them. It felt like his was, too.

After half an hour, I was dizzy, though it had felt like no time at all. My only proof it had been a while was my racing heart, uneven breathing, and swollen lips. He looked like he was in the same shape.

"I don't want to leave," he said, holding me tighter.

I knew I needed to check the time because it was getting late. I glanced at my watch; I had to end the night. "I really should get in. I try not to abuse my privileges."

He sighed. "I'm gone next week. My family's going to San Francisco for this Thanksgiving holiday of yours."

"Touring the States while you're over here?"

"Something like that."

"Then I'll see you when you get back." I was thinking that a week apart would be good. Maybe by then everything that had happened that night would sink in.

"Just let me walk you to your porch," he said stroking my cheek.

We held hands walking to my door, and I wanted to pinch myself to make sure all of this was real. When we reached the porch, he kissed my cheek. "Look after yourself whilst I'm gone."

"You too," I whispered.

With a tousle of my hair, he turned and walked to his car. I closed the door behind me and rested my back against it. Going against my better judgment, throwing caution to the wind, and leaving my sanity behind, I was grinning.

Chapter Thirteen

Waking up the next morning, I immediately smiled, though I probably had never stopped smiling from the night before. I felt the need to say it out loud as if to confirm the reason behind my happiness: "I kissed Adam Kincaid last night. More than once—like, a lot. Like, a lot a lot."

Hearing it aloud still didn't make it seem possible, but then I remembered his words to me: "*You don't know how long I've wanted this.*" My heart jolted, which caused a fit of snickering. Trying to smother some of my giddiness, I threw my pillow over my face, but that didn't control my feet tapping the mattress in excitement.

Unfortunately, my private party was abruptly interrupted by an annoying knock on my door from Mom. I wasn't about to kill my buzz any further by getting up to answer.

"Yes?"

"Good morning, Nicki. You were out late last night."

"Just at Tom's." I rolled my eyes. I had privileges, but my actions were monitored closely.

"I need to do some errands, so I'll be back in a couple of hours."

"Okay." I smiled at the good news. The house would be empty.

In less than twenty minutes, I had Rachel and Lisa in the living room with me. Rachel giggled. "Well, look at Miss Happy Face. We haven't seen that in a while. Well, maybe not since David was on the scene."

"Give it up now, girl," Lisa said with a smirk.

I was still grinning as I grabbed a pillow for emotional support. Was my mouth going to hurt after all this smiling? I quickly remembered that I needed information from them before I told them anything. "I need to know what you think first. What did people do when they saw me lying on him?"

Rachel looked unimpressed with the question. "All Tom said was 'Finally,' and I said, 'Amen.' We just kept watching the movie after that."

"That is such BS, Rachel," said Lisa, tossing a throw pillow at her. "We were trying not to laugh too loud. As for everybody else, well, most people just smiled or ignored it. Except for Lance…"

Lance. Bitchy, queeny, lovable Lance. The memory of David between my legs in Lance's backyard came to mind. *Uh oh*. He was a problem. "So…what did Lance say?"

"Lance made a comment like, 'It looks like Nicki has a thing for the entire Kincaid family,'" said Lisa. She waved her hand dismissively. "You know how he is."

Rachel wrinkled her nose. "He said it kind of loud, but Adam just laughed it off. You were dead to the world."

"Thank God." I considered it for a moment and said, "All in all, it sounds like I made out okay, though."

"Speaking of making out, how did that go?" asked Rachel.

"How do you know about that?" I sucked at playing dumb, so a giggle escaped, which annoyed Lisa.

She rolled her eyes. "Get real. Like you didn't spend the rest of the night making out in his car."

"Yeah." They were my best friends, but for some reason I felt shy talking with them about Adam. Why was that?

"Come on," she said more nicely. "You've been smiling since we got here, so I assume it was good."

Rachel answered for me. "Of course it was good! Like Adam Kincaid is going to be a bad kisser."

"She has a point." I giggled.

"Too bad he's away for a week," Rachel said.

"Yeah, it sucks. Last night was fun." I still had to ask the question, though. "So what do you think about it? Good or bad?"

"What?" Rachel sounded baffled. "Of course it's good. He's great. You've spent the entire semester like a lovesick cow. And the only person who is happier than the two of you is Tom. He's felt like he's been in the middle of this drama, so he's very happy to have it over. He didn't understand why things were so difficult for you two. Maybe it's because things have always been so easy for us."

That soured my mood a bit. "Well, nothing seems easy for me."

Lisa's face softened. "Oh, Nicki. This year has been really hard for you. It's really nice to see you happy."

She glanced at Rachel and took a deep breath. "Listen, Rachel didn't want me to say anything, but I feel that I have to say something—as a friend."

I stared at her, frightened. She flashed a look at Rachel, who scowled at her.

"What?" I gulped.

"Okay. Well, you know I'm judgmental."

"That's an understatement." It had come out super dry, so I added, "But it is one of the reasons why we love you."

First smiling at my response, Lisa then held up her hands as if to shield herself. "So, take this with a grain of salt. I worry that you're only going to get hurt by him. I think his dick rules his mind, but all guys are that way, so…whatever. And I know you're really into him, and I can understand why. He's leaving, though. It may be fun right now, but I don't think he will be good for you in the end."

She might as well have spoken her last words in Russian because I didn't understand them at all. It didn't compute. Adam? Adam would be bad for me? After last night, that seemed impossible.

It took me a moment or two to respond to her. "Thanks. I know you mean well."

"Oh, good. I'm happy to have that off my chest," she said, placing a hand to her heart. "You should know that regardless of everything, I'm glad that you're happy right now."

"So am I."

After they left, Mom came home, and she caught on almost immediately. "You're unusually cheery today. What's going on? Is there a new boy?"

Ugh. I didn't want Mom involved until the last possible moment. Yet I also didn't want her to be totally in the dark. Then she'd make too big a deal of it when she did meet him.

More than ever, I wished Lauren were here. She would've made the discussion light for all of us. I could hear her saying, "Aw, Mom, leave her alone. She's got a crush." Or she'd spill the beans all at once: "Mom, he is so cute, and he's got an accent, and he's even smart—well, at least smart enough for Nicki, maybe not for me." Instead, it was just Mom and me in all of our awkwardness.

"Someone new?" I shrugged. "Maybe. Not sure yet."

Mom raised her eyebrows and turned away, but I caught her smiling. Oh well. It made me smile, too.

Just as Lauren and I always had, I spent Thanksgiving with Dad while Mom went on a beach vacation to Mexico with some friend. Dad always flew his mother in from Austin for the holiday. My Grandma Johnson was much older than my other grandparents. Even though she was warm and loving, she was kind of a mean old biddy. It made her pretty funny because she always said what she thought, which meant she said lots of rude and inappropriate things. Lauren had adored her.

She was also very, very Catholic and hated the fact that my parents had divorced. Any time it came up in a bad way or even when it was just mentioned without too many people around, Grandma would always say under her breath, "Never would have happened if Joseph were alive." I bet she was right.

Grandpa Joe had been a very stern man who'd always had a hold on Dad, even when he was an adult—Dad was an only child and devoted to his father. But Grandpa Joe had died a few years before the divorce, after a long battle with cancer. Looking back, his death had seemed very natural to me because he'd been so old, and the cancer had just slowly taken everything away from him. I couldn't really remember a time that he hadn't had cancer. Grandma Johnson had never gotten over it, and I couldn't tell if Dad had.

When Dad picked me up at the airport again, he gave me a clingier than usual hug. "I'm happy you're back."

"Me too," I said with a smile. Amazingly, it felt like the truth.

When I saw Grandma Johnson, I noticed at once that she looked tinier than the last time I had seen her. She gave me a big hug and whispered, "You look too thin. I don't care what the style is these days. Men like breasts."

"Right. Got it." It was hard not to be bitter, even though she was only stating facts. So I grumbled another fact. "But thanks to Mom, I don't have a lot to work with."

"It's okay," she said, patting my back. "I've been cooking."

"Of course you have. I'm looking forward to it."

Things were quiet in the house while the turkey roasted, so I decided to steal into Lauren's room. It looked untouched since the last time I'd been there. Once again, it was so pretty with all the different shades of blue as the light hit the walls. And once again, my heart called out to her. I immediately teared up. I sat on the bed with my hands between my legs and whimpered.

I wanted to tell her how everything had changed—about how Mom had this new crazy side; how Dad seemed a little more interested in me; how even Michelle was now nice; and how I had kissed this boy who seemed like a dream, yet I was worried the other shoe was going to drop.

Was I sad that Lauren was dead purely for my own selfish need of a friend?

No. I missed Lauren as my sister and friend, but I missed *her*, too. Lauren had made my life better just because she was here. I gasped, and with a tear of my heart, I went to the place that I absolutely forbade myself to go. I started to wonder what life would be like if she were alive.

What would she be doing right now? What would we be doing? How many funny stories would she have made up about her teachers? What great grades would she have gotten? What boy would she be crushing on that she wouldn't tell me about?

Then my questions went further. What would her future have been like? Where would she have gone to college? Would she have gotten married? Would she have had kids? Would our kids have played together?

When I imagined two wild little girls chasing each other—something that would never be—I really started to cry. Big, ugly crying. Because whether I was crying for me or for Lauren, she wasn't there, and my life wasn't going to turn out like it was supposed to. In a way, my life as I knew it was over. I was going to have to start a new one.

My blubbering only began to subside when my sleeves got so wet from my tears that I had to search for a tissue. I couldn't find one in her room, and with tears still streaming down my face, I knew I needed to get the hell out of there or my crying jag wouldn't stop. As I closed the door, I saw Grandma Johnson shuffling down the hallway. Only a blind person wouldn't see that I'd been bawling. A grandmother would probably sense it once I opened the door.

She walked over, gave me a big hug, and I cried on her shoulder. "Grandma, when does it get better? When is it not so painful…so hard…all the time?"

"I suppose everyone is different," she said, pulling away. I knew a friendly lecture was coming. "At times, your grandfather's passing is as hard for me today as it was the day he died, but the pain isn't as constant anymore. I can go days and even weeks of going along in my life with nothing. Then it can hit me out of the blue, and I feel the grief all over again. Other times, you *know* when a bad patch of pain is coming…birthdays, holidays…things like that. You can brace yourself."

It still didn't quite make sense, but I nodded, which instigated another hug from her. "Oh, Nicki, I wish I could tell you something different. Unfortunately, you're going to have to find your way on this one without much help."

"Yeah. That's the one thing I've kinda figured out."

Stroking my hair, she smiled and said, "The bright side is the wonderful memories are always there waiting for you, right beside your heart."

Chapter Fourteen

Of course it was misting as I walked to school on Monday morning. My hair was probably expanding in frizz with every step, and I knew I'd look frightening by the time I got there. The weather fit my gloomy mood. I was anxious after running through all the scenarios that could happen that morning.

What if Adam acted like nothing had happened? Very likely. Typical guy behavior. What if everything that Friday night with him had been just a dream? Unlikely. I wasn't *that* psycho. What if he decided that it had been a mistake? Possibly. Guys could be fickle.

But none of those things happened. Before I got even near the lockers, Adam craned his neck to spot me and smiled. I waved, and my stomach started to tighten with nerves. When I was close enough, he reached out and grazed my forearm with his fingers. "It's good to see you again."

My heart jumped at his twinkling eyes, which seemed happy — so happy that I had to look away for a second. "Hi…It's good to see you, too."

Adam leaned against his locker as I started getting my books out. "Did you get tired of eating turkey?"

"A little. How was San Francisco?"

"Foggy and rainy. It felt like home."

"Did it make you more homesick than usual?" Why did I ask a question that I didn't want the answer to?

"No. I wouldn't say I was homesick. And Christmas is coming." He shifted his weight before saying what sounded like an admission. "We're going home until after the New Year."

"That will be nice."

That's not what I thought, though. England. His ex-girlfriend. Ouch. My soul sank along with my heart. I closed my locker door and glumly announced, "Time to get to class." How did my happy day go south so quickly?

Adam suddenly looked a little forlorn, too, but then he smiled. With a wordless nod, he placed his hand on the small of my back. It felt like reassurance as he guided me into the classroom. Equally silent, I responded by leaning somewhat into his warmth; it felt like the right place to be. My body told me that the micro display of public affection was an extraordinary event—a visible, shared sign of something we both felt.

And that began a day of school for me unlike any other. We met at our lockers after every class and would talk and laugh. There would be some moments of awkward but electric silence. Occasionally, he would touch me with either a hand on my shoulder or my arm. At first, I avoided looking at him when it happened. Then before fourth period, he put his hand on my shoulder, and I stared at him. His eyes held mine, and his whole face turned into a naughty smile. I had no idea what he was thinking about, but I was sure I'd enjoy it. I spent most of the day in hyper-anticipation about what might happen next.

Through drama class and lunch, Tom would look at me and grin. Finally, in the middle of lunch, I had to ask, "Tom, why are you smiling at me?"

"Because two of my good friends who haven't smiled in quite a while are very happy today."

My face must have been as red as the Chinese flag. My mouth opened up, but nothing came out.

"Don't worry, Nicki," said Rachel. "The entire school hasn't figured it out yet—just a handful. The rest would know more if anyone listened to Lance."

I smiled but squirmed in my seat. I never really thought about people gossiping about me. Why would they? Other than the accident, there wasn't anything worth talking about. *Oh, God.* I could just hear the reactions of people like Brittany Taylor and Cici Arnold if they heard anything about Adam and me. I was spitefully happy.

After school, Adam asked, "Can I give you a lift home? It's bucketing down."

"Thanks," I said, my stomach flipping with excitement.

When we stopped in front of my house, however, I frowned—it was the end of our day together.

"I'd invite you in, but my mom has a rule that she first has to meet the guys I bring into the house."

"Has she rejected any?" He smirked as he said it. He had to know that he would pass any mother's test.

"Not really."

"What about your dad? Has he?"

"Well, because of where Dad lives, he really hasn't met many of my guy friends. But when he does, he likes to remind them that he used to work in law enforcement. I'd say he was joking, but he's kinda not."

He got the picture. "Hmm. Something to look forward to. Maybe we should just stay here until the rain stops. Tell me about your holiday."

"Nah, I want to hear about your trip first."

After he told me about his travels, he got quiet and looked at me through his thick lashes. "I was a bit worried this morning that maybe you had changed your mind—that you thought last Friday night was a mistake."

I so wanted to kiss him again when he acted all shy. "I worried myself about you."

"I suppose with good reason. I'm sorry, Nicki. I really was horrible to you."

"You weren't horrible." His apology was making me self-conscious, so I decided to put him on the spot instead. I wanted to get to the bottom of things. "So, what happened between you and Meredith?"

"I've been asking myself that, too."

"How so? I don't understand."

"I don't know. I fell into going out with her last term." He smiled and nudged my shoulder. "*You* already had a bloke."

"Whatever…" Of course, I was dying that he'd noticed I had dated someone back then.

"It's true. But what happened between *you* two?"

I shrugged. "John and I broke up after the accident. He already had plans to work at a summer camp until August, and then he was going off to college. It wasn't a big deal."

"It wasn't?"

"At that point, I didn't really care about much," I said bitterly. "Anyway, we were talking about you and Meredith."

"Right. As for Meredith, she was nice to me from the start when I didn't know anyone."

"And she's beautiful." I wanted to take it back immediately. It made me sound just like the jealous girl I was.

Adam rolled his eyes. "Yeah, that too." Then he took my hand and began rubbing my arm where my scar was. "When I heard about your accident, I was really sad for you. We didn't really know each other, but I always thought you were great and you seemed…different. When my mum came back from your sister's funeral, she was pretty gutted. She said your family was devastated, and you and your mum were in bad shape physically. But what struck me most was that she was worried about you—that you seemed numb."

"You can tell her that I was on some awesome drugs." I tried to smile but quickly looked away. I didn't want to talk about this anymore, and I hoped he got the point, so I added, "Go on."

"When I saw you at that party at the beginning of term, I was curious about you and how you were doing. Here you were, this beautiful, clever girl, but you seemed so removed from the world. It was heartbreaking. And then as I got to know you, we got on well, and I really started to fancy you. I knew that I had backed myself into a corner when I looked forward to spending time with you more than Meredith."

"I don't know…It looked to me like you and Meredith were enjoying yourselves." I gave him a dirty look. "Sometimes in front of my locker."

"I'm really sorry. I was such a prat. I talked with Tom, who filled me in on your side of things—that I was trying to have my cake and eat it with you and Meredith. That you were nice to talk to, but I didn't want to be seen with you when I had Meredith instead. Total bollocks. I still can't believe you thought that."

"All empirical evidence aside."

Shaking his head, he looked out the window. "You're right. Of course you're right that it must have looked that way. But please believe it wasn't my intention. I was so bloody stupid about it all, but you called me out on it. I deserved to be told off."

I looked out the window, too. I don't know where the tears came from, but a few rolled down my cheeks.

Adam's mouth flew open when he saw my face, and he said softly, "I wanted to get things straight with you, but you wouldn't talk to me." He shook his head like I just didn't get it. "I was really depressed, and I knew I should dump Meredith. I made excuses all the time not to see her. Things kept getting in the way, though, like Homecoming. You were right that it was a big deal for her. Then, I had set up that stupid date when David visited. Speaking of whom…" He smiled at me. "Tell me about David. What was that all that about?"

It was my turn to divulge some things. I tried to make light of it. "He's a great guy, and…well, no one had paid any attention to me in a long time. He was really, really nice to me."

Laughing, he playfully banged his head against the steering wheel. "That was it? You liked him because he was nice to you? That's all that it took? Do you know how insanely jealous I was? From the moment you two started talking at our lockers."

"If you were so jealous, why did you go to Lance's party?"

Adam found my hand again and, looking down, replied, "When I saw how happy you were with David, I thought I should do what I could to help. I swallowed every bit of jealousy because I knew I deserved it." I lifted my other hand to get the hair out of his eyes. He looked at me intently. "I thought I'd blown it with you anyway. When you curled up next to me last Friday, I was worried you might wake up and run away."

That was my green light. I took a breath, leaned over, and gave him a kiss. It took all of ten seconds for us to reacquaint ourselves with one another before sliding into a series of successively deeper kisses. He let go of my hand, put both of his around my waist, and pulled me to him. We made out for a while just like we had before, but things became even more heated. I began to notice all the discomfort of making out in a car. Too many things in the way, too many hard angles.

Adam must have noticed it, too, because he murmured, "Hang on a sec." I felt his hand move off my back and reach below his seat. As he moved his seat backward, he pulled me onto him saying, "I want to hold you."

There was only one proper answer to that. I smiled, crawled into his lap, and planted a giant kiss on him. His hands began to roam over my sweater — avoiding all those places to be avoided if you were trying to avoid certain things during an initial grope session — but still finding their way around. He got hard in less than a minute. My unconscious and shameless response was to move so that I was no longer sitting in his lap but right on top of his erection.

When I pressed against him, he groaned that groan that guys make when they want more and can't have it. "Bollocks. Why are we in this car?"

"Sorry." I didn't want to be a tease, but that's where things had been heading.

He smiled and pressed his forehead to mine. "Christ, don't be. I'm wound up because it feels so good being with you."

"I feel the same way," I whispered.

After another long kiss, I looked at my watch and saw it was after five. "Oops, I need to go inside. My mom will be home soon."

"Too bad."

"You're more than welcome to come over later and meet her."

"I am?"

"Sure. You'll get a pass at least for the first meeting, just because she knows your family."

"No. I want to do this right. Will you go out with me on Friday?"

My heart said, *Yippee!* But of course, I just smiled. "That would be great. You can meet her then."

"Brilliant." He kissed my cheek. "For now, I'll walk you to your door."

"But it's still pouring. I'm the only one that needs to get wet."

He was out the car before I finished my words, and he opened my door, saying, "Let's make a dash for it."

We ran to my porch and were dripping wet by the time we got to it. He laid each of his hands on the sides of my face and kissed me. I could taste the rain on his face. We said our goodbyes, and I walked inside, confident that I had left a part of myself on the porch.

Everything about that week should have been depressing. It rained every day, and I'd just come off an emotional weekend up at Dad's. Also, it was Christmastime, and I could tell that the Lauren stuff was going to be ten times worse than even her birthday on Halloween. It was December, and Mom and I hadn't even talked about what we were doing for Christmas yet. It was that bad.

But I wasn't depressed—I was elated. Adam drove me home from school each day, where we spent half the time talking and half the time making out. I felt like a giggly girl with a sweet boyfriend. Mom totally sensed something was up.

When I mentioned I had a date on Friday, she smiled. "I look forward to meeting him." She didn't ask who it was, which was good. I didn't want her cluing in too quickly that she knew Adam's mom.

By Wednesday, Adam had started going out of his way so that he could walk me to all my classes. It was really then that I started to see the look in other people's eyes when they saw us together. It was an expression of curiosity like, as if they were wondering why he would dump Meredith Daniels to date *me*. Despite the majority of gawkers, there were a few friendly faces whom I didn't really know that well but who gave me a big smile. I loved them. It felt like some sort of underdog solidarity.

One afternoon, Adam and I were again outside my house in his car, talking as the rain beat down around us. Our neighbors across the street already had their Christmas lights on their house. He pointed to the decoration and said, "We leave for our Christmas holiday on the last Friday of school."

England again. The old girlfriend. I felt like I was physically deflating; it was such a downer. I mustered up, "That will be nice." It couldn't have sounded sincere because it was the same thing I had said the last time he'd brought it up.

"What are your plans?"

Not that question. It sounded so simple, yet that was a question that got to the root of just how screwed up my life had been since Lauren died. What did boxers call it? The bob and weave? That's how I needed to avoid answering him. I was just tired of doing it.

When I didn't answer immediately, he prompted me. "Nicki?"

"I don't know."

His brow furrowed. He should've been confused. Most people, *normal* people had this sort of thing worked out. After all, Christmas was less than a month away.

I started and stopped, then started again and finally said, "Well, things are really hard for my mom. She's avoiding a lot. She hasn't brought Christmas up yet, so I haven't either. I'm guessing we'll go to Baton Rouge to see my grandparents. Then we'll come back, and I'll go see Dad."

Adam nodded, but he again had that look that made me comfortable saying more. I added, "As to whether or not we're getting a tree or exchanging gifts, I have no idea. I mean, I'd be happier not doing any of it, but I wouldn't mind my mom actually talking with me about it first."

"So your mum hasn't always been this way? She talked to you more before…"

Not wanting to look at him, I focused on our neighbor's shrubs. I didn't know if I was ready to get into it. Yet here was the opportunity to talk with someone who wasn't my seventy-five-year-old grandmother or my dad's girlfriend. I choked up as I got out the simplest sentence that still explained it all. "Everything was different."

I wiped the tears from my eyes as I looked at Adam and forced a half-smile. He actually looked somewhat pained. "I'm so sorry, Nicki."

"You're not going to want to spend time with me if all I do is cry on you."

"I'm finding myself not wanting to spend time with anyone else." He gave me an encouraging grin.

"Thanks. I…um…like spending time with you, too." I was bashful again, just like the stupid skunk in *Bambi*.

At that, he leaned over and kissed me on the mouth, but quickly moved to kissing my face where it was wet from tears. "We won't have a tree at my house either, if that makes you feel any better," he said in between the kisses.

I giggled and pulled him closer to me. "It actually does."

And then I threw myself at him. What caused me to do it? I didn't know. But there I was, all over the guy. Everything in my life felt easier with Adam, so I only wanted to feel more of him. It seemed like he felt the same way—like we couldn't get close enough to one another. Clothing stayed on, but for the next ten minutes we lost ourselves in each other. It was wet and warm and hot and beginning to feel very, very good — uncomfortably good.

When he slipped his hand under the front of my sweater, I at first didn't really notice because my body was too busy responding, but soon I panicked in self-consciousness. He made me forget myself so much that only then did I remember he might see what I look like. He might be disgusted by my scars — not to mention that my chest had to be a disappointment after Meredith. I tensed up immediately.

"Sorry," he said, withdrawing his hand. He looked a little embarrassed. "I got carried away."

"It's just that…" I stopped speaking because I actually didn't have a good reason.

He smiled and looked outside with a tinge of regret. "Not the best time."

"No," I said in relief. "Not the best."

"I can't wait to see you on Friday." He placed a kiss on my cheek.

"Me too," I said with a grin.

Chapter Fifteen

At eight that Friday night, I was still putting on my tights when the doorbell rang. *Damn.* He was punctual. I wanted to beat Mom to the door, but that wasn't going to happen. After throwing on the handiest unwrinkled blouse and my short — but not too short — brown skirt, I looked in the mirror and saw that most everything else was in place. We were supposed to see a movie, so I grabbed an old cardigan of my grandfather's and headed downstairs.

By the time I made it to the living room, Mom was already in the middle of her interrogation. I sat down next to Adam on the sofa and didn't interrupt, as it took about thirty seconds to see she was totally taken in by him — just like every other American female.

She talked about traveling in the United Kingdom when she was in college and was so cheery that Adam had to know he was ahead in the game, but he still played his ace as he said, "And you may know my parents from church." I don't think I said a word for ten minutes, and Mom was all smiles when we said goodbye.

He clutched my hand as soon as we left the house. I squeezed his and smiled at him in amazement. "Mom was eating out of your hands. Very good work."

"I like your mum. She's funny, and my mum was right for once. She's lovely."

"Were you hitting on my mom?" I laughed.

"God, no way." He snickered. When he opened my car door, he sneaked a kiss on my cheek. "Especially not when I have a date with her daughter, who is twice as attractive as she is."

I rolled my eyes as I got in the car. After he got in, he commented, "You two don't look that much alike, though. Do you take after your Dad?"

"Yeah…a lot." I took a breath before adding, "Lauren looks…I mean, looked…like my mom."

"I resemble my dad as well."

I could tell he was trying to make the conversation easier for me, and it worked. I was able to say something that I'd been thinking for months. "It's funny, because looking at my mom reminds me of Lauren, but somehow it doesn't make me sad." I shrugged, but it actually felt good having said it.

Tucking a stray hair behind my ear, he said, "Well, she's your mum…You love her, too."

"I guess that's right." I turned away. Sometimes the things he said just sang to my heart. He was such a nice guy. No wonder Meredith was so torn up by their split; I would be, too. Then I remembered my predicament: I *will* be, too.

Taking advantage of the noise of Adam starting the car, I silently contemplated my situation. I was falling hard for a guy who I'd most likely never see again after the first week of June. Adam would go back to his old life, and I'd be stuck here without him but with reminders of him everywhere—just like with Lauren. It would be déjà vu all over again.

Yet here he was at my side. We had fun; he always seemed to know what to say to me no matter how sad I was, and I couldn't stop thinking about what it would be like to be naked with him. I knew there was only one thing to do. I couldn't think about the future or it would only protract the pain. I couldn't dwell on what was *going to* happen. No, I wouldn't go there—not yet, not until I absolutely had to. So I made a life-changing, snap decision: with one sweep of my mind, I packed all the angst away until I had no choice but to face it.

Somehow it was liberating. I turned to him and smiled. "So what do you want to see tonight? I'm open to anything."

"Well, if it's all right with you, I thought we might get the bloody parental thing out of the way. How about we go to my house and watch a video there? My parents have rented a few, and they're not all rubbish."

Panic. Adam's parents? I immediately looked down at what I was wearing. I was completely covered and somewhat conservatively dressed. I exhaled. "Okay. But there is no way that I can outdo your performance with my mom."

"You'll be fabulous. She already likes you."

When we walked into the large foyer of his house, Sylvia was at my side at once. "I'm so happy Adam brought you over."

"Thanks for having me."

"She's not here to see you," Adam said, full of brotherly annoyance.

Sylvia retaliated by giving him a dirty look and sticking her tongue out. It was really funny, so I had to laugh. When she saw me smile, she grabbed my hand and began dragging me through the house. "Mum! Nicki's here."

Both his mom and dad greeted me as we walked in the kitchen. They were washing up dinner dishes. His mom dried her hands and happily announced, "It's nice to see you again, Nicki. Maybe you want to sample some of the famous Kincaid spotted dick?"

My eyes bugged open. *What the hell? Did she really just say "dick"? She couldn't be talking about her son, could she? Like his dick has freckles?* I didn't know who to look at, but I glanced quickly at his dad. He looked uneasy. I then turned to Sylvia, and she giggled. Finally, I looked at Adam, and he blurted out, "It's a pudding."

"Oh. Sure. Thank you." *Whew.*

His mom was pleased and directed Sylvia to get plates. Adam whispered in my ear, "Sorry about that. My mum…well…she just doesn't always get it."

As the five of us sat at their kitchen table eating a strange spongy thing with raisins and custard, Adam's dad carried most of the conversation, asking me about my family—what my father did, where he lived in Chicago, where my parents had grown up. He was nice enough, but with each answer I felt like I was failing a test, which made no sense to me. My parents were educated, my family was upper-middle class, and we'd traveled internationally before. We shouldn't seem like stereotypical "ugly Americans." What was his problem?

Maybe his posh accent added to the judgmental vibe, and ironically, he ended his interrogation by saying, "You have a distinct Texan accent. Have you always lived in Texas?"

"Always," I said. "I'm sort of stuck here I guess."

Sylvia groaned. "That's how I feel about Cambridge. I can't wait to leave. I want to live in New York."

"You would leave your poor mother and father behind?" Adam's mom said it jokingly, but she was a mom. You could tell she meant it.

"Sorry, Mum," said Sylvia. "But I want to be where the action is—somewhere cosmopolitan. London would do as well."

"Bloody right. I've had enough of the countryside," Adam said, helping himself to another serving of dessert.

"Well, just as long as you don't stray too far," Mrs. Kincaid said, "I'll be fine with it."

Adam shook his head. He seemed to be lost in his own thoughts. "Don't worry about that. I don't think I'm cut out for living abroad."

My heart heard every word of what he'd said, and it ached. He was never coming back. I took a deep breath. Remembering that I had decided to forget the future, I quickly swept it away with all my other feelings.

After we ate, his family wandered upstairs. Well, his parents did. Sylvia hung around for a while, until Adam pointedly asked her, "Don't you have somewhere to be?" She was nice to me as she left, but she still walked off in a huff.

Adam's home was much larger than mine. There was a big TV room off the kitchen with French doors shutting it from the rest of the house. We settled in there with a couple of Cokes, and he showed me the choices of videos.

"You know that I'm going to sleep through half the movie, so you should pick what you want to see," I said.

"Okay. Then it will be *The Mambo Kings*."

I snuggled up next to him, but still in my own space, and he frowned. "That's not any fun."

With a giggle, I nudged my way closer as he put his arm around my shoulders. I couldn't have been more comfortable.

When I woke up in his arms, I remembered having seen the opening to the movie, but that was about it. He kissed my cheek and mischievously smiled. "You know my mum walked in about twenty minutes ago."

My eyes widened at the thought of her seeing me asleep with her son holding me. "Did she say anything?"

"No. She just smiled."

Of course I was wide awake for the second half of the movie, which had some hot sex scenes with more than one pair of naked breasts. Given I was cuddled up with Adam, it was hard to ignore being completely turned on. At one point, we caught each other's eyes, and I saw where his mind had been as well.

In seconds, his lips found mine, and it was just like our times in his car — long and hot, with neither one of us pulling away. Then I remembered where we were. "I don't want to ruin my goodwill with your mom. Is she going to walk in here again?"

"You would have to do a lot worse than kiss her son to ruin the soft spot she has for you. Besides, I think she suspects that we've snogged already."

"You think so?" I giggled.

He gave me a quick peck before he reassured me, "When she turns the lights off in the kitchen, you won't see her again until the morning. The same with my father. And Sylvia knows better."

I glanced at the doors, which were as dark as the kitchen behind them. When I turned back to Adam, he gently caught my head and pulled my mouth to his while our bodies mashed against each other. This was a kiss like no other. It was full-bodied and direct, and he punctuated it with a murmured "I've finally got you alone."

I gasped, "Yes," and without any forethought, I hiked my leg over his hip. My skirt crept up to my hips, leaving my entire lower body exposed if not for my tights. I couldn't have cared less; I was too busy grasping onto the muscles of his arms. When my crotch bumped into his hard-on, it felt incredibly intimate. I jerked my hips back as if I had touched something hot, which I had. Then he startled me. He skipped a base.

His left hand was no longer on my waist in the expected position for heading toward first base. Instead, his hand ever so gently stroked me right between my legs. There was only sheer nylon between his hand and me. His fingertips first just tickled me down there, which drove me wild, but then the tip of his index finger explored and bingo. He hit the spot.

He pressed into the nylon of my tights and began quickly touching me just like I did every night in bed when I was alone thinking about him. I went nuts, involuntarily bucking and mewing. I was so excited that at first I didn't notice his other hand had started pulling down the waist of my tights. When it did register, I snapped out of it straightaway.

"Uh, Adam. I'm not sure—"

"It's okay. I've got something," he said in a husky voice.

Something? Like a condom? Oh my God. He thought we were going to have sex. I had planned on eventually telling him I was a virgin, but I didn't think we were at that stage yet. Why hadn't I prepared for this?

I found some courage and sputtered, "This is a little weird because of what we've been doing…but you need to know that I haven't had sex before."

When he stopped touching me, I dreaded what was next. *Oh no.*

"Really? You've never…" His voice was quizzical.

"Yes. Why is that hard to believe?" Then it dawned on me. "Do you think David and I had sex?"

"No. I just thought you and your last boyfriend were very close."

"We were…until we weren't."

"I understand. It hasn't been that long for me. My first time was with my old girlfriend Kate."

With that little bit of disclosure, I thought maybe I could get some more information out of him. "So how many girls have you slept with…if that's not too personal a question?"

"Not too personal at all. The answer is two, unless we're going to count you falling asleep on me, which you've done twice now. Then it would be three."

"Very funny." I grinned and punched him in the arm. Two—that meant this Kate character and Meredith. Somehow I felt a little more at ease.

"I thought it was very funny," he said, rubbing his arm. His smile told me it didn't hurt, and he soon pulled me to him. "Come here."

Brushing the hair out of his eyes, I tried to explain myself. "I'm not saying I don't want to be with you…just not in that way…not yet. I'm not ready." I looked down. I hated bringing the subject up, but it was an issue. "I'm kind of damaged goods right now. I'm kind of…well, I'm already a mess…and…"

"Nicki," he said with the kindest eyes. "I don't think you're damaged at all. And the sex thing really doesn't matter to me. I just want to be with you." I gave him a suspicious look, and he laughed. "Okay. That's not the whole truth. It does matter to me because I've fantasized about you only about a million times."

Adam Kincaid fantasized about me? My heart jumped out of my chest right there, but I recovered and said, "I'd be a little worried if it didn't matter to you at all. Maybe you should go out with Lance, then."

Before he could say anything else, I leaned over and gave him a kiss. He pulled away. "Please just tell me if I'm doing something wrong or that you don't want."

"I can't imagine that happening." I laughed.

Things got quiet after that as we both watched the end of the film. And when Adam dropped me off at home with a much less passionate kiss than we'd had in days, I got a little concerned. Had he begun having second thoughts? Had I blown it? I tossed and turned most of the night worrying.

Chapter Sixteen

The next morning, I awoke to a note from Mom announcing she was out running errands, but that she expected me to clean the house while she was gone.

Great. What a fun day.

Unfortunately, the housework only occupied my hands; my mind was free to concentrate entirely on me screwing things up with Adam. Why'd I have to have a scruples attack the night before? If Adam didn't call me by school on Monday morning, I was in serious trouble. My gut wrenched at the thought.

As I moved the vacuum cord from one outlet to another, I heard the doorbell. Yikes. I wasn't really presentable this morning. I hadn't showered because I knew I would sweat while working around the house. My hair was on top of my head in a ponytail, and I was wearing my usual housecleaning garb — one of Dad's wife-beaters and a pair of boxer shorts.

Peeking into the peephole, I saw Adam standing there looking toward the street. *Uh oh.* My heart raced. This had to be bad, and of course, it was happening when I looked and smelled like shit. I took a deep breath and opened the door.

"Good morning," Adam said with a grin.

I must have looked ridiculous to him. He, on the other hand, looked unbelievably hot—unshaven with his hair kind of wild like he had just rolled out of bed.

"Hi." I smiled and tapped on the door. "This is unexpected."

"I'm sorry for not phoning. Do you have a minute?"

Anxiety punched my gut. A tense date the night before had led to an unannounced visit in the morning. The situation had all the warning signs of terrible. I swallowed hard. "Yeah, come on in. My mom is out."

Closing the door behind him, he said, "You look adorable."

Was he nuts? "Er…thanks. I should warn you that I haven't showered. Do you want something to drink?"

"Cheers. I'll have some water." He reached over and touched my ponytail. "I like your hair like that."

"Why?" I asked, laughing. "Do I look like a cheerleader?"

"No, actually. Better."

Tingly warmth and anticipation came over me. Trying to stay even-keeled, I said, "Let's go to the kitchen."

He followed me there, and as I filled a glass for him, I said, "So, what's up this early? I thought you might be the Mormons."

"Mormons? The missionary boys?" He smirked and tugged at the waist of my tank top. "It wouldn't be very kind of you to address those nice boys in this."

I looked down. *Oh God.* I hadn't really thought about what I was wearing when I'd opened up the door. I was braless, in a see-through shirt with gaping armholes. You could spy my breasts from the side, and through the cotton my nipples were visible and, of course, erect. My cheeks heated with a blush, but it felt like it spread across my entire upper body. I handed him the glass of water. "Yeah. Let's go in the living room."

After we sat down on the sofa facing one another, Adam took my hand. "I wanted to see you this morning because it felt like things got a little bit off-kilter last night."

"Don't worry about it. You were understanding…all things considered. I wasn't really clear."

"I didn't like the way things ended. I thought I'd rather apologize to you in person than on the phone."

"Well, there's nothing for you to apologize for." I smiled and gave him a kiss on the cheek. "Although I'm happy you dropped by, even if you are seeing me and smelling me at my worst."

He leaned in to sniff my neck. "You're just as pretty…maybe a little bit musky…in a nice way." Looking into my eyes again, he continued, "I just wanted to make sure everything was okay."

"Please don't worry about it. Because if you do, I'll start to worry."

"Okay. I've said my peace, then." He pointed to my chest. "So, how often do you wear men's undergarments?"

"Only around the house."

After studying my shirt for a few seconds, he crooked his index finger and ran it along my stomach. "What's this?"

My scar. He could see my horrible scar through the thin fabric of my shirt. I crossed my arms over my middle. "That's a scar…I've got a few, as you've probably noticed. They're from the accident, but…well, the ones on my torso are mainly from the surgeries. They're pretty hideous compared to the others." I grimaced. "When I said I was damaged goods, I wasn't joking. I'm kind of permanently disfigured. Luckily, people don't see these."

"I bet they're not as bad as you say." He shook his head with sympathy. "Show me one."

I froze for a moment, but soon I accepted reality. He already had a pretty good view of most of me. I lifted up my shirt with my right hand to right below my breasts. My scary scars were exposed. I pointed to the ugly abstract pattern of purple slashes across my torso. "This is the main one here, but there are more. They cut me open because of my ruptured diaphragm, but then they did more surgery because of some internal bleeding. So the big scar starts up here but goes all the way down here. I also had some gashes and little cuts, so I've got random stitches here and there."

I pulled my shirt back down and lowered my boxers to show my abdomen. The worst scar extended around my belly button and covered most of my stomach. I summed it all up. "They're gruesome." Finished with the show, I pulled up my boxers and wrapped my arms around my front again.

Adam nodded, his expression grim. He pulled me to him and set me on his lap. Kissing my forehead, he said, "I'm sorry."

"Thanks," I whispered. He was so kind that I had no words, and really what else was there to say?

"Can I see them again?" he asked.

Unfolding my arms, I leaned back again and lifted my shirt just a bit. He gently touched the scars, and God, did it feel good. His brow slowly knitted together in thought, though, and he stopped. Taking my hand, he asked, "Can you tell me what happened to you in the car?"

The story. Adam wanted to know the story that I hadn't told anyone other than Dad, and I'd only done that when I was doped up on painkillers. I looked at Adam and sighed. I knew I shouldn't trust this unknown boy so much, but when it came down to it, I wanted to. So I told him. I told him everything—from the bickering about dinner to the Jaws of Life to waking up to Dad and Grandma. I didn't talk about the funeral or Lauren, really. I kept it to just the facts about the accident, but that itself was hard enough.

He was quiet as I spoke, only occasionally asking a clarifying question. When I stopped talking, he asked softly, "When did you find out about Lauren?"

Looking down, I teared up, and I bit my lip to keep it from trembling. When I looked up again, I choked out, "I knew it before I heard it. I knew it almost immediately."

Then I cried a steady, wet whimper on his shoulder.

"Oh, Nicki," he said, stroking my hair. "I'm so sorry. I didn't mean to make this worse for you. I shouldn't have asked that."

"It's okay. Actually, I feel a little better. I just haven't talked with anyone about it."

"What about your family—your mum or your friends?"

I wiped my eyes but still shed a few tears as I shook my head. "Lisa and Rachel never even ask. I think they feel it's their job to make things easier for me, so we avoid talking about it. And my family… that's a long story." There was no way I could talk about the accident *and* Mom and Dad in one morning.

He kissed my forehead. His face was a little scratchy from his stubble. Eventually, I stopped crying and laughed as I wiped my eyes. "I'm really the worst date."

"No, you're not." He played with my ponytail. "And this isn't really a date, right?"

"Uh. No." I smiled. "I try to dress better than this on a date."

"I'll come over any time when you're dressed like this," he said with a wink. Then he gave me a look like a warning, and he raised my shirt up a bit and began tracing my scar.

Uh oh. It felt too good, and I floated away in silence on another mood swing while he continued caressing me. Eventually, I had to say something. "That feels very, very nice." I tried being calm, but he had to have noticed my staccato breathing as I spoke.

He didn't stop touching me, and his eyes and smile became bright. "I sort of like this. It's a bit like a map painted on a beautiful body."

My cheeks were on fire—as was my entire pelvic region. I reached up and gave him a kiss. "Kind of a funny map."

Tickling my tongue with his, he pulled up my shirt a bit more. That I could expect, but when he moved his lips to my stomach and began kissing my scars, I was in shock. Yet somehow I instinctively felt safe enough with him to lean back and watch this beautiful boy kiss all my ugliness. The kisses were wet and soft. So many emotions whirled around me, but I was also incredibly aroused.

He followed the scars down my stomach, but stopped at the top of my boxers. As his mouth went lower and lower, it took all my willpower not to squirm, and I had a twinge of disappointment when he reversed direction upward. Wanting him to continue, I started stroking his hair and neck, urging him on.

When his mouth got near my sternum, he looked up at me and asked, "Can I?" I knew what he meant. With only a smile, I lifted my top over my head and dropped it on the floor. There I was, totally exposed to him — 32A boobs and frightening scars. He seemed unfazed, though, because he smiled as he moved his mouth from my scars to my breast.

With a hand on each one, he squeezed them and alternated tonguing and sucking on each nipple. It was hot as hell. He looked like he was enjoying it, and I most definitely was.

"God, you're gorgeous, Nicki, and you smell…you smell so sexy."

"Are you kidding me?"

"No. Why do you say that?"

"I'm a prime candidate for plastic surgery between my scars and my boobs, and I stink. Most guys would be scared off by now."

Shaking his head, he snickered and gestured to his dick. "Total rubbish. Do you see this? I get a stiffy after one bloody kiss when you've got all your clothes on. It's a little bit embarrassing, actually. So imagine what's it's like for me now that you're naked and letting me touch you."

"It feels great," I whispered.

"You're going to have to do better than have a few marks on this fit little body of yours to scare me away. I'm not leaving. No way." Leaning in to kiss me, he added, "And I like the way you smell."

Was he saying that just to get laid one day? I didn't care. I found his chin and tilted it up so I could kiss him, but really, I also wanted to touch him like he was touching me.

We kissed hard and wet for the next few minutes before I finally demanded, "Take your shirt off, too. I don't want to be the only one topless."

He complied with a smile, and there was a half-naked Adam Kincaid sitting on my sofa with me—all lean muscles with some soft golden chest hair that darkened in color as it disappeared into his jeans. I rubbed my hand all over his pecs and followed the trail well past his belly button and then back up again.

"This. This is very nice."

"Yeah?" He raised an eyebrow, and his whole body tensed when I touched his happy trail again.

"Oh yeah."

At once, Adam wrapped his arms around me, and I straddled him. Pressing into him, I tickled my own nipples against his chest hair as I kissed him with everything I had. He groaned in response and grabbed my butt, pulling me flush with his erection.

And then I heard a car pull into the driveway. "Shit! It's my mom."

Adam was discombobulated. "Fuck. Uh…my shirt…your shirt."

Hopping off him, I tossed him his shirt and headed for the stairs with mine. "I need more clothes." Mom would flip if she knew I'd let Adam in the house when I was wearing so little.

Luckily, she was getting things out of the car, so it gave me enough time to throw on sweats and a fleece. But as I rushed out of my room, I caught a view of my face in the mirror. *Shit!* My ponytail was a mess, but even worse, my lips and chin were red. I obviously had been making out with a guy with stubble.

By the time Mom walked in, Adam and I were standing at the door. He greeted her, and she responded happily, if a little surprised, "Adam, it's nice to see you again so soon."

Adam got a smile from her. I only got a knowing look, which I ignored. "I'm just walking Adam out," I said.

When the two of us got to his car, he gave me a kiss behind my ear. "Thank you for talking to me."

"No, thank you. It feels good to have told someone."

Then he let out a throaty laugh. "And I really like that map you have. I…like the directions."

"You do, now?" It was impossible for me not to flirt with the guy.

"I do." He winked and got in his car, leaving me with a final "I'll call you tomorrow."

Walking back to the front door, I sighed. "Oh my…"

The wait had gotten ridiculous. Christmas was less than three weeks away, and Mom still had not talked with me about it. So, at the beginning of that week, I took it on myself to bring it up at dinner. I tried to do it as casually as possible.

"So, Mom, what's the deal with Christmas? Where are we going to see Grandma and Grandpa? Here or Baton Rouge? I want to know so I can make plans with Dad."

With her head stuck in the fridge, she had her back turned to me. "I'm so glad that you asked, Nicki." She slowly turned around. "Grandma and I just finalized it today. We're driving to Baton Rouge on the twenty-third and going to New Orleans for a few days. We'll have a very low-key Christmas. Just little presents this year, no tree, no big deal. Then we'll be back here on the twenty-sixth. That will let me get some work done over the break."

I looked at her like she was insane, because she was definitely acting that way. Did she really expect that I wasn't going to notice what she was doing? I was pissed. I slammed my silverware down on the table.

"Mom, this is really fucked up."

Her eyes flashed at me with disapproval. "Nicki, your language."

"Whatever. This is really screwed up."

"I don't know what 'this' is. Be specific when you speak."

"*This* is your obvious attempt to avoid Lauren stuff."

She stared at me and pursed her lips. She was ticked. "I don't like your tone, and I don't know what 'stuff' you're talking about."

Why was she lying to me? "I'm not stupid, Mom. I can tell what you're doing. You're never home. You've basically put Lauren in a box somewhere in the attic. You refuse to talk about her with me or, I'm guessing, with anyone else either, but I don't know. You've obviously put off even thinking about Christmas until the last minute, and now you and Grandma—who seems equally fucked up, too, by the way—have concocted this…this Anti-Christmas."

I teared up as I got even madder. "Do you ever even think about me? About what I may be going through? Because I really can't see that you have."

"I won't have this conversation with you like this. Until you calm down, it's not up for discussion."

Fuck it. I stomped away to my bedroom. I was pissed and pan-icked and devastated. Mom would never have treated me that way in the past. Had she gone over the edge? Or worse, was it as I'd always suspected? Lauren was her favorite, and she was mad that Lauren had died and not me? I knew it was irrational, but I was so upset that I wondered.

After a few minutes, Mom knocked on my door. I cringed, but her coming to me *was* a good sign. "You can come in."

Without saying anything, she sat on my bed beside me and put her hand on mine. She waited a moment before declaring, "I'm… actually, you're right. I'm not dealing with things very well."

Leave it to this new mother of mine to sterilize the most emo-tional of situations. I kept quiet. She must have gotten the hint. "I haven't been thinking about you as I should."

Looking at her out of the corner of my eye, I felt terrible. I had made my mom cry.

Wanting to console her, I gave her a hug, but it just made me sob. "Mom, I'm sorry if I was mean. I guess…I guess I miss you. I mean…I miss Lauren so much that my heart…like, hurts, but I miss you, too—the old you."

Was that okay, what I said? I'd just told her she had changed and for the worse.

She didn't say anything for a moment, but then said into my shoulder, "I'm sorry, Nicki. I'm trying…but it's hard."

She broke our hug and wiped her tears. "You've given me a lot to think about. I just want you to know that you should never feel like you can't talk to me. I can't have that with my daughter."

"It's okay, Mom."

Thinking of what was going on, I began to laugh. "You know… right now Lauren would say something to you like, 'It's not a big deal. It's not like she ever talked to you before.' Lauren always knew what to say."

Mom let out a little gasp and laughed. "She really was a bit of sunshine around here." Her smile stayed as she said, "I'll call Grandma and rearrange Christmas. We should have it at their house with a tree in Baton Rouge. But I would still like to come back early for work and some other things. I'm sorry that I haven't been here as much, but it does help me to be out of the house."

"That's fine. Thanks, Mom."

Seizing upon my weak moment, she went in for the kill. "So, we haven't talked in a while, and we've never had a talk about Adam. He seems very nice. And from what I know of her, his mother is very kind. How do you feel about him?"

Cringe again. Uncomfortable. She must have been saving that question since Saturday morning when she'd caught us; she had said nothing about it that day.

But even though I had just told her I wanted to talk, Adam was still not up for discussion. "Er…yeah, Mom. Can we go back to not talking again?"

"Sure." She smiled and sighed. "I wouldn't want to talk to my mother about anything like that either."

Chapter Seventeen

The fun thing about dating the guy who has the locker next to you is that the school day is like one long date, and Adam and I took full advantage of that. We both arrived to school early, stayed late, and then he drove me home, where we'd spend half an hour in his car talking and making out—or, as he called it, *snogging*. The first time he called it that, I told him it was a goofy term for a pretty fun activity. He laughed hard at that, and with his eyes still twinkling, he gave me another kiss and slid his hand inside my shirt.

Though I'd been there before, I was anxious as we walked into Adam's house on Wednesday. Mrs. Kincaid was in the kitchen and happily got us Cokes, asking us to sit down. After a few minutes into the conversation, I realized I'd been ambushed so she could grill me about my family. Adam looked at me apologetically; it seemed he was an unwitting accomplice. You could tell she was trying to parse out what was going on with me. All the while, she was complimentary of Mom, but she asked a few questions that made me wonder what she was getting at. Why did she care if Mom slept or not?

After about twenty minutes, she left, announcing she was going to a meeting at church before picking up Sylvia at the art studio. Adam immediately reached over and pulled me to him.

"She left us alone in the house. That's a very good sign."

"How so?"

"She'd rarely do that even with Kate, and our parents are good friends."

Kate again. I was quiet. Didn't he know I felt weird when we talked about her?

"Well, you should know my mum is a counselor, and whilst she says she doesn't do it, she ends up analyzing everybody. Believe me; it drives Sylvia and me mad."

That was unexpected. "So, you think she's going to practice on me. She wants to…fix me."

"Maybe, but she does like you. I think she thinks you're good for me. I don't know. That's the problem when you have a mum who's a counselor. She's always trying to figure you out, so you end up always trying to figure out her motive."

"Okay. Good to know. I'll watch out and won't be offended if she probes too much." I ran my fingers through his hair. "It's nice to see you outside of school."

"I agree." He whispered in my ear, "I did my trigonometry homework last night and had the hardest time not thinking about your map…"

"You're teasing me," I said, poking his chest.

"Without a doubt. It's fun."

He was smiling at me, but I was skeptical. "Don't you think that all this map talk might make me even more self-conscious than I already am?"

"I hope not. That's not my intention." With his forehead knitting together, he reached out and touched my hair. "I was hoping it would have the opposite effect."

"I know you mean well. Don't worry about it. I was also teasing a little. It's not a big deal. I'm just not very comfortable in my new skin, so to speak."

"Well, I'm more than comfortable with it. You're gorgeous, and you make me want to rip your clothes off."

"You are blind, then."

"Utter bollocks!" With a quick peck, he announced, "Let's go upstairs. I'll show you my room."

He grabbed my hand and started pulling me forward. I needed that lead. Going to a guy's room when his parents are gone is kind of a dicey thing to do, but away I went.

Most of his room was like that of any normal guy. It had a blue comforter on the bed, a large pile of clothes in the corner that were probably both clean and dirty, lots of Liverpool Football Club posters and stuff, and a big stereo and CD collection. The drafting table was atypical, though, as were all the cartoons and caricatures he had up around the room. I could tell that he had done them, because they were similar to ones I'd seen him draw at school. I was impressed.

"Oh my gosh, all of your work! This is great." I went up to the one closest to me to study it.

"Oh, that's a bad one of Boris Yeltsin." He looked down. I could tell he wanted to show me, but he was also shy about it.

"I think it's awesome." I smiled and continued to walk around the room, looking at all the different characters: Margaret Thatcher, Prince Charles, the Pope, Yasser Arafat — and those were just the ones I could identify. "In fact, they're all really cool. So you really do want to be a political cartoonist."

Shrugging, he said, "It would be fun, but I should probably go to university, then become a reporter first. You know…the traditional route."

"Well, I'm impressed."

For the first time, Adam was the one blushing. As if to change the subject, he kissed me on the cheek and declared, "You're kind."

He was in such close proximity, I fidgeted, and he must have known I was a little nervous being in his room alone, because he said, "I swear I only brought you up here to show you my room. We can go back downstairs."

"*Only?*" I laughed.

"Maybe it wasn't the *only* reason I brought you here." He wore a sheepish smile. "But, I'm perfectly happy being wherever you want to be."

The truth was, I was painfully attracted to him. It wasn't like I didn't want the guy touching me, and I absolutely wanted to touch him. The past Saturday on the sofa together had been hot.

I looked at him slyly and moved over to his bed. "Okay. Let's sit here."

Adam's face was covered in surprise. I kicked off my shoes and sat on the middle of the mattress cross-legged. He joined me and leaned against the wall on one of his pillows. I could tell he had no idea what to expect from me.

I pointed to the walls. "So tell me more about your work."

With a huge smile, he pulled me to him in a big hug. We spent the next half-hour talking about his cartoons — who the people were and what he liked and disliked about them. He seemed so happy and engaged as we discussed them.

"I can't believe it. Not too many people are interested in this sort of thing."

"I don't know. I'm into politics, and I always look at the cartoons in the editorial section of the paper. Political cartoons are kind of cool. They tell about current events but in a way everybody can understand."

Whatever I had said, Adam must have really liked it. He squeezed me tighter to him, grinning so appreciatively that I had to look away. I spied a brand new copy of *Catcher in the Rye* on his desk.

Nodding over to the book, I asked, "Are you starting on that book early? I thought we were reading some short stories first next semester."

"Unfortunately, I've got a couple long flights ahead of me. I thought I'd get a head start."

"You know, I might actually read that one again. I'll probably get a whole lot more out of it now than when I was eleven."

Looking again at his desk, I noticed a small corkboard with photos to the right of his drafting table on the wall. I pointed over to it. "Are those photos of your friends from home?"

"Oh…er…yes. Do you want to see them?"

"Sure."

He went over, pulled down the board, and brought it to me. Starting clockwise at the top, he described his "mates," naming them and telling me a little about each one.

But I wasn't listening. I was staring at a girl, who had to be Kate, in a group photo at the top. She was really pretty—not in the Meredith sort of beauty pageant kind of way—but in the fresh-faced, willowy, J. Crew model way. She was fair with light eyes and perfectly coifed, straight blond hair. *I cannot compete with that*, I thought.

When he finally pointed to her, he said flatly, "And this is Kate." To his credit, rather than playing it down, he then pointed to another group photo at the beach. She was in the front and at his side, both of them smiling as happy as can be. She wore a one-piece. *Thank God she's got small breasts.* I couldn't handle any more perfection.

"She's very pretty." What the fuck else was I supposed to say? I couldn't add my next thought: *Are you still in love with her?*

"Yes, but then so are you." He kissed my cheek.

I eeked out a nervous laugh. "Not like that, though."

Dropping the board beside him, he looked a little befuddled. "Nicki, you're beautiful. Why do you say that? And you're a different person. I like it. I tried to tell you before, you're…you're so much more. She's still a friend. That's why she's in the photos."

Since I was already feeling awful, I thought I might as well get it all out on the table. "So, do you get to see her over the break?" I tried to make it sound as cheery as possible, but I failed miserably.

Adam was now obviously uncomfortable with how the conversation was going. "Probably…we have mutual friends. And our parents are friends—her father lectures at Cambridge as well. We grew up together and…um…we're still in touch."

Great. She's gorgeous and probably brilliant, and they talk or write or whatever, and have some sort of lifelong bond that I'll never know anything about. I said nothing. I felt sick.

When they saw each other, would he want to be with her again? Would he have sex with her? They had only broken up because he'd left. It's not like they hadn't still loved each other. I felt like an idiot. What had I gotten myself into? I couldn't think of anything to say.

Running his hand through his hair, he said, "Oh, Nicki, this isn't how I wanted…wanted to explain things about Kate to you. Honestly, I'd forgotten she was even in these photos."

But did I really have any right to an explanation? He wasn't my boyfriend; I wasn't his girlfriend. At that moment, I hated myself. Why had I put myself in such a vulnerable position—telling him all these deeply personal things about me and knowing so little about him? Was I that desperate for attention and affection to put myself at such risk? I was pathetic.

But I needed to respond. I wanted to play it down because I had to take my feelings for him down a notch. "You don't have to explain. You don't owe me anything." I hoped I sounded convincing.

I must not have. He sputtered out, "But I want to…I have wanted to. I was waiting for the right time, but I also didn't know about how you felt. Things have gone so fast in the last few weeks, but it hasn't been that long. And—"

"And" whatever. That was it for me. The conversation was going nowhere good, and I didn't want to be there anymore. I kept my voice perfectly even and straightforward. "Maybe we should talk some other time." Thank God I could deliver lines well when I really needed to.

"No, Nicki." He shook his head. "Please. Please don't shut me out again."

Was that what I was doing? He was right. But shutting him out was the safest thing to do.

"I should go. We can talk later."

"I don't want things ending like this today. Please let me give you a lift."

I knew if I said no to him things would be really bad the next time we talked—maybe irreversibly so. I nodded. "Okay. Thanks."

Silence stayed between us until we got to my house. From the corner of my eye, I could see his mouth was in a hard line. He was obviously thinking. When we pulled in the driveway, he turned off the car and faced me. "Please listen to me."

"Yeah?" What on earth was he going to say to make any of this better?

"I really fancy you." He shook his head just a little, as if it hadn't come out right. Touching my hair, he sounded more sincere. "You are so special…and you're so special to me—like no one else, not even Kate. Just being around you makes me happy." With a guilty smile, he said, "That's probably why I can't keep my hands off of you."

He was so wonderful that I let out a giggle, but then his face became serious as he talked about what we never talked about: "But the fact is, I'm leaving in June."

I gulped at that. Obviously, he was letting me down easy, so I had to be tough, but I had no words. I could only muster, "I know."

"No, no! That's not what I meant." He craned his neck down to look me in the eye and tipped my chin up. "The last thing in the world I want to do is stop seeing you. I feel so close to you, and I don't know what that means, but if we end it today, we'll never know."

I took a deep breath before I responded. What could I say? I felt the same way, and I wanted to be honest. "Well, you don't know how happy you make me. I feel…very close to you. I tell you so much, but I'm a mess, and I feel exposed. Don't think it's because I don't like you when I act this way. I'm just trying to protect myself."

Adam laughed, breaking the ice. "Get yourself over here," he said as he pulled me across the car and onto his lap. He moved the seat back so that I wasn't crammed against the steering wheel. Before I could think twice, I put my head on his shoulder and into the crook of his neck. Then he kissed my forehead. "I promise to do my level best to not cause you any more pain. Kate is irrelevant. You're the one I want to be with."

I could tell he meant it, so I whispered, "And I want to be with you."

I looked up to see his reaction. I only caught a glimpse of a smile before his lips hit mine. And what a kiss it was. If it was designed to make me feel special, it did the trick. I wanted him to feel just as special to me, so I placed a hand on the side of his face. The combination of his five o'clock shadow and kiss made him feel both manly and loving—just what I wanted in a guy. He responded to my hand with a soft moan, but he stopped the kiss after a moment.

"Nicki, can we just not talk about my leaving in June? Can we bloody ignore it for a while?"

"Gladly." Until that afternoon, ignoring the reality that he would be gone all too soon had been working for me. I was happy to live in willful ignorance again.

Adam told me he wanted to see me both days that weekend since he was traveling the following week. So that Friday night, he brought me over to his house, saying he had good news and bad news.

"The good news is that my parents are at the opera, and it's a really long one. The bad news is Sylvia is still home."

"But I like Sylvia."

"I like her, too, but she gets in the way."

When we arrived, Sylvia bounced across the living room. "Nicki!"

"Hey, Sylvia."

"I just ordered pizza for us, but it's going to take a while to get here."

"That's okay. Thanks."

"In the meantime, come and see my room." Sylvia took my hand and started tugging me upstairs.

"Great." I turned around to see Adam's reaction. Rolling his eyes, he trudged along behind.

Given that Sylvia rarely wore any other colors but black and white, I was prepared for a Goth room of band posters and crucifixes. What I wasn't prepared for was the profusion of pink mixed in with it all. Her door should have tipped me off to Sylvia's weird brand of Girly Goth. There was a Siouxsie and the Banshees poster on it, with her name written in cursive with pink puff paint on top.

Inside her room, the largest Joy Division poster I'd ever seen was placed above her bed, which was covered in pink, frilly bedding. She had a large crucifix on her wall, but on it was a pink boa. In the corner of her room, there was an open pink parasol with an Asian bird design hanging from the ceiling. Sylvia did have flair.

When I saw the easel and paints also in the corner, I said, "I didn't know you painted."

"Yeah. I spend most of my time at the art studio at school."

"Wow." I turned to look at Adam. "You're such an artistic family."

He smiled shyly, but Sylvia laughed. "Adam? Artistic? You mean his goofy cartoons?"

"I think they're really good and clever."

"Let me show you some of my stuff." Sylvia went toward some canvases—all with very abstract designs. "You'll like them better than Adam's."

"Shut it, Sylvia," Adam said with a scowl. "Call us when the pizza arrives."

I followed his lead to his room, but not before smoothing things out with Sylvia. "You can show me later, okay?"

"Brilliant!"

I smiled to myself and whispered to Adam as we walked out. "Is she always this chipper?"

"Chipper? Is that what you think she is? How about fucking annoying?"

"She's nice. Well, to me she is, but I'm not her brother."

"She wants you to be *her* friend as well." He grabbed me by the waist. "I don't want to share, though. Can I take you to my bedroom? I want to show you something."

"Sure." His room again. *Ugh.* I was nervous considering what had happened there the other day, but he held my hand. After he closed his door, he took me immediately over to his drafting table. He took the bulletin board with the photos down and moved us over to sit on his bed.

Pointing to the board, he said, "No more Kate. Okay? She should never have been there."

It was true. Kate had been eradicated from the board. He looked so contrite and honest, and I wanted to kiss him badly. I ran my fingers through his hair. "I'm sorry if I overreacted."

"Your reaction was completely reasonable. I'd be crushed if you had pictures of John up in your bedroom."

The grimace on his face gave me the nerve to bring up the question that had been eating at me since Wednesday. "So, you're going to see her soon?" I held my breath as I waited for a reply.

"Yes, but please don't worry about it. Kate's moved on, too. She's seeing some new bloke I don't know. I'll probably see her when I go out with my mates. She's just a friend now." He waited a few seconds before adding with a smirk, "When I'm alone in my room, I think about you, not Kate."

Was it just that I wanted to believe him, or did I really think he was being honest? My gut said he was sincere. I smiled and asked playfully, "You think about me?"

"Yes."

Adam inched toward me for a kiss, but I landed mine on him first. Maybe if I kissed him hard enough, things would be okay between us. By the way Adam responded, it must've worked; in no time, we were rolling around on his bed.

The buttons on my blouse stayed closed for all of five minutes before he began unbuttoning them. I certainly wasn't complaining. I was too busy nudging his thigh between my legs so I could rub myself on it.

When Adam spread open my blouse, he grinned. "My map!"

I rolled my eyes until I felt his lips on my torso. Oh my God. It felt good. Then he stopped kissing me and got this delighted smile when he saw I was wearing a front-closure bra. I only wanted to encourage him, so I said, "Let me do it," as I popped it open and then wriggled out of it.

With my breasts now exposed, he whispered, "You're so beautiful, Nicki."

"Let's take off your shirt, too. I liked that."

For a moment, I stepped out of my body and watched with some detachment as the perfectly sculpted, half-naked Adam Kincaid licked and fondled my breasts. But as soon as his mouth was on mine again, I was back in the moment, and he knew it. It was like he could tell I was frustrated rubbing against his leg, because without any hesitation, his hand wandered into my leggings and then my panties.

I let out a little gasp when his fingers touched me. He asked huskily, "Is this okay?"

"Uh…um." I tried to be coherent. "Definitely okay."

"Then let's do this." He smiled as he tugged my leggings and underwear to below my knees.

Yes, I was more naked than not on a guy's bed with my ass bare and my legs spread open, but I didn't care. I kissed him hard. His hand was now fully exploring all of me, and it was driving me nuts. After a few seconds, I think he got the lay of the land, as I felt a finger slip inside of me. I wasn't sure why he groaned because I was the one who felt it in my core. Then I realized why — I was absentmindedly rubbing his erection through his jeans.

Time passed without me knowing it as we fooled around. I hadn't been with many guys, and those that I had certainly didn't know the ins and outs of my body or I doubt any girl's, for that matter. Adam plainly did. I was on fire, and in a minute my legs began to quiver. I had to grab hold of his comforter.

Bucking my hips, I unintelligibly sputtered his name and some other gibberish about God or something, and my body rose into a wonderful orgasm. Afterward, it took me a minute to catch my breath and realize what had just happened.

When I looked up at Adam, he was smiling at me with a mixture of surprise and pride. Unsure of what to say, I squeaked, "Hi."

"Hi, gorgeous."

It was stupid of me to be embarrassed, but I was. I kissed him immediately, just so that I didn't have to talk. After that, though, I wanted to return the favor. Adam was kissing me forcefully, and my hand followed the hair on his body from the base of his neck down to the button of his jeans. When I started to unbutton them, he moved his hips so I could have better access.

And then Sylvia's voice could be heard from what had to be downstairs. "Pizza's here! I'm setting the table."

In complete exasperation, Adam yelled, "Fuck!"

Sylvia replied, "What?"

"Nothing!"

I felt badly for Adam, but I giggled. "We have terrible timing."

"Yes, we do." He laughed as well. "See. I told you she's annoying as hell."

Throughout dinner, the banter between Sylvia and Adam kept me laughing. At one point, he chided her about her grades, and she nonchalantly shot back, "Whatever. I can't be bothered about school like you are."

"And your marks show it."

"Why are you so mean to me?" Then Sylvia turned to me and, obviously without thinking at all, asked, "It's not right to be so mean to your siblings, is it, Nicki?"

The funny thing was that I was ready to answer like any normal person would. I knew what it was like to have a sibling. It didn't matter that Lauren was dead. I was fixing to make a joke like, *Teasing should be encouraged.* But before I could say it, I glanced at Adam, whose eyes had narrowed into a glare that went beyond sibling teasing.

A mortified Sylvia apologized all over herself. "Oh, Nicki. I'm so sorry. That was awful. I wasn't thinking. I didn't mean to say something like that. I'm so sorry."

"Just shut the fuck up, Sylvia." Adam's eyes were still shooting daggers at her.

I didn't want this to become a bigger deal than it should have been. "No, no. I'm okay. It was funny, Sylvia. Don't worry about it."

"Please forgive me." She fidgeted with a look of dismay. "I can't believe I said that."

"Really. No big deal. Let's talk about something else. Tell me about what you like to paint."

With a hesitant smile, Sylvia began to slowly tell me about her love of Mark Rothko. I was only half-listening to her, though, because I looked again at Adam, who was still pissed. But when he caught me watching him, he smiled apologetically and found my hand for a quick squeeze under the table.

That was when I figured it out: Adam wanted to protect me. Sure, he liked me the way high school guys like girls. Yet there was something else in the way he acted around me. It was like he felt some sort of responsibility for me. As my realization sunk in, I smiled right back at him and squeezed his hand. The last thing I wanted to do was discourage the feeling.

Chapter Eighteen

"That's it," Tom proclaimed as he snapped a cap onto a marker, punctuating the loss for his team. "The next time we play this game, Nicki and Adam aren't allowed on the same team."

Everyone in the room looked at Tom and then over to Adam and me. I sat there wondering how a game of Pictionary had caused such drama.

"Why is that?" Adam asked, grinning at him. "Why can't Nicki and I be teammates?"

"It's an unfair advantage." Suddenly, Tom stopped being Tom the Actor and gave me a wink and a smile. "You both are repositories of useless trivia, and you seem to know what the other is thinking. I'm not going to lose again."

"It's just that Adam draws well," I said. Unfortunately, it sounded defensive. This was our first real outing as a couple with our friends, and with all the eyes in the room focusing on us, I was a little embarrassed.

"No way. It's not that simple. He draws something, you mumble an idea, he looks at you, and you blurt out the answer. You two are simpatico," Tom said.

Lisa looked at me and sniggered, apparently amused by Tom's observation about Adam and me. I rolled my eyes in response, trying to deflect the attention away from us. In reality, I was tickled that someone had noticed. I was about to smile at Adam—to let him know how I really felt—but out of nowhere, his lips landed on my cheek.

"It's not a bad thing, Nicki," he said, pulling away.

Just as he always did, Adam made me forget myself. Ignoring all our friends, I gave him a quick kiss. "You're right. It's a good thing."

As I arrived at the lockers on Monday morning, the sight of Adam made me so giddy that I gave him a kiss on the cheek before we even said hello. His face lit up, and he wrapped his arms around me, lifting me off the ground.

He whispered, "I missed you yesterday."

"And I missed you."

He put me down, and we reported to one another about our Sundays as we got our books. After a moment, he touched my shoulder and smiled down at me. "I need to see you this week before I leave on Friday."

When he said things like that, it was so difficult to know what to feel. The thought of him leaving made me sad, yet the fact that he was so adamant about seeing me made me happy. It was the conundrum of my life.

Not wanting to dwell on it, I simply replied, "Sure. When?"

"I've a French essay and a physics test this week. And, unfortunately, I've got to do well on it. I fucked up the one last month. Can I see you on Thursday?"

"Sure." A little alarm bell went off in my brain. "On Thursday, Mom won't be home until really late. It's her work holiday party; they always go out afterward. You should come over."

I was subtle, but Adam knew exactly what I was implying. We'd have whole night alone together—something we'd never done before. He just nodded and played with my hair. After a moment, he said with grin, "That sounds…nice. You know, it reminds me I've been meaning to talk with you about something."

"What about?"

His eyes darted to the side for a moment like he was thinking, "Well, about that map I like so much…"

"That again?" I smirked. "I just don't think that map is very interesting."

"Oh, I don't know about that." Adam chuckled. "My girlfriend and I had a very good time following it the other day."

I was stunned. Adam's big smile seemed to have a taunt about it. We both knew what he'd said. My face was in flames. I didn't know what to do, so I fixated on my locker combination for a moment.

"So, do I know this girlfriend of yours?" I peeked over to him. "Would I like her?"

He leaned against his locker, gazing at me with those light brown eyes. My heart couldn't handle waiting for his response, so I stuck my head inside my locker. I couldn't see him, but his voice had a smiling sound to it: "I believe you do know her. I like her…a lot… more than I think she knows."

Oh my God. Adam Kincaid really had just called me his girlfriend. Fortunately, he couldn't see my mouth hanging open. I started to say, "I think…" and then I stopped because I didn't know what I wanted to say. I didn't even know what to think.

After a few seconds, I heard him ask, "What do you think?"

Closing my locker door, I breathed deep before answering, "I think you're right. I do know her, and she's just…" My voice was about to falter, but the glint in his eyes was reassuring. I happily admitted, "She's crazy for you."

Internal cringe. I had just quoted a Madonna song to this beautiful new boyfriend of mine.

Luckily, he didn't seem to notice, as his smile became even brighter. He tucked some of my hair behind my ear and declared, "I'm glad to hear it's mutual."

"You know, she's happy to hear it, too."

Leaning down, he gently rubbed his nose against mine and whispered, "Good."

I held my breath, debating if I should give in to an overwhelming urge to crush my body and lips against his.

He must have known what I was thinking, because he asked, "Is this an appropriate display of affection at eight in the morning in the middle of a school hallway?"

"Um…yeah. It is." I didn't add that I wouldn't mind being pinned against the wall by his hips again—appropriate or not.

It felt like everything had changed between Adam and me that day. Of course, I still had that heady feeling just being around him; I doubted that would ever end. But with the boyfriend/girlfriend pronouncement, everything became more comfortable. Adam seemed happier and less cautious when he spoke to me. And I felt like I could be more myself around him, rather than being on guard the whole time. I also stopped trying to second-guess him so much, especially about Kate. It no longer felt like the other shoe was about to drop.

On Thursday, my heart and stomach were aflutter as Adam and I walked into my house right after school. As I'd predicted, Mom had confirmed that morning she would be gone until ten. So there we were. No parents or Sylvia, no friends, and not outside in a car. We would be all by ourselves for six hours.

Adam and I got some Cokes and were standing in the kitchen talking. There was a natural pause in the conversation when he asked, "Will you show me your room? I'm curious to see what it's like."

"Okay." I smiled, trying to remember it was a normal request.

The moment he saw my room, he said, "This is cool."

I had tidied it up that morning, but the walls remained fully covered in newspaper articles, photographs, posters, and general crap. He walked around studying and reading, eventually asking, "How long did it take you to cover the walls?"

"I don't know, maybe a year or so."

"Brilliant. It's interesting. Do you put up whatever takes your fancy?"

"Pretty much. Mom hates it, but that just makes it more fun."

Adam then turned to my music. First, he glanced at my CDs, then he zoned in on all my old vinyl. He thumbed through a stack of records, which appeared to pass muster. "You've got some good stuff."

Walking around the room again, he nodded toward the bathroom door. "A loo off of your room. That's handy." He peered in and then looked back at me. "That other door can't lead out to the hall. What's through there?"

I gulped. "That's Lauren's room…or was Lauren's room."

"Oh." Adam's face became serious. "I'm sorry. Nicki, I…"

"Oh, no. Don't worry about it." On impulse, I announced, "I'll show it to you. There's nothing in there."

Adrenaline from courage or stupidity took over, and I led him into the bathroom. Lauren's door let out that same crack as the last time I had walked in. The new-paint smell had only faded slightly. Adam's face remained somber. He didn't say anything, but suddenly the words flew out of me.

"I don't like it." I sighed. "My grandmother—Mom's mom—did this. I hate it, really."

I didn't cry as I spoke, but Adam immediately pulled me to him, and we sat on the floor in the middle of the room. It felt so safe in his arms that everything spilled out of me.

I told him all about my nutty family—about how Grandma Stuart had boxed up Lauren's life and hid it out of sight up in the attic; how Mom was so loco herself that she hadn't thought twice about me when Grandma had done it; how Dad had been thoughtful and saved Lauren's room for me, all because of his girlfriend who I used to hate; and lastly how Grandma Johnson had helped me.

It felt really good, not just to finally tell someone but also for the first time not cry as I spoke about my life. I felt more in control. Adam would ask a question here and there, but mainly he just listened.

When I ran out of steam, he kissed my forehead. I took his hand in both of mine. "Thank you for listening to me. It feels good to be able to talk and not cry. I think it's because I've been talking with you so much. It really can't be that fun for you."

"Rubbish. I'm happy you would share that with me." He grinned. "I've got something for you."

"What's that?"

"A Christmas present." He smirked, clearly knowing he'd caught me off-guard.

"We said no gifts!"

"Well, I changed my mind."

"But I don't have anything for you."

"I don't care. And it's not a big deal. Come with me."

We went back downstairs, and I sat on the sofa while he took a small flat package wrapped in red tissue paper from his jacket. He must have snuck it in.

He sat next to me and offered it, looking a little anxious. "Adam…" I tried to protest, but I was too touched. A guy just wrapping a present for you could clench the coldest heart. As I slowly unwrapped the paper, it was apparent that it was a small book, so I expected to see a novel he thought I might like.

I didn't expect what it was—a beautiful brown leather journal, wrapped with a matching cord of leather. My fingertips brushed across the soft material, which smelled so nice. "It's so pretty."

"Look inside."

As I undid the cord, the pages fell open to beautiful illustrations of flowers and vines edging every page and done by his own hand. I was stunned, though, to see what was pasted into the first page. It was a fine sketch of a woman's profile from a slightly turned angle. Despite the halved image, I knew at once who it was.

"This is me?"

He nodded shyly. "Yeah, I drew you in lessons…around the time you weren't speaking to me. You never looked at me, so you were a good model."

"Oh, Adam. No one's ever done anything like this before. I don't know what to say."

"Do you like it?"

"Like it? I can't believe you made it for me. I love it!"

"I'm so glad. I was worried you wouldn't like it. I tried to pick the best sketch." He looked down shyly. "I had a few to choose from."

"Well, I didn't talk to you for a while. I'm sorry about that." I threw my arms around him, holding as tightly as I could. I hoped he could tell how my heart felt, because the only words I found were, "Thank you."

For the next few hours, Adam and I hung out downstairs, laughing our way through bad TV. Eventually, we got hungry and ordered a pizza. Then around seven, we started a heated debate about the cover of the Clash's *London Calling* album. I swore it was a take-off on one of Elvis's old records, and he didn't believe me. I swiped Mom's Elvis, and we ran upstairs together to check out the Clash album.

He laughed breathlessly at me. "I don't know why I bother arguing with you. You're usually right."

"About some things."

His eyes twinkled, and he pulled me onto my bed. Right as we hit the mattress, we were shamelessly all over one another, and this time clothes started flying off. Somewhere along the week, I had lost all my inhibitions with the guy. I knew I still wasn't ready to have sex, but my fingers itched to touch him again. So I made the first move and had his shirt and sweater off in a snap.

As soon as I saw his skin, my hands and mouth were all over his lanky muscles. I followed them up and down and all around, and every time I hit a patch of his curly brownish hair, I squirmed below. It must have been obvious, because soon after I'd gotten him half-naked he said, "I think this is unfair to both of us."

"What is?"

"I haven't seen that map in a while."

I giggled and looked down at my blouse. "Well, help me with the buttons."

He got to work on the buttons and muttered, "I like your men's vest better. It was easier." But when my bra was exposed, he said, "Actually, I take that back."

Of course, my lacy bra with front closure was premeditated. He smiled and made a throaty sound in appreciation as he first traced my scars and then the lace around my breasts. "So beautiful." I knew I wanted the sensation again of him kissing my body, so I unfastened my bra as fast as I could.

That elicited a groan and such quick action from him that I was flat on my back before I knew it. He was kissing and sucking on my right nipple while massaging my other breast. His mouth was wet and warm, bringing my body to life. I arched toward him, only wanting more. I got so worked up that it took me a bit to realize his mouth was headed south.

As much as I wanted whatever Adam was planning on doing down there, I wanted to feel him first. I had left this boyfriend of mine with blue balls too often — not to mention I was dying to see what he looked like. So I pulled him up for a kiss and then rolled us over so that I was on top of him.

I could tell he was curious by what I was doing and probably thinking I was slowing us down. But he appeared almost baffled when I smiled and reached down to the button of his Levis. I always loved the fuzzy belly above a guy's jeans, so I stroked it a few times before I started to unbutton them. In a quick breath, he exclaimed, "Oh my God."

Enjoying my few minutes of complete power over a guy, I toyed with him. "Is this okay?"

"Fuck yeah."

With that, I unbuttoned his jeans and started tugging them down along with his boxers. I was a little uncertain as to how far they should go. Down to his thighs? To his knees? Off altogether? Adam decided for both of us. He quickly kicked off his shoes and stripped down. The sight of him fully naked gave me a start.

For as much as John and I had fooled around, he'd never been totally nude in front of me. This was my first time being with a guy like that. I felt a little thrill. Being in the presence of a perfect male form reminded me of visits to the Menil Collection or the Museum of Fine Arts. I wasn't just seeing something beautiful in a book; I was present and fully experiencing it.

"I'm…uh…" Adam said.

When I raised my eyes to his, I saw he looked uncomfortable, maybe even distressed.

"Well, in the UK, they don't…" he continued to mumble sheepishly.

Then I realized what he was so shy about — he was uncircumcised. Meredith's friends had said she didn't like it. Yet, I hadn't noticed at all. His penis looked perfect — just like the rest of him. It seemed to be about the same size as John's; I really wasn't sure if that was large or small. And yes, there was the difference of a foreskin, but because I had seen more classical art and statues in my life than American porn, his foreskin looked like it was supposed to be there.

"You know, you look like Michelangelo's *David*," I said with a smile.

He grinned when he heard it, appearing both relieved and pleased, and he pulled me back on top of him for a forceful kiss. I didn't let that go on for too long, though. I wanted to play around, so I moved down his body. The relatively small amount of experience I'd had with guys had taught me one universal truth — they were simple. If you put your hand and especially your mouth on their dick, they were instantly happy. If you made them come, they were ecstatic. And if you let them come in your mouth, they were downright overjoyed.

Afterward when I looked up at him, he was still shaking and panting, but he started to smile. He pulled me up as that guaranteed overjoyed grin spread across his face. "That…that was fucking fantastic."

Whatever I had done earned me a long, passionate kiss before he rolled me on my back. He extended the kisses down my neck and around my breasts. Venturing downward, he brushed every one of my scars with a kiss as he went lower and lower on my stomach, causing me to hold my breath in anticipation. I didn't hold it long, though, because he continued kissing me as hooked both his hands on my skirt and yanked it off along with my panties.

I squirmed a little out of embarrassment. I was lying there completely exposed. I hadn't even been that naked in front of John. And now Adam had the complete ugly view of the scars across my body. I was going to say something about not wanting to scare him off, but Adam groaned—a low, sexy groan. He went back to work kissing my scars, and this time he started going lower and lower, below my belly button. I was playing with his hair the whole time, feeling every kiss on my stomach deep below as well. When he reached the top of my pubic hair, kissing along the edge of it, my breath hitched. Was he really going to do what I thought he was? Indeed he was. A few minutes later, my hips started bucking, and there was no controlling me from repeatedly mashing myself into his face, eventually releasing into the best orgasm ever.

When I caught my breath and came back to reality, I giggled—a little out of embarrassment and a lot out of happiness. Who was I to say men were simple? I was just as easily pleased. I pulled Adam's face up to mine and placed both of my hands on his cheeks, kissing him. I could taste and smell myself on him, but I didn't care, and he didn't seem to mind either.

"I'm glad you liked that." He laughed and rubbed his nose against mine. "And that was just my first go."

We ended up lying under my covers talking and laughing for the rest of the evening. It took a while for me to realize that it wasn't perfectly normal for Adam to be lying naked next to me with his head on my green paisley pillow.

But as the night wore on and I saw that it was getting perilously close to ten, I knew we had to break up our little party. It felt like I had crashed into a wall of sadness. Adam was quiet, too.

Despondent, I said, "You should probably leave soon, before Mom gets home."

He nodded. "We're leaving so bloody early tomorrow anyway." Then he turned his head on the pillow to look at me. "I'm going to miss you, Nicki. These last few weeks have been…wonderful."

My heart was folding in on itself, and there was a giant lump that felt like a boulder in the back of my throat. I couldn't say everything that I wanted to. Instead, I whispered, "Yeah. Me too." I rolled my head away from him as a tear left my eye.

"Oh, Nicki, don't cry."

Turning back to him, I could feel more tears on my face, so I tried to smile. "I won't. Send me a postcard, okay?"

He kissed my wet cheeks. "Of course. I'm back on the second. Can we go out that night? I'll ring you as soon as I can that day."

"I'd like that." I wiped my tears. "I think we both need some clothes now."

We laughed a little as we helped each other get dressed. Looking around the room, I realized that before Mom got home I should also straighten up. Most importantly, I needed to make my bed.

I knew if I walked him out, my tears would come on even stronger. I hugged him and kept my forced smile. "You should let yourself out. So I can clean up my room and wash my face before Mom is home."

He looked a little disappointed but nodded.

"Thanks again for my present. It's really beautiful. You shouldn't have."

"But I wanted to." He leaned down and gave me one more long kiss before he whispered, "Cheers, sweetheart."

I whispered goodbye, too, mainly because I was holding back a gusher of tears that wouldn't let me speak clearly. After kissing my forehead, he walked out the room.

Sitting on my bed, I cried as I heard his car drive off, but I smiled through my tears. The guy was adorable. He'd called me sweetheart!

Chapter Nineteen

I trudged through the next day at school. No Adam to make my day better. No Adam for weeks to make the holidays better.

His absence did provide an opportunity for me to catch up with Lisa and Rachel, though. That Saturday, my mom said she was going out with friends for dinner and a movie, so I begged Rachel to leave Tom for the night and come over with Lisa. She ended up bringing Lisa, pepperoni pizza, and beer she'd scammed from her dad's endless supply.

Lisa started counting. "It's a good thing that you brought one, two, three…damn, Rachel, you brought half a case. How am I supposed to drive home?"

"You won't." Rachel giggled. "We'll just crash here. Nicki's mom won't care."

"I'm in. I should call my mom before I start slurring my words, though."

Being with them again cheered me up. "We haven't done this in a while. I've missed it."

It was true. We hadn't spent the night together since Lauren had died. It had always been so much fun, especially with Lauren lurking around trying to figure out what we were keeping from her about guys and sex. She would spend an ungodly amount of time in the bathroom pretending she was peeing, brushing her teeth, or taking a bath. Out of nowhere you'd hear, "Wait…where were you and John?" or something like that. I'd then scream, "Lauren, get the hell out of there now!"

As soon as we sat down to eat, Rachel immediately got to the point. "I'm guessing you haven't had sex with Adam, because you would have told us immediately, right? So what's been going on?"

"Ask me specific questions, and I'll answer them specifically within reason." I really didn't want to say too much about Adam.

Rachel started a rapid-fire interrogation. "So have you had sex?"

"No."

"Okay. Then we'll start at the beginning. Has he touched your breasts?"

"Yes."

"Shirt on or off?"

"Both."

"Very nice. Has he touched your vagina?"

"Yes."

"Ah!" Lisa jumped in, "Have you touched his penis?"

"Yes."

"Oh my God! And is he really uncircumcised?" asked Rachel.

"I think you know the answer to that," I said, flashing her a look.

"How exciting! So have you touched his penis with your mouth, too?"

"Yes." By then, I was giggling like the silly girl I was. Rachel's eyes got big as she asked, "And has he touched your vagina with his mouth as well? Please say yes."

"Yes." It came out sort of proudly.

And then even Lisa was excited for me. Gripping a pillow, she asked, "And did you have an orgasm?"

I nodded and continued giggling, while Rachel screamed and bounced up and down. "Oh my God! Awesome!"

"All right." Lisa grinned. "That's a wicked good reason for abandoning me since Thanksgiving."

"I'm sorry about that, Lisa."

"Not a big deal, really. Anyway, what is oral sex like? I keep being with these lousy guys who push my head down on them but won't touch me."

"I hate that." Rachel shook her head in disgust. "Nothing pisses me off more than a guy who pushes my head down to his dick. It's so demeaning. I never give a blowjob to a guy who does that to me."

"I guess I'm lucky." I giggled.

"Yes, you are!" said Rachel.

Lisa then asked the question everybody, including me, wanted to know the answer to. "So, when he gets back in January, will you have sex with him?"

"You know. I haven't told y'all about how great he's been to me… how kind he's been about…about Lauren and my family and stuff… or how much fun we have together."

"Wait. Are you in *love* with him?" asked Lisa, her eyes wide.

"Like I was saying," I said. "I really like him, but I'm pretty sure I'm not in love—at least not yet. I think that's got to be more than a couple weeks of good times."

"Smart girl," said Lisa.

"And sex?" asked Rachel.

"I'm not having sex with him until—"

Rachel interrupted, "Until you're in love with him?" She was so eager for an answer she leaned in as far as she could in her chair.

"Until I have my shit together and I'm in love with him. I mean he's wonderful and gorgeous and so much more, and the way he makes me feel is just special, but…I'm still messed up. I don't know if it's a good idea for me to do something like that when I'm still like I am, but believe me I've thought about doing it with him a lot."

As if she was letting out a great secret, Rachel announced, "Well, I'll tell you what I know."

My eyes widened. I'd forgotten that Rachel might have some information from Tom about Adam's feelings for me. My heart skipped a beat.

"I've been holding back on this even though it's not much. Tom says he's never seen Adam happier." Rachel got a big smile on her face.

My heart swelled. I may not beat Kate, but he cared for me more than Meredith. I got some satisfaction from that.

Then Rachel hit me with the shocker. "But the bigger thing is that Tom said he heard Sylvia tease Adam about you. She said something like, 'Just because she's the love of your life doesn't mean she can't be my friend, too.' Anyway, Tom thinks that he's…well, that he's in love with you but doesn't know it yet or doesn't want to say it yet or something like that. You know how guys are."

Adam in love with me? Like *in love* in love with me? I thought about the journal he made me and him calling me sweetheart. Even though it was such an innocent thing to say, it had felt like he'd meant more when he'd said it. My heart was bursting with happiness, but all I could say was, "Wow."

"Does this change how you feel?" Lisa asked.

I was still shocked—too shocked to cogently answer that very good question. "Well, it makes me happy—like, kind of giddy, but I don't think it automatically changes how I feel. I'll get back to you."

For the rest of the night and into the morning, I stayed absolutely elated by what Rachel had told me. I'd memorized her words and parsed through them repeatedly, even when eating breakfast with Mom. Unfortunately, she took my silence as an opportunity for a big talk.

After taking a couple sips of coffee, she cleared her throat. "Nicki, I think it's time we had a talk."

"Yeah?" The tone of her voice put me on red alert, but there was no way I was looking at her.

"It's about Adam. I see how you are with him…how he is with you…how much time you two spend together. You do spend *a lot* of time together—all day at school, afternoons, weekends. It wouldn't bother me if I hadn't talked with his mother the other day. I didn't know about his family leaving in June. That's going to be very hard for both of you, but especially for you."

Her voice became taut. "This has been a hard time for you. I just don't want you to get hurt. You've been through enough."

All ecstatic thoughts about Adam escaped me as my heart deflated into a harsh reality. "I don't want to get hurt either."

"Nicki, please. Just listen to me. I speak from experience. He's very nice, but there will be many more boys in your life. Don't get too wrapped up in him."

If the last several months had taught me anything, it was that pain could be pushed aside for a minute if you made a joke. You could put yourself above it all—maybe find some power when you're otherwise powerless. I bit my tongue, though, because the joke I wanted to make wouldn't have sat well with my audience. I wanted to say to Mom, *Glad to see you've decided to be my mom again.*

Instead, I sat there as her sound parental advice brutally pummeled my heart and then logically registered in my brain. Mom had dutifully cautioned me not to fall for the guy, but not wanting to be harsh, she'd also added the proverbial there-are-other-fish-in-the-sea consolation. She probably expected to repeat it again when Adam left.

I considered what she'd said for a moment and realized that it was most likely universally held, conventional wisdom. A picture popped in my mind of Adam with his family at their dinner table in England. The image was fuzzy at first because he'd never told me what his house looked like. Based on the few British films I'd seen, I could only envision a giant table in a palatial dining room or a rickety table in a dark, thatched cottage with rats underfoot. Nowadays, there had to be something in between, but I couldn't think of it, so I went with the palace.

Then the picture took shape of Adam in his fancy house, with his fancy parents telling him he shouldn't get too caught up in that Nicki Johnson. Mrs. Kincaid liked me for some unknown reason, but in the end, she had to think I was just another girl with a crush on her perfect boy. I was even less desirable, though, being an American with an awful Texas accent.

They would tell him that, yes, they were going back to the United States in a few weeks and he could see me again. But they would be leaving soon enough, and realistically, he would be back with Kate by the summer. They might even suggest he let me down sooner rather than later. I realized the scene was so predictable that it could have been playing out simultaneously to my own at that very moment. And it was so painful that just thinking about it made my eyes cross.

I tried to will all thoughts about my futureless relationship with Adam back into their locked compartments in the back of my mind and pit of my stomach, but I couldn't deny reason and reality. I was just about to throw my hands over my face to hide my welling tears when Mom declared, "But because I *was* once seventeen, I know you're not going to listen to me."

But I actually was listening to her for once. Confused by everything, I scratched my head. "Huh?"

Reaching into her pocket, she took out a business card and put it in front of me. "I just wanted to let you know that if you need birth control, please call my OB/GYN's office and set up an appointment. It's a large practice, and you don't have to see my doctor. They have my insurance, which you're covered on. I think it would be wise to do it over the break."

I peered down at the business card, which seemed to demand action from me. *She wants me on the pill ASAP?* I was beyond confused then. First, she'd put me through an emotional wringer by telling me to cool it with my boyfriend, and then she'd started a sex talk that amounted to passing me a business card. I wasn't expecting it at all, but I was happy to have it end like this.

"Oh…okay. Thanks, Mom." It sounded curt, but what was I supposed to say—*That's really thoughtful?*

She wasn't done yet. She pressed, "If you're going to be sexually active, you should be on the pill. The last thing I want for you is to end up pregnant right now. You should also use condoms because of AIDS and other diseases."

So being in high school and pregnant was worse than AIDS. Only a mother who'd married too young could think that. Not wanting a lecture, I said, "Got it, Mom. Are we done?"

"Sure. So will you do it?"

Ha! So that's what she was getting at. She must have known I'd been a virgin before I'd started seeing Adam. Now, she wanted to know if I'd already had sex with him or if I was planning on it. What was my answer to that?

Too much silence on my part made her antsy. She asked again, "Will you?"

Rachel and Lisa had asked me the same thing the night before. That conversation may have been an interrogation, but this felt like I was on the stand—like I needed to make a decision. *Will I or won't I? Yes or no?* I thought of my overwhelming urges to touch Adam and to have him touch me. Then I thought of him calling me sweetheart. *Jeez. Who am I kidding? It's just a matter of time.*

"Yeah. It's probably a good idea." In a pathetic attempt to seem like less of a horny teenager, I said under my breath, "Just in case."

You couldn't fool Mom on matters of the heart, though. She saw right through it and smirked. "'Just in case.'" Parenthood took her over once again, though, and she ended the talk more motherly. "Good. I won't be worrying, then."

Chapter Twenty

If Adam had left for two weeks at any other time of the year, I would've continued to bumble around my little self-centered universe, wondering what he was doing and who he was doing it with. But those darker thoughts were kept at bay because it was my first Christmas without Lauren. I was glad that we were going to my grandparents in Baton Rouge, because being at home sucked. I hadn't felt that lonely since the summer, and the only antidote was to look through the book Adam had made for me. It made me smile every time.

On the drive to Baton Rouge, I promised myself that I would bring up Lauren's name a few times while I was there. Ignoring her might be my grandmother's way of dealing with her death, but it wasn't going to be mine. I wouldn't say anything inappropriate, but I simply wanted the family to acknowledge her, especially at Christmas.

I dropped her name once or twice, and no one said anything, so I decided to make a big deal of it at Christmas dinner. With the full holiday spread before us on the table, Grandpa Stuart always started off with a toast. Lauren and I had always liked it because we got a tiny bit of wine so we could join in. Even during this totally crappy year, Grandpa found things to toast—his most recent golf scores and Grandma's lump-free gravy.

After everyone took a drink, I piped up, "And to Lauren because we miss her."

There was a moment of silence before Grandpa broke it with "Hear, hear." He smiled at me, and I looked at Grandma, who appeared sad as she looked down.

I turned to Mom, and she declared, "Yes, to my littlest girl." She looked at me with a small smile and tearful eyes, but I wasn't crying. She had made me grin.

"My littlest girl" was Mom's nickname for Lauren. I was so proud of her. I'd never expected to ever hear her say that again.

We flew back home the day after Christmas, and the following day I went to Dad's. I wanted to be back in Bellaire for New Year's Eve—not that I was going to a big bash, but I wanted to spend it with my friends instead of with Dad and Michelle. Plus, I had the OB/GYN appointment that week.

While I was at Dad's, he asked me to join him on an expedition to the liquor store for his New Year's Eve champagne. Maybe he thought I was bored.

But as he was pulling out of the driveway, he announced, "Your mom says you have a boyfriend."

This was bad. As far as I knew, Mom and Dad only really talked when there was something to discuss about Lauren and me. Everything was civil between them, but Mom always said, "We only talk about what's important—you two."

I was trying to figure out why they might have talked recently. I desperately hoped that I could just sweep the story aside with "Yeah. He's nice." I changed the radio station for added effect. Then my eyes darted over to Dad, who returned the side-eye.

"So, tell me about him," he said.

Dad had to have heard the anxiety in my voice as I offered information on Adam that amounted to his name, rank, and serial number. Why was Dad doing this to me?

"Your Mom thinks you two have become pretty serious, pretty fast," he said.

Somehow Dad was managing to simultaneously stare at me and drive the car. I needed to make a joke. "Dad, don't expect to be paying for a wedding for at least ten years, and at this point I wouldn't bet any money on him being the groom, okay?"

Dad's eyes went back to the road. He exhaled. "Nicki, you know I don't think something serious right now would lead to a wedding. That's not what I'm getting at."

Oh God. Dad was going to have a sex talk with me. He had always left these things up to Mom. Humor hadn't worked before, so I tried gratitude to get him to back down. "I appreciate your…um… concern, but Mom and I talked. Don't worry about it."

"I know." He side-eyed me again and then looked back at the road. "Your mom told me about the…er…doctor that you're going to see. I wanted to talk with you about something else."

He smiled after he'd said it, but it didn't work on me. I was not at ease, and he didn't appear to be either. Dad talking to me about something like a gynecological appointment was way weird and totally embarrassing. I looked at him apprehensively. "What do you want to talk about?"

He acknowledged my suspicion by focusing only on the road. "Listen, I'm a realist. It's not like I think you'll wait until you're married. I just would like for you to have some history with someone over a considerable period of time. I don't like it that he's leaving in a few months."

Turning to the window, I mumbled, "I don't like it either." I refused to go back to that well of darkness, though. I had done my best to stay out of it since Mom had dumped all over me before Christmas. I looked at him squarely and nodded. "Got it, Dad."

But he wouldn't give it up. "Just do me a favor and…when you're with him…stop before things get out of hand. Make sure he's the right one."

I went back to the window, lost in the conversation. In a very low voice, I pondered to myself but still aloud, "What exactly constitutes 'out of hand'?" I was pretty sure that whatever "out of hand" was, Adam and I were about to get there soon.

"Nicki, what are you asking?"

Turning to Dad, I saw he was startled. My eyes widened with some embarrassment. "Sorry, Dad. I was talking to myself. I forgot you were here."

He looked relieved and chuckled. "Well, I'll still answer the question without getting into specifics. I would say 'out of hand' is somewhere between not wanting to stop and not being able to stop…and closer to the latter. As for what exactly is…going on at that point…I'll let you be the judge of that."

I nodded. "Got it." My mind ran through my encounters with Adam, and I quickly decided that nothing had gotten out of hand yet. But I couldn't imagine really ever *wanting* to stop anything with Adam. As for him being the right one, well, as Rachel would put it, I could do much worse.

We sat in silence for a moment.

When we got to a red light, Dad faced me full on. "Nicki, I'm sorry if I'm sounding heavy-handed and intrusive. Since I'm not back there often, I haven't met the guy to —"

"To scare the living shit out of him?"

Dad laughed hard — so hard that he didn't seem to care that I'd cursed. "Yes. Scare the shit out of him. That's exactly what I would do, and more."

Later that afternoon, I curled up on Lauren's bed. If anything was out of place in her room, it was only because I'd left it that way the last time I'd been there. Yet it felt like so much else had changed in my life since Thanksgiving. I thought about Adam — the big change in my life in the last month. He'd made me happier, but not fully happy. He helped me, but he couldn't fix me.

If Lauren were alive today, I wouldn't be talking about Adam with her that much. I'd be just as alone in my thoughts about him as I was right now. The age difference between Lauren and me usually didn't matter, but I knew that a lot of my relationship with Adam was not age appropriate for a thirteen-year-old. I certainly wouldn't have told her about that conversation with Dad. It's not like I would never have talked with Lauren about that stuff, but definitely not for a couple of years.

But now that Lauren was dead, did she know everything anyway? Was Lauren's soul hanging out around me? I looked up at her ice-blue ceiling and wondered exactly where she was. No divine revelation occurred, though. No angel or Saint Lauren descended from heaven.

Just me, crying alone and thinking out loud again. It was the new normal that I had to get used to.

I got home to Bellaire in the late morning on New Year's Eve. Mom got me settled at home and then went shopping. She said something about a party she was going to that night, which seemed a little more festive than I'd expected from her, but that was a good thing.

When I flipped through the letters and advertisements, a postcard fell to the floor. I smiled immediately because it was a detailed map of the London Underground.

Adam sent me a postcard of a map! He's so clever. I eagerly turned it over to see what he'd written:

I miss you, Sweetheart.

He hadn't signed it, but the card was addressed to me in his distinct handwriting. I sank to the floor, smiling a huge, giggly smile.

Chapter Twenty-One

From the moment I opened my eyes on Saturday morning, I was nervous. Was Adam going to call me today?

When he did call in the late afternoon, he sounded like he was happy to talk to me but also exhausted. My heart did a little dance when he said that he still wanted to see me, despite being so tired.

Adam opened the door to his house before I even got up the walk. We met halfway, where he grabbed me close and kissed my hair. Like his postcard, he said, "I missed you, sweetheart."

I got on my tiptoes to say in his ear, "I missed you, too." I pulled away and smiled. "You didn't have to come outside, you know."

"I'd rather say hello to you out here than in there under my mum's eye." As if to prove his point, he gave me a slow, sweet kiss.

Afterward, I asked, "Are you as sick of your parents as I am of mine?"

"More. Traveling with them wears you down. But at least they're both going to bed before long." He sighed. "Sylvia, on the other hand…"

He had to have had a premonition of her because her voice rang from behind us: "Nicki!" Then in annoyance, she called, "Adam, can you bring her indoors?"

After kissing my forehead, he grumbled, "Yes, Sylvia."

We walked inside and talked a bit with his parents and Sylvia about their trip and my trips to Baton Rouge and Chicago. It wasn't long, though, before his parents and even Sylvia wandered upstairs, leaving us alone in the family room. But in one minute, she came bounding back down the stairs.

"I have a present for you, Nicki!"

"Oh, thanks. But you didn't have to do that." I glanced over to Adam, looking for him to confirm what I was about to say. "I haven't really been celebrating Christmas this year. I'm sorry I don't have a gift for you."

"I'm sorry," he whispered in my ear. "I told her not to, but she did anyway."

Sylvia heard what he'd said and scoffed, "Since when do I listen to you?"

With that, she handed me a perfectly wrapped box with a gorgeous bow of different satin ribbons. I was impressed. "Wow. The box alone could be a present; it's so pretty."

"Thanks. I'm glad you like it." She stood a little straighter with pride. "I did it myself."

Adam made a face like he was going to puke. "Can you leave now?"

"Not till Nicki opens her gift."

I opened the present as best I could without destroying the decorations. Sitting inside the tissue paper was a beautiful black woolen scarf with a modern silk patchwork design on it. It looked like stained glass. "Sylvia. Thank you so much!"

She raised her eyebrow to Adam. "See. I told you she'd love it. I know these things."

Wrapping it around my neck, I traced the intricate design. "It's really cool."

"I bought it when we went to London."

"Well, I do love it." I gave her a hug. "Thanks. Let's go to dinner sometime so I can thank you."

Sylvia's eyes popped open. "Oh, really? That will be fun!" She turned to Adam and smiled. "I'll leave you two alone now." She gave me one more hug, and I wished her goodnight before she pranced up the stairs.

"I like her," I said, taking off the scarf.

Adam rolled his eyes but quickly pulled me to him. "I like *you*."

We ended up in his den again, and he put in a random Hitchcock movie that his parents had lying around. It wasn't like we were going to watch it; the movie was just an alibi.

I'd only seen the FBI warning before we were all over one another. For one brief moment, I thought maybe I should actually talk with him first to find out what had happened with Kate. But somehow I had a feeling that everything was okay, and frankly, I didn't want to talk. I just wanted to keep kissing him and feeling his hands on me and mine on him.

Adam was the one to pull away, though. He smiled. "I actually have a little present for you as well, but Sylvia kind of spoiled it with hers."

"But you already gave me a gift, and I haven't given you anything at all."

Reaching over to the side table, he picked up a small, soft package that was wrapped in white tissue paper. "It's not a big thing. Just a souvenir from England."

I took the parcel from him and opened it up. I laughed as a red and white wool scarf fell out. It had "Liverpool" written on it and a logo with a shield—just like the scarf he had in his room. "You want me to be a Liverpool football fan?"

"Normally, I'd say you couldn't be prettier," he said, wrapping the scarf around my neck. "But this scarf just might do it."

"Thank you, I guess." I giggled.

His expression softened to a more thoughtful one. "You're welcome. I just wanted you to have something from home." He looked aside and added, "For when I'm not here."

I swallowed hard. "I thought we weren't going to talk about that."

"I don't want to," he said, shaking his head. "I don't think it will do us any good. I just thought about things a lot whilst I was away."

I nodded. I had, too. About him. About me. About Lauren. If I wanted to think, I had a lot to think about, but thinking got tiring. That was one of the reasons that I loved just being with him. I didn't have to think so much.

He pulled me tight to him and began to speak. "The first night at home, I was sitting watching TV with Mum. She mentioned it was good to be home, and I agreed. Then she said, 'But you miss Nicki.' I asked her how she knew, and she said she could just tell. Plus, I was clutching a cushion."

"She *is* a psychologist."

"Exactly. Anyway, she likes you—a lot. She said she understood how we'd got so close so fast. She didn't say anything more. I guess the good side of her being a counselor is that she's not very judgmental." His smile soon turned to a frown. "My dad, though. He's a scientist, and he's quick to judge. He also has a different background than my mum. He likes you and everything, but he sat me down and warned me about getting too serious with you."

I knew it. I just knew it. With some trepidation, I asked, "Because?"

"Because we live in different countries."

"Anything else?"

"Oh, he just has these ideas about the type of girls I should be with."

My back automatically stiffened. *Proper English girls.* Hoping my bitterness wasn't on display, I asked, "And?"

"And it doesn't change anything." He kissed my forehead in reassurance. "I'm not going to stop going out with you."

I felt some relief and exhaled. "I got a couple of those talks from my parents, too."

"I expected as much." He added with some chagrin, "I'm not a very desirable suitor."

"*I* still like you."

Leaning in for a kiss, he declared, "I more than simply like you, Nicole Johnson."

That made me tackle him. If we were going to do some kind of Romeo and Juliet thing and defy our parents, I was all for it. Any questions I had about Kate escaped me entirely. I clung to him and kissed him hard. I thought he was as into it as I was, but he pulled away again.

"There's something else I need to tell you."

"What's that?"

"Well, I saw Kate."

"Oh." My heart had to have stopped. Something bad was coming. My thoughts raced backward for a moment to think about how he'd acted with me since he'd gotten home. He wouldn't make out with me repeatedly, say all those adorable things, and *then* tell me he cheated on me, would he? That would be so shitty and really not like him.

"I saw her twice, actually. The first time we went out to dinner—just as I told you we would. It was good to see her. We caught up. She asked me questions about you first, but I could tell she bloody well didn't like hearing about you. I think she saw how I feel about you. She had just broken up with that guy she'd been dating and was pretty naffed off."

I didn't like what I was hearing. Weeping ex-girlfriends were very dangerous things. I tried to ferret out the issue Adam was obviously dancing around. "So she cried on your shoulder, and then what happened?"

"Nothing." He shrugged. "I hugged her goodnight. That was it. Then I saw her again when a group of us went out on our last night. I didn't expect to see her at the pub, but she showed up with another friend."

A bar. Drinking beer. An ex-girlfriend who wants him back. My eyes must have had terror in them. Adam noticed. "It's okay. Nothing really happened. Kate just got smashed, and I had to pull her off me. She demanded I take her home, but there was no way I was doing that. So David made sure she got back."

I stared at him for a moment without saying anything, just thinking about the phrase "had to pull her off me." Did that mean she'd tried to kiss him? Or did it mean they actually had kissed? Or more? Did I want to know? No, I didn't want to know…I felt nauseated… my stomach felt like it had turned inside out…but I had to know.

I ventured, "So, when she was all over you…what exactly happened?"

His eyes told me that he comprehended exactly what I was asking. He didn't flinch. "I said no. I didn't touch her."

I nodded. There was no need to clarify what he'd said no to—Kate had wanted to have sex. Still, she might have touched him—might have tried to kiss him. I still looked at him warily. "Is that it?"

He played with my hair. "Yes, that's it. I suppose most guys wouldn't have told you, but I…I don't know. I felt like if I didn't, I would be misleading you somehow."

Smiling in relief, I touched his hair as he did mine. "Thank you. I appreciate it."

"Oh, I forgot. There was something else." He grinned mischievously.

"What's that?"

"David says hello."

He knew he was being a smug little jerk, so I punched him in the arm. "I think you're being a wanker, right? That's what they call people like you in your country?"

"That's right. But he still says hi. And he's glad you followed his advice."

I smiled at the thought of what *that* conversation had been like between the two of them. "I should thank him for it one day."

"Better not thank him too much," he said.

"*Pfft*. Don't be silly."

"So, can we go back to our previous topic?"

I laughed at him. "What topic? We weren't talking. We were kissing."

"I know. Let's start that again."

We messed around for another hour—as best as we could on a couch with his family upstairs. Later, things were quiet between us as he drove me home. I figured it was just because he was so tired.

So when he stopped the car and turned off the engine at a random street corner, I was surprised. He grinned at me and demanded, "We should get out."

"Why?"

"You'll see."

Thinking he was up to something very odd, I opened the door and got out. "It's starting to rain. Why are we out here?"

With the same goofy grin, Adam came around the car and took my hand. "So, do you know where we are?"

I looked around. *What in the world?* I pointed to the street sign over his head.

"This is where you told me to sod off a few months ago."

"I guess that's right." I squeezed his hand. "Sorry about that."

"So, I thought this might be a good place to say something I've been thinking about."

My eyes widened, and my heart sped. Before I could think my next thought, he grabbed my other hand.

"I love you, Nicki. Truly, I do. I know that it hasn't been that long that we've been together, but I can't help it. You're so special to me—more special than anyone I've ever known."

My racing heart stopped. There was nothing else I wanted to say but exactly what I felt at that moment.

"I love you, too."

Then we both had goofy grins and leaned into a kiss that was full and warm. I pressed myself against him as firmly as I could, but still not as close as my heart wanted. Everything became fiery between our bodies until a car came down the street.

We stepped apart, and Adam gave me a peck on the cheek, saying, "I'm feeling much better than the last time I was here with you."

"Well, I know I *certainly* am." I giggled.

When I got home, I was relieved Mom was already down for the night. I didn't want to talk to her; I needed to think. After closing the door to my bedroom, I leaned against it. Had Adam Kincaid really told me he loved me? I thought about it all objectively, and it really seemed so unlikely that he would ever feel that way about me. Yet, I'd been there. He'd said it on the street corner and again on my doorstep.

I was elated, but I wasn't bursting to tell anyone. I wanted to keep it to myself. It was something I wanted to cherish a bit just for me.

Chapter Twenty-Two

It was bound to happen, even in a high school as large as Bellaire. Eventually, Adam and I would run into Meredith.

Nothing was really different that Monday morning in front of our lockers. Adam was trying to make up for teasing me by nuzzling my neck. Then Meredith walked by with her new boyfriend, Jared. Jared played basketball and towered over the school. He appeared to be telling her a story, but she wasn't looking at him. She was looking at me.

It would've been rude not to acknowledge her, especially since I hadn't seen her in weeks, so I was friendly. "Hi, Meredith."

Nodding, but with no smile, she said, "Hi…and hi, Adam."

He glanced up and greeted them both as they continued walking by us. "Morning, Meredith…Jared."

When he looked back at me, he appeared bothered by the exchange, so I asked, "Was that bad?"

"I couldn't care less." He shrugged before a smile returned to his face, and he leaned back into my neck. "Now, where was I?"

That afternoon, Adam and I were enjoying some hot and heavy dry humping on my couch. All the thrusting and rubbing made me wonder if it bore any similarity to actual intercourse—it felt pretty darn good.

When we finished our daily messing around, we got our clothes situated just in case Mom found her way home early. That morning's encounter with Meredith also still lingered in the back of my mind. I wanted to ask a question that had been bugging me for so long.

I went about it in a roundabout way. "So, what do you think of Meredith and Jared?"

"I don't know. Good for her." He shook his head and sighed. "I didn't really treat her very well, so I hope Jared does."

"What do you mean?"

"I stayed with her when I shouldn't have…maybe out of guilt." Then he looked at me sideways. "And because you wouldn't give me the time of day."

I rolled my eyes. "Yeah, right." Then I probed further, "But what do you mean by guilt?"

His eyes went up to the ceiling. "Things went badly with Meredith. I'll never let that happen with you."

"You don't have to give me details." The thought of specifics made me want to puke, and yet I was curious. "I probably wouldn't want them anyway, but what do you mean?"

Adam glanced at me for a moment, obviously deciding what to say, but he soon cut to the chase. "Meredith and I should never have had sex, mainly because I wasn't that into her. We never clicked; I carried on seeing her only because things were easy with her. Then this one night we were both drunk—you've never seen me that way before. She was the one who started it, and the way she was with me…I never thought for once that she was a virgin, for God's sake; otherwise, I'd like to think things wouldn't have gone so far." He grimaced and continued with the question that answered itself. "But who knows?"

Gone so far? Like gotten out of hand? I'd heard that before. "That doesn't seem so bad…I mean…not unusual." Remembering what had happened between him and Kate at Christmas, I thought to myself, *After all, girls seem to throw themselves at you all the time.*

Adam frowned. He seemed to choose his words very carefully as he agreed, "I suppose it's an old story. The problems came later when we continued going out even though I didn't feel anything for her any more. In fact, I liked her less and less." He brushed the hair away from my face. "I was falling for you, and I was too fucking daft to realize it."

So that was it. He'd never loved her, but she had loved him. Stupid Meredith must have said she loved him, but he'd never said it back and continued to fuck her because that's what guys do.

Still sounding sad, he said, "I'm sorry it took so bloody long for me to sort things out. We could've had more time together."

Time. Right. The thing we didn't have a lot of. As usual, I ignored it. "Don't worry about it. I wasn't ready for anything anyway."

He leaned and gave me a peck. "I love you." And as if to lighten the moment, he poked me in my side. "It wouldn't be like that with you."

"Oh really?" I laughed. "How would it be?"

"It would be fantastic," he said with eagerness and, with a gasp of breath, added, "I can't think of anything better."

Really not knowing how to respond to that declaration, I kissed him and didn't let it stop. I'd never had intercourse before, but if sex with Adam was going to be anything like kissing him, it probably *would* be fantastic.

I wondered if I should tell him that I'd started taking the pill, but it seemed kind of goofy. I didn't want to have sex right then, and it wouldn't be effective for a few weeks anyway. I also didn't think I could handle any kind of planning for our first time—too much pressure.

Eventually, I replied with what summed everything up: "I love you, Adam."

For the rest of the week, we saw each other every afternoon.

One day at his house, he gave me a hard look, though his voice was casual. "You know, I read *Catcher in the Rye* whilst I was away."

"Yeah."

"Are you going to be okay reading it?"

"Yes…I told you I read it years ago."

"Nicki, it's about—"

"It's about a depressed teenage guy. I remember he gets kicked out of school and ends up with a prostitute and eventually in a mental hospital."

"Yes, but what is Holden depressed about?"

My eyes got wide. I'd forgotten about Allie, Holden's dead little brother. I frowned. "Oh. I hadn't really thought about that part."

"How could you not remember it?"

I didn't say anything as the book came back to me—and not just the mentally unstable, sexually frustrated, and parentally neglected Holden Caulfield. *Uh oh. Some similarities there.* I also remembered Allie Caulfield, the younger brother who Holden couldn't get over.

Looking away for a moment, I at last stated emphatically, "I'm not Holden Caulfield."

It sounded sort of stupid after I'd said it. After all, it was obvious that I wasn't Holden Caulfield. I was grieving for a sibling, but it wasn't like I was going to end up in a mental asylum like Holden.

Yet Adam's face didn't change. He instead began to stroke my hair. "No, you're not Holden, but you're in a similar situation."

I could tell the conversation made him anxious—that he was probably worried the book would set me back and make me depressed.

I scowled at the thought, so I dismissed it. "I'll get through it."

Adam tousled my hair and gave me a kiss. "I'll help."

He really was too kind to me. I looked down, knowing I did want his assistance—but with something else. I had to ask because I couldn't do it by myself, and I really wanted to. I needed to.

"I do need some help with something."

"What's that?"

"Will you help me get some of the boxes with Lauren's stuff down from our attic?"

"Of course." Surely he knew, though, that I wasn't asking just for his ability to move boxes.

So, Adam went up into the attic for me, and I stayed at the bottom of the ladder. He soon called down to me, "Nicki, none of these boxes are marked. There's got to be at least forty of them up here. Do you want me to help you up?"

"Sure."

"Grab a jacket first. It's freezing."

We tromped around the musty, dirty attic searching for her things. Once I figured out her stuff was in the most non-descript office boxes, I saw there were only three.

We sat down together in front of them. Adam was obviously waiting for me to do or say something, but I just stared at the containers. The sight of them made me incredibly sad. "So, Lauren's life amounted to three boxes."

"She was young." Putting his arms around me, he kissed my hair. "You don't need a lot of stuff to remember who she was."

Of course he would say the right thing to me. I turned to him and looked into my favorite eyes in the whole world. It was such an odd time for me to think about us, but it happened.

My life was intense. Everything about it went way beyond what my friends dealt with on a daily basis. Adam brought lightness to my life that hadn't been there in so long. I felt more like my age again. He wasn't simply a distraction, though; he didn't simply take my mind off things. Being around him made me more at ease, made it easier for me to deal with all my shit. He made life fun and gave it more meaning.

Would I have felt the same way about him if Lauren hadn't died? Maybe not as quickly, but I was sure I would've ended up right in the same place—completely in love with him.

I knew Adam was the one for me. Mom was right that there were other guys out there. They could be substitutes, but they couldn't replace him. We'd only been together for a couple months, but it seemed much longer. It felt like I had a rare connection with him, and remarkable as it was, I was confident he felt the same way about me.

What did I do in response to this revelation? I placed my right hand against his cheek and laid a giant kiss on him, full of all my emotion. Adam immediately responded, pulling me to him.

When my hand wandered down to find his dick, he murmured, "Is this what we came up here for?"

"Sorry about that. I—"

"Don't apologize." He tousled my hair. "I just thought we might take the boxes down and go to your bedroom."

"Um…we can't." I shook my head both to say no and shake off my arousal. "Lauren's stuff should stay up here where Mom won't find it. She's much better now, but I don't want to push her. I mean…

even if she was totally fine, she may not want to look through this stuff for years."

"Or maybe ever."

We plowed through the boxes. I'd come across things that would make me cry, like Lauren's maimed and threadbare teddy bear, Mr. Bear. Other things would make me laugh and remember the best of her, like her book reports and really bad art projects. I found her diary but stopped reading it after a page. It was so personal that I felt like a snoop and quickly put it down.

It was great having Adam at my side while I remembered all that was Lauren. As he had pointed out, though, it *wasn't* all of Lauren, just the physical reminders. He helped me through the whole thing. He hugged me when I got blue and was interested when I would show him certain items. But after an hour, I worried that Mom would come home soon. It was time to decide what I wanted to keep.

Mr. Bear was the obvious choice. It was a little trite and maybe silly to take her favorite stuffed animal, but Mr. Bear had made her really happy. She'd been inseparable from him most of our lives, more so when we were little, but he'd still always been there on her bed, even when she'd gotten older. I explained it to Adam, and his face became concerned.

"I don't think it's silly. It's very personal. But, what will happen when your mum sees it?"

"Oh…I hadn't thought of that." I looked down at the little guy. "But, I want him. I'll hide him for now. Maybe later it won't be a big deal."

I wanted to tell Mom that I'd been up here, though, simply to show her that I was brave enough to have gone through the boxes.

"You know, I told her I wanted to look through the boxes specifically for a notebook. Maybe I could bring one down."

Adam pulled one out of a box. He opened it, and we saw it was totally blank inside.

"Perfect," I said, both of us smiling.

Chapter Twenty-Three

That Saturday night, Adam and Tom went out for a guys' night out. I took it as an opportunity to repay Sylvia for her gift by taking her out to dinner. She was ecstatic even though I was just taking her for Chinese.

For the first half of the meal, she was jumpy and happy, telling me all about her art and why she wasn't going to college. "Daddy wants me to, but I told him to sod off. I'm going to be an artist, not an academic."

She then cocked her head and made a statement that was more of a question. "So you and Adam talked about what you shall do."

"Do when?"

"After we leave."

"Uh, no." There went my appetite. "We're kind of ignoring it right now."

"What?" Her usually perfectly arched eyebrows knitted together in concern. "He said he was going to talk to you."

"Who wants to talk about that?" I thought it was pretty self-explanatory.

Sylvia straightened up in her chair, like she was taking command of the situation. "Well, I'll do it, then. He thinks you should go to university in Britain. I do, too."

Huh? What? I didn't say anything as I absorbed what she'd said.

She used the time to talk more. "He's going to have to cram two years' work into one so he can get the grades he needs to get into uni. He's missed the chance to apply this year because we've been here. He doesn't know where he'll be going yet. Maybe you could decide together."

I'd never even thought of that because I never *would* think of that. But I considered it for a moment, and fate quickly slapped me in the face.

"I can't. I can't be that far away from my family. My grandmother is getting older. I've thought before about going to school at UT because she's in Austin. If she moves to Illinois to be near my dad, I'll try to go to Northwestern. I think I could get in." I grimaced as the hardest fact came out. "I really don't want to be away from my parents. I'm all they've got now."

All the spirit in Sylvia seemed to leave. Clearly, she and Adam had talked at length about it. I always had suspected that underneath all their bickering they were good friends. And they'd decided this was the answer, but they hadn't thought about me.

She was quiet before saying, "I'm sorry. We should've thought of that. I think you should talk to Adam."

"Yeah, I guess so." That was the last thing I wanted to do. Face reality? No way. A distant glimmer of hope came to mind, though. "What about him coming here?"

"Impossible." Sylvia pursed her lips and shook her head. "A lot is expected of him. My dad wants him to choose 'Oxbridge'—you know, Oxford or Cambridge—or at least Exeter or Canterbury. Daddy would never pay for him to study abroad."

Again, fate wasn't on my side; no stars aligning for me in this life. "*Daddy*" would certainly never pay for Adam to go to school with me. I bet he wouldn't even like to hear his kids had talked about me going to school over there. Pressing my lips together, I tried to stop them from quivering and to keep my mouth shut. I wasn't going to cry on the shoulder of Adam's little sister.

After a moment of silence, she spoke. "You two need to talk."

"I know." Of course we needed to talk. There just wasn't much to say.

When the fortune cookies arrived at our table, I told Sylvia to take her pick. By now, I figured I had little control of my life; my fortune would be decided for me.

She read hers aloud: "Stay true to yourself." She laughed. "Well, that's never been a problem for me."

Laughing at her spirit, I pulled the paper strip out of my cookie. I read it and shook my head. "I hate fortune cookies that aren't fortunes. You know, the ones that are just platitudes."

"What do you mean?"

"Mine says, 'Happiness is made.' That tells me nothing."

"Don't you think it's true?"

"Yes, but I also believe in luck." Pulling out a twenty from my wallet, I thought, *And luck is something I don't have.*

As soon as I saw Adam on Monday morning, I knew he'd spoken with Sylvia. They must've done it when he'd gotten home the night before. He was just as sweet to me as ever, but he seemed down. I didn't ask him about it because I knew the reason.

Although it was the conversation neither of us wanted to have, he wasted no time raising the issue when we were alone after school. I tried to deflect it by starting our daily make-out session in my living room, but he only kissed me for a minute.

Pulling away, he announced, "I talked to Sylvia."

"And?"

"And I don't know. Your reasons are completely understandable, but my dad will never let me come to school here. I think that's one of the reasons I got a talking to over the holidays."

Finding both of my hands, he held them tightly in his. "I love you. I just don't know how we can work this out."

"I love you, but I don't know either."

There was silence. It was obvious neither of us wanted to rehash our problems.

After a minute, he said thoughtfully, "Maybe we need to lower our expectations of the future."

Lower my expectations? After the year I'd just had, I had no expectations for my future. How could they be any lower? A lovely boy had walked into my life; he made me feel more special than anyone on earth, and now he was going to walk out of it. To use one of Grandpa's golf expressions, it was now par for the course.

What had Adam meant by that, though? That we were just going to be friends or something? With what I felt for him, that seemed impossible, entirely impossible.

More to myself than to him, I finally replied, "I don't expect anything anymore."

"Oh God, Nicki. This is killing me," he whispered as he stroked my cheek. "Let's not do this right now. We've got a few months. Let's see how things turn out."

It looked like I was going to have to be the realist. Maybe that was my new duty in life. "We'll have to face facts at some point."

"Yes, but not now. It's not going to do any good fretting and worrying now." He smiled. "I have too good of a time with you to waste it doing that. Let's worry about it in spring—not say a word until April at least."

Sticking my head in the sand for a few more months sounded good to me. I simply nodded. "April, then."

It was a stupid decision, yet it was the best decision. Starting immediately, we never, ever talked about the future. We were only in the present, and we were only out to have fun. We found ways to see each other even more than usual, and we'd even started talking on the phone—something Adam hated.

All the while, I checked my calendar every morning to see how many more days I had left until my pill was effective. I still hadn't told Adam. The fact I'd gone and done it—at my mother's urging no less—felt embarrassing and presumptuous. I also remained committed to not planning some big sex event. I just wanted it to happen.

Valentine's Day was on a Sunday, and Adam was very secretive about what he had planned. All he told me was to be prepared for a short hike. The weather was warm for February, and the sun shone brightly as if to give us a blessing.

When he picked me up, I asked, "So what's on the agenda?"

"A picnic." He added sheepishly, "Not very original. I know."

"We live in Bellaire. How creative can you get?"

We ended up far outside of Houston, along the coast. I had to ask, "How do you know about this place you're taking me?"

"Research," he said and smiled.

The "short hike" was definitely off the beaten path, although still on a trail. It was kind of a pain because I had his bulky present in my backpack. But when he announced, "We're here," I understood at once why he'd taken me there. It was a beautiful stretch of undeveloped beach—a rare thing along the petrochemical Mecca of the Texas coast. There were even enough trees around it that we were alone.

"Wow," I said, looking around. "This is really pretty."

"I'm glad I picked the right place," he replied as he spread out the blanket.

Lunch was very fancy—so good that I assumed Sylvia had to have helped him out with it. Afterward, Adam rummaged through his backpack and pulled out a small box; it was obviously a jewelry box.

He presented it to me, grinning. "Happy Valentine's Day, sweetheart."

"Aw. Thanks, Adam." I glanced over at my own bag. "I've got something for you, too."

"Well, you open yours first."

Giggling at the suspense, I opened up the tiny box, and my heart both danced and caved when I saw the contents. A silver filigree heart on an intricate chain rested inside.

As I took out the necklace, Adam commented, "Sylvia helped me. I didn't know if you'd want white or yellow gold, but she insisted that white gold was more classic."

Gold? No one had ever given me gold before. Silver, but not gold. I winced at the tears that came from his thoughtfulness. "I love it. It's beautiful."

"I got it for you because you're my sweetheart," he said with a grin.

I grinned back. He was adorable and corny and everything you'd want in a boyfriend. Handing it over to him, I turned around. "Help me put it on."

The necklace was long, falling just above my cleavage. When I turned back around, he admired his choice, but soon his face changed. His voice was earnest and a little rough. "I...I also wanted you to have it because you'll always have my heart."

He'd alluded to the future. At first I was taken aback that he had broken our promise, but then I realized I was about to do the same thing.

Just as earnestly, I confirmed, "And you'll always have mine."

I quickly grabbed my bag and handed him my little present, not saying anything about it.

After he opened up the flat package the size of a piece of paper, he smiled at the framed print of a drawing from the Menil Collection. I swallowed hard. "Something from here."

"It's perfect. Something to remind me."

That was my breaking point. I couldn't handle the bittersweet any more. My only answers were to blubber in front of him or kiss him. I chose the latter, and boy, did he respond.

We were mashed against each other in seconds. In no time, we were rolling on the blanket, and then he hitched my leg so we could really feel one another. It was crazy and hot, and the emotions I felt were like nothing I'd had before.

I thought I might be alone in my feelings, until he pulled away breathlessly after a few minutes. He rolled on his back, and after a few seconds of silence, he talked to the sky. "I want to be with you, Nicki. I want to be your first. I know it's silly and stupid, but it would mean so much to me."

Of course, I was going to say I wanted to be with him, too, but I had to laugh to myself. What he'd said was such a guy thing to say. What was it with taking a woman's virginity?

When I didn't immediately respond, he looked over at me. "But I understand if you don't. If you want to wait…for someone who will be sticking around."

Sticking around? Why would I want to wait for that guy—if that guy even ever came around? I only wanted Adam.

I smiled to put him at ease. "I want it to be you. Now."

"Now?"

"Now."

He looked back and forth at our open surroundings. "But we're outside, and you'll get cold."

"I don't care, and no one is around. We're in the middle of nowhere."

Making sure he had his wallet, he guiltily remarked, "I have something…"

I got excited to tell him my surprise. "We don't need it. I'm on the pill."

"You are?"

"Yeah, for a while now."

The prospect of condomless sex must've startled him. "I've never… done that before."

"Well, then you'll have a first, too."

That brought out a giant grin and then a big kiss as we picked up right where we'd left off, with my leg hitched against him. He was rock hard in less than a minute. As I kicked off my shoes, he quickly started to strip me of my jeans. Then things slowed down.

He sweetly kissed me as he began to stroke my belly, then my thighs, and then in between. I smiled and urged him on by placing his hand at my vagina. Kissing me again, he first slid one and then two fingers inside as if to prepare me.

He stopped kissing with a cute warning. "I should tell you that I may not last long."

"Whatever." I laughed. "I'm hoping we do it again."

"Fuck yes!"

With that, he undid his pants, and I helped him get them down to his knees. His dick bobbed in full erection. He seemed almost giddy as he lined himself up between my legs. Despite his joy, he asked one more time, "Are you sure?"

I tried to swat him on the butt. "Yes, just do it, damn it."

It had to be some kind of sexual instinct because straightaway I raised my hips up to him so that it was his move next. With a determined smile, he looked down so he could properly place his dick against me. Then, he gently pushed in. The first couple inches didn't feel like a big deal, but the deeper he got, the more pressure I felt. It wasn't painful, but when he finally got all the way in — or at least as far as he was going to get, it was uncomfortable.

I didn't want him to think I didn't like it, though, so I smiled at him when he asked, "Are you okay?"

"More than okay."

He then slid out and back in again, repeating it over and over and going a little deeper each time. I couldn't say it was orgasmi-cally pleasurable, but I could see how it would be in the future. We were naked, physically joined, and our hearts were in it. He was in a much different place, though; he looked like he was about to explode with lust.

"So good. You feel so good. Shit, Nicki. I'm not gonna last."

"Then don't."

It wasn't like he was asking for my permission, because he grunted and launched into me, hitting me deeply. *Yowza!* I flinched hard, and he yelled my name with a curse or two. Then he crashed onto my chest panting and, after a moment, said, "I love you, sweetheart."

I kissed his hair. "I love you."

He looked into my eyes as if to get an honest assessment. "Did I hurt you?"

"No, of course not. It was fun."

He announced, all too seriously, "I wanna make you come, though."

"Well, I'm all for that." I giggled. "Let's try again."

"Oh, Nicki." He shook his head and snickered. "We are going to try and try again."

"You promise?"

Reaching up to my face, he happily rubbed his nose with mine. "I promise."

Chapter Twenty-Four

That night, I restrained myself and waited a whole thirty minutes after I got home before I did a three-way call to tell Rachel and Lisa the big news about the end of my virginity.

Rachel was unimpressed. "It's about time."

"You know I didn't want to have sex until I knew the pill thing was okay."

"If that was true, it would've happened a few weeks ago. You were holding out for something big—which is fine," said Lisa.

After I told them the details, they became more excited.

"You lost your virginity on Valentine's Day, on the beach, with a hot British guy," Lisa said. "Maybe it was worth the wait just for that."

"It's a story to tell your grandchildren."

"Um…right, Rachel." I rolled my eyes. "That's just what I was thinking—not!"

The following day, everything was perfectly normal between Adam and me with no mention of what had happened between us the day before. It was only in English when we were supposed to be listening to Mrs. Anderson that he acknowledged it. Sensing his eyes on me, I turned to look at him. He grinned and winked at me, and I smiled back bashfully because I knew exactly what he was thinking.

I'd already wondered what was going to happen when we got to my house after school; after he winked, I knew. When we pulled in my driveway, we wasted no time kissing in his car. Instead, we were laughing at each other because of how quickly we were trying to get inside the house.

As soon as we got in, he picked me up off the floor. "I'm taking you to bed."

"I can walk, you know."

"This is faster." As if to prove his point, he gave me a kiss while taking me up the stairs.

When we got to my bed, I pulled him on top of me, and our clothes were gone in no time. The mechanics between us were better than the first time, though still a little awkward, but the simple act of sex with Adam was fun. I smiled, taking in all of its pleasures — the connection, the arousal, and the playfulness. We both enjoyed it, and eventually Adam showed me how much with a cursing, grunting, and altogether animalistic orgasm.

Afterward, we cuddled and laughed for a while before I noticed my ratty hair and our pervasive scent. I giggled. "Uh, I think we smell like sex."

"I suppose we do."

"I think my mom may notice."

He looked at me devilishly. "Then maybe we should have a bath."

"I don't think I've taken a bath with anyone since I was six." I giggled.

Raising his eyebrows suggestively, he nodded toward the bathroom. "Me neither."

For the next few days, Adam and I went at it like rabbits. We did it whenever and wherever we could. Adding new positions each day, we also got better and better at it. Our times together were so carnal and fun, but I was also taken by the intimacy.

It was Thursday of that week, and we were moving in unison on my bed. Adam was on top of me, resting on his elbows and holding my hands slightly above my head. Our fingers were interlocked, binding us together. Occasionally, Adam would look down to watch himself slide in and out of me, but mostly our eyes were focused on one another.

When our mutual orgasms peaked, I got spooked. There was something about the look in his eyes and the feeling of our bodies being connected that was too much. Everything about being with him felt impossibly special, but was it? In a way, I didn't care if the actual sex was as good for him as it had been with Kate or Meredith; he appeared to enjoy himself just fine. But did it *feel* the same way for him?

Only allowing him to rest on my chest for a minute, I turned over onto my side. I felt the need to protect myself, but I also wanted to know the truth — at least I thought I might. Timidly, I asked, "Is… is it always this way? When you're with someone?"

He pulled me back toward him. Looking me straight in the eye, he somberly shook his head. "No. It's never been like this for me." Kissing my forehead, he ended the discussion. "I love you, Nicki."

It was bliss — or as blissful as you could get for two high school students living with their parents. For weeks, Adam and I existed in our own bubble. We spent most of our waking hours at each other's side. Soccer season had started for him, which cut into our afternoons, but I made it to all of his games.

And other than an occasional slip, we kept our pact not to talk about the future. Sometimes we would be out with friends or at a party where we couldn't control a conversation. The talk might turn to summer jobs or vacations, but that was rare. Our close friends knew to steer clear of any subject that forced us to talk about our separate ways.

But as the month of March wore on, the foreboding I had kept at bay for all those months began to gradually seep into the forefront of my mind. Maybe it was because everyone started mentioning April in passing all the time. April was the month we'd delayed all of our talks to. Now April was right around the corner. It was as if the sand in which I'd happily stuck my head was now receding all around me.

I didn't really think about what Adam and I would do when he left; I was still absorbing how it was going to feel. Regardless of what we did together in the future, he would be gone from my everyday life. I would miss him desperately—just like I did Lauren. I would be alone again, and loneliness was paralyzing to contemplate.

I kept my troubles away from Adam. Instead, I saved my gloom for when I was by myself, or at least alone in my thoughts.

One night at dinner, I was lost in this teenage wasteland of thought when Mom loudly snapped, "Nicki! Do you hear me?"

"Uh…yeah. I'm sorry. What did you say?"

"I was asking if you were interested in a summer job at the Bellaire library. I heard they're hiring, and I thought you might want me to call my friend there."

"Sure. That would be fun." I smiled apologetically. "Thanks."

With a determined look, she said, "I want you to be busy this summer."

"Why?" Right as the word came out of my mouth, I knew it was stupid to ask.

"Because you're going to be lonely."

I stared at Mom. She'd come a long way in the ten months since Lauren's death. She seemed more present in our everyday life—no longer like a zombie going through the motions. Most importantly, she looked after me more.

The way she'd told me I'd be lonely reminded me of how she used to answer when I'd ask why I needed a coat on a spring day. She would say, "Because you're going to be cold"; it was a fact I wanted to ignore. As I'd grown older, however, I accepted her reasoning. She was right. So I responded just as I would've if she'd told me I'd get cold without a coat. Reluctantly, I said, "You're probably right."

"I am." Her voice became soft. "It's what happens in these situations."

"What kind of situations?" I asked it like Dad would if he was in court. It was a leading question because at that moment I wanted her to lead me through what I was feeling, what I was going to face, and what I didn't want to face by myself.

"When you're in a long-distance relationship."

"Is that what I'll be in?" I'd never considered it might have a label.

"Well, I think so." Her brow furrowed as she confirmed, "You two are staying in touch, aren't you?"

"Yeah, I guess. We haven't talked about it."

"You need to. You need to have a good understanding of what each of you expects."

"Because?"

"Because…" She stopped with a frown and placed her hand gently on my arm. "Because these things rarely work out. Long-distance relationships are difficult for adults—even for married couples. When you're so young, it's doubly hard. If you don't know what you expect of one another, you'll get hurt, although—"

My eyes locked onto hers. "I'll probably get hurt anyway."

"It's going to be painful regardless." Then she tried to spin it. "Who knows, though? Through it all, you two might have a lifelong friendship."

Friendship. Only a friendship, because there was no happily ever after for two teenagers from opposite ends of the Earth. We could merely be friends—pen pals, maybe. If we were lucky, that's what it would come to. There would be a few letters during the year. The highlight might be the rare phone call, but because it was international, it would be expensive and super scratchy sounding. That's it. Was that what Adam had meant when he'd mentioned lowering our expectations?

My heart went numb. How could I just be friends with Adam? Yes, he was my friend—my best friend, really, but I couldn't imagine sharing him with another girl. Would I have to hear about whom he was dating? How happy he was with her? What they did together?

I thought about him saying that Kate hadn't liked hearing about me. At the time, I'd taken a bit of pleasure in it, but there was none now, only sympathy. Very soon I could be in her same situation.

Faking a small smile, I mumbled, "Thanks, Mom. I'll think about it. I need to go study now."

Mercifully, she let me go.

The year before Lauren had died, Tom had hosted a movie night where we'd watched *The Three Faces of Eve*. It had always stuck in my mind, and somehow I identified with it now. It was like I had multiple personality disorder.

I didn't tell Adam about my conversation with Mom; what good would that have done but to start our painful talks early? With Adam, life was playful and fun, and I smiled all the time.

With Mom, I was utterly despondent. There was no use trying to fool her after that downer conversation. She knew what was up.

And with Lisa and Rachel, I went back to acting just as I'd been before Adam and I had gotten together; I was melancholy and sort of half-hearted about life. I'd still hang out with them, but I wasn't as cheerful, and I begged off when I could.

Of course, it didn't take them long to figure out what was going on with me. The first signs were a couple of knowing looks that passed between them. Then there was mention of a trip to Galveston right after school got out. The timing obviously coincided with Adam's departure.

When I looked at a calendar, I realized that it was also near the anniversary of Lauren's death. I had been so absorbed with my Adam crap that I hadn't thought too much about it being almost a year since the accident. It was the one good thing about Adam leaving: I had expanded my inventory of things to be depressed about.

When Rachel and Lisa finally spoke to me directly about everything, we were sitting in my living room, eating popcorn and watching videos on MTV. I knew eventually they would confront me, and I'd expected a coordinated intervention. So I was surprised when they casually stumbled into the conversation.

During a commercial, Rachel announced, "I heard a secret today."

"Really? What?" Lisa asked with a raised eyebrow.

"Well, I can't say. It's about Adam and Nicki."

I looked at her quizzically. What could she possibly know that I didn't? "What's that? Why can't you say?"

"I'm not supposed to know." Rachel shrugged. "But I overheard Tom and Adam talking when I was in the bathroom at Tom's. It's a surprise for you."

Lisa was sardonic. "But you bring it up anyway? Like you're not going to tell her…"

"I couldn't decide, but then I thought that maybe Nicki should be prepared." But first, she scolded me. "I don't think you and Adam have talked much about the future."

I shook my head; I couldn't imagine what Adam was up to. "Is it a good surprise or a bad one?"

"Well, I'd say an all-expense-paid vacation to England is a good surprise," Rachel said giddily.

"Are you kidding?" Adam and I had never talked about me visiting. I considered it a taboo topic.

"Nope! Not kidding. He's going to buy you a ticket to visit him this summer. He wants you to stay for a month or so."

"Oh my God. How would he pay for it?" I couldn't imagine he had that kind of money.

"You know his family is loaded, right?" said Rachel. "His dad is the heir to some giant estate."

I had to shake my head again. At least in Bellaire, Adam's family didn't live that differently from mine. His house was bigger, but it wasn't like they drove fancy cars. An estate, though? My vision of his family at dinner in a palace hadn't been that far off.

"Wow." I couldn't verbalize another response.

"He's been fighting with his dad over it." Then Rachel wrinkled her nose in distaste. "His dad thinks you two are young and you'll break up — like it's not worth it. But Adam's mom is on his side, and his dad finally gave in."

As happy as I'd been, my heart sank. Adam's dad still didn't want us to be together; he probably didn't even want us to be friends after they went back to England. Just like Mom, he thought it was a futile relationship, except he was practical. He wanted a clean break.

I envisioned being in some giant mansion for a whole month with Adam's dad watching over us the entire time. His father had always been nice to me, but I could predict that the scene would be awful. Just thinking about it made me feel like shit.

"It's not that his dad doesn't like you." Rachel frowned sympathetically. "I think he— "

"He likes me okay, but he probably thinks if Adam and I are going to break up anyway, we should just stop seeing each other altogether — like, why prolong it?"

"You think that's it?" asked Lisa.

"Sure." I shrugged. "My mom's said something like that. From their perspective, it makes sense."

Lisa looked at me warily. "What are you saying, Nicki? Do you feel that way?"

"I don't know. I don't know what we should do. Maybe his dad is right. Maybe there's something to just ending things." As the words came out of my mouth, I became confident that Adam's dad could very well be right.

"What does that mean? 'Just ending things.' Like breaking up with him permanently? Like not talking again once he leaves?" asked Rachel.

"Maybe. It's a thought. Maybe it would be easier," I said.

They were both shocked, but Lisa exclaimed incredulously, "Nicki, he's your boyfriend! You would just let him leave and never see him again? That would be horrible for both of you."

"You would really, really hurt him," Rachel said in a warning tone. "He loves you."

"Yeah, but how much? We're supposed to have a long-distance relationship? For how many years? Everybody knows those things don't last." In that instance, quoting Mom made sense. She knew a hell of a lot more about failed relationships than me.

"But you could be friends," said Lisa. "Listen, you know I haven't always liked the guy, but even I can tell how much he cares for you. You care for him. You're good friends. Why would you throw that away?"

"Even if you're not *together* together, don't you want to at least give it a shot?" asked Rachel. "Otherwise, you'll never know."

"I know the odds, and the odds aren't with us." I looked at my best girlfriends' pleading faces and decided to tell them the truth. "And besides, I can't bear to think of him with another girl. And I know him; I know he would be. I'd die of jealousy. I wouldn't be a friend. I'd be a pesky, jealous old girlfriend while he was off with some new girl."

"Oh, Nicki. I'd feel the exact same way. I'd hate the bitch, but is that really worse than not speaking to him?" asked Rachel.

"Of course both of you would date other people," Lisa said in a practical manner. "But not talking to him ever again would be incredibly painful."

That irritated me, and I couldn't see how they were on my side. "I think I know something about pain — more than both of you. I know what I can handle."

I'd played my trump card, and they knew it. Their faces were aghast.

After a moment, Lisa said cautiously, "Let's say you two are guaranteed to break up. Wouldn't it hurt worse to have it happen suddenly? Wouldn't it be easier for you if it happened over time?"

It was a good question; it got to the root of what I'd been debating. Mulling it over, I thought of Lauren. She'd left me suddenly. Would it have been better if she'd had cancer and was sick for a year before she died? I would've been with her another year, but watching her die would've been excruciating.

The difference with Adam was that if I broke up with him, I could have some control in my life. I'd be making the decision. I would be devastated either way, but at least I could make the call and decide when it happened.

My eyes shifted between Rachel and Lisa. Both of them looked alarmed and depressed. I knew I shouldn't talk with them anymore about it, especially Rachel. I was putting her and Tom in an awful position.

I smiled. "Don't worry about it, okay? I'm just thinking."

They seemed relieved, and Lisa said, "That's fine, but you tell us before you do anything."

"Yes, please tell us," Rachel said. "I won't say anything to Tom. It's not my place."

"Sure. I trust you." Then I looked away and lied, "And I'm not going to do anything. I've got plenty of time."

Chapter Twenty-Five

I didn't have a lot of time before Adam left, and I panicked at the thought of having to talk to him about visiting that summer. When he didn't mention it after Rachel and I had talked, I was sure his father had changed his mind. I felt relieved, but I was still sad thinking that his dad was right about it all. *We should just end things.*

My multiple personalities began to fail. Since I'd talked with Rachel and Lisa, the three faces of Nicki started to merge into a single melancholy one. The morning of April first, I changed my calendar and sighed as the word *April* shouted at me. Then I noticed what day it was: April Fool's Day.

Great. It's April, and I'm the fool. I've got a great boyfriend, but he's leaving forever. The joke is on me.

I tried to be happier around Adam, but that day he must've seen through it. After school, we were lying in my bed after having our usual round of afternoon sex, but I was quiet. Adam stroked my hair and asked, "What's wrong, sweetheart? You seem sad today."

Remaining silent for a moment, I debated what to do. Grandma Johnson was a big knitter. Sometimes when she got frustrated with a project, she would just tug on the end of the yarn. The sweater she'd been knitting—often after she'd spent hours on it—would unravel right before my eyes. I knew if I brought up Adam's leaving and the possibility of us breaking up, I'd start a chain reaction like dominos falling. Was I ready for that?

I'd wanted him to bring up the topic of our future, but it was stupid to wait for him to get around to it. If I was going to decide what happened to me, I needed to face the music myself. I needed to be strong. I decided to simply broach the subject but not dwell on it.

Nodding over to my calendar, I said, "It's April now."

A huge smile appeared on Adam's face. "I know. I've been waiting for today. I've got a surprise for you."

Oh God. The ticket. I stuttered, "What's…that?"

"I want you to come and stay with me at home this summer. I'll buy your ticket. You can stay as long as you want. My parents are good with it, and of course Sylvia is ecstatic."

I tried to play coy, hoping to drag out the conversation so I could switch topics. "Oh my God, Adam. That's unbelievably generous. How can you afford that?"

"Oh, I've got some money saved up. My grandfather gave it to me. This seems like a great way to use it."

"Your grandfather? What does he do?"

"Um. Not much anymore. He's getting on a bit now."

"But what about when he was young?"

"Well, he was in the Royal Air Force, and after that he took care of the family business."

"What kind of business?"

"We have an estate," he said nudging in closer to me. "My father's family is an old Scottish one."

"Is he like some kind of lord?"

"Something like that."

"Seriously?" I'd been joking. No matter how rich you are in America, you don't have a title. "So does that mean one day you'll be one? Like you're in line to the family throne?"

"I wouldn't call it a throne, but, yes, eventually, technically, I'll have a title. It's not a big deal, though."

"Do we have anything in common?" I shook my head in disbelief and smiled.

"What? Of course. That's only the Kincaid side of my family, not my mum's. Her family had to work hard to give her and her sister a good education; she wasn't privileged like my dad. You might've noticed her accent is a little different, more like David's."

I smiled, trying to wrap my head around it all. When I was quiet, he added, "I promise you I don't live in a castle. We're utterly middle class. You'll see. Won't you come and visit?"

This was it. My answer to this would decide everything. I knew what I needed to do for myself. I took a big breath and started the chain reaction that would detonate the nuclear bomb.

Shaking my head again, I sullenly told him the deep feeling that underpinned my entire decision. "I love you, Adam, but I can't. It's so kind of you, and it just makes me love you more, but I can't do it. If I go, it's only going to make everything harder."

"What do you mean?" He looked at me like I was crazy. "I don't understand."

"Adam, I love you, but I don't think that's enough. Let's be real. We're not going to really have a relationship after you leave."

Frowning, his brow furrowed as he played with my hair. "Well, yes, I suppose things might change over time, but why worry about that now?"

I pursed my lips before answering. "I can't *not* worry about that."

"What do you mean?"

"I mean it would kill me."

"I wouldn't like it either, but…" He pressed his lips to my hand. "But we could be friends. And you never know what's going to happen in the future."

My heart felt like it was beating outside my chest. In total panic, I sputtered, "I can't do that. I can't watch our relationship die a slow death. I think we should break up when you leave." I gulped in air before my finale. "I don't think we were meant to be. I think this is it."

Adam was stunned; he even looked a little angry. He was silent for a moment before he let it rip. "Are you mad? You think that because we've got…geography problems, that we should just split up?"

Nodding, I started to cry. "I think it would be easier."

"That's complete bollocks. How long have you been thinking about this?"

"A few weeks." I started bawling, and my feelings tumbled out of me. "I can't do it, Adam. It's too much. It will be easier for me if you just leave. If I don't have to talk to you when things are impossible between us, it will hurt, but not for so long."

His eyes narrowed at me. I'd never seen him so upset. "I can't believe I have to say this to you, Nicki, but you're being fucking selfish as hell. This solution may be easier for you—although I doubt it is—but it would be hell for me. There are two people in this relationship, not just you."

"Well…" He had a point that I'd dismissed when I had talked to Lisa and Rachel, but it was harder to reject it coming from him.

"You just said you loved me, for Christ's sake!"

"I do love you," I said defensively.

"How could that be true if you don't even want to be my friend?"

I stopped crying because I realized we were having our first real argument and we were naked. It seemed odd to have him so exposed and furious at the same time.

I tried to calm him, explaining, "I think it's the best thing for both of us. Our parents are right. We're too young. We live too far away. And now I hear we're too different. We should just enjoy what we've had."

Adam jumped out of bed. He looked livid as he started pulling on his boxers and pants. "This is bullshit. I'm going home. We can talk later."

I smiled apologetically and asked, "Will you call me tonight?" I was sure he would say yes.

He ran his hands through his hair as he deliberated what should've been an easy answer of yes. "No. I don't think that's a good idea. I need some time."

My eyes widened at his rejection. "Oh. Okay." I looked away for a moment. *What have I done?*

He gave me a peck while he buttoned his shirt. "We can talk tomorrow."

"I still love you, Adam."

He looked at me suspiciously and then sighed. "And I love you."

When he left my room, I realized what I'd done. I had thought I'd suggested that we break up right before he left. Instead, I was pretty sure that in his mind the break-up had started right then.

The next few days proved my theory. There was no longer flirty laughter with hugs and kisses at the lockers. We were brooding and uncomfortable around one another at school. Neither one of us wanted to talk about things there. Then when we'd get to my house after school, we'd have sex just as usual, but it felt wrong, like we were demanding something physically from one another that we weren't getting emotionally. Then we'd have the same ugly argument about what to do when he left—or we just wouldn't talk at all. Things got progressively worse between us the next week. When it became uncomfortable saying "I love you" to each other, I knew things were really bad.

It wasn't long before Rachel accosted me in the hallway at school. "What the fuck is going on, Nicki? What did you tell Adam?"

"Leave me alone. I know what I'm doing," I said and stomped away.

The truth was, I was only eighty percent sure I knew what I was doing. I really didn't need anyone reminding me that there was a one-in-five chance I would regret what I'd done. I felt horrible, but I just kept telling myself that it would only be worse in the summer if I didn't do it now.

I questioned myself again when Adam wouldn't come into my house that afternoon. I couldn't believe it and asked frantically, "You don't want to come in?"

"I need to study for my French exam."

Right. That was a lie if I'd ever heard one. I stared him down for a few seconds just so he understood I knew he was lying to me. He simply glared back with the same hurt and angry look he'd had all week. I gave him a kiss on the cheek saying, "Have a good night," before I got out of his car and didn't look back as he drove away.

My stomach did flip-flops after I shut the front door behind me. I gasped for air as I walked up to my room. Throwing myself on my bed, I started bawling into my pillow. I was quite certain that Adam and I were over.

I stayed in my room even after Mom came home from work, only barking through the door to her that I didn't want dinner. When I heard a car pull up in the driveway, I peeked out the window. It was Adam.

Running to the bathroom, I saw I looked like absolute dog shit. *Great. He'll always remember me looking like a hag when we broke up.*

When I went to open my door to meet him downstairs, a knock and Adam's voice startled me. "Nicki?"

He walked in and closed the door behind him. No wonder Mom had just let him waltz into my room. He obviously had been crying. He looked like hell, too.

"Adam, are you okay?"

"No." He grabbed me into his arms and pressed his head against mine. "We just heard my grandfather's died. We're leaving tonight."

It was as if the few days of excruciating pain had never happened. I was all over him, caressing and soothing him, "Oh, Adam, I'm so sorry."

The pain wasn't over for him, though. As if he remembered he wasn't supposed to touch me anymore, he stiffened up and announced, "I don't have much time. I wanted to let you know that I'll be gone for a week. I'll be back next weekend."

"Sure. Sure." I nodded. "Please tell your family how sorry I am."

"I will. I really need to go."

Everything about the situation felt awful. I tried to salvage it by standing on my tiptoes and kissing his forehead. "Have a safe trip. I love you."

Placing his hands on my shoulders, he pushed me away while saying once again, "Yeah, right. I love you, too."

As he walked out, he said, "I'll call you when I get back."

Chapter Twenty-Six

The week Adam was gone was horrible. I missed him terribly. That was awful enough until I remembered that I'd be feeling the exact same way in less than a couple of months, only then he would never be coming back. It was a crushing thought.

I still hadn't told Rachel and Lisa about anything that had happened. I refused to discuss Adam with them because I knew they'd be pissed I hadn't talked to them first. Without spending time with Rachel and Lisa, it felt like I had no friends at all.

By the middle of the week, the longing I had for him was so painful that I reconsidered everything. Maybe a friendship that withered on the vine one day wouldn't be such a bad thing. At least I'd get to talk with him.

The following Saturday he called me in the middle of the day, just as he had when he'd come home from Christmas. This time was different, though. He didn't ask to see me that night. Instead, he said he was too exhausted and asked, "But your mum will be at church tomorrow morning, right?"

"Yeah. You can come over then."

I was disappointed that he didn't want to see me immediately but happy that he wanted to see me alone. Yet something gnawed at me about how he'd said it—like maybe he wanted to be alone so he could tell me something. As the following morning drew closer, I was convinced something bad had happened. I didn't know what, but it was bad.

When I nervously let him in the house that morning, I did a double-take. He had a black and bluish ring around his left eye.

I gave him a kiss on the cheek and asked, "Hey, sweetheart, what happened to your eye?"

"Er. Yeah. So you can still see it, then?" He seemed very embarrassed.

"I'd say. What happened?"

"I'll tell you later." With a big smile, he hugged me, "I'm so happy to see you, Nicki. I missed you so much."

"I missed you. Come on in."

As we walked toward the living room, I became a little hopeful that maybe things were back to normal. But when I turned and saw him anxiously running his hand through his hair, I was worried again. I sat us down on the sofa and faced him directly.

"So, tell me about it."

Adam opened his mouth and then caught his breath. There was no doubt about it now that whatever he was about to say was bad. He spoke morosely, "Nicki, I have to tell you something."

"What's that?" I asked in a quavering voice.

I'd never seen him look scared, but that's how he appeared — a frightened boy. He slowly declared, "I've always told you the truth."

"Yeah?"

"I want to be honest with you. Please know that."

"So?"

"I was..." His Adam's apple bobbed with a giant swallow of air before he continued, "I got together with Kate when I was home."

I was silent. There was too much to take in. First, the words had to register in my brain. I wasn't sure what they meant exactly, but the general meaning was clear. He'd hooked up with Kate.

I was bewildered. I couldn't comprehend a world where Adam would hurt me. *That* I'd never expected.

Eventually, I whispered, "What?"

"Oh, Nicki. Christ, I'm so sorry. I'm such a fucking wanker. I love you. I never meant to hurt you. I was drunk..."

Everything he said seemed like standard cheater bullshit. None of it told me anything. "Why?"

"I don't know. I was drunk." He mumbled, "Kate was there. She knew my grandfather. She's familiar."

Ouch. That hurt. She'd consoled him; I hadn't. Me—who had spent the last year grieving and crying on his shoulder—I hadn't been the one to console him about his grandfather's death. Kate the Bitch had.

Then, starting to tear up, he roared in what sounded like self-defense, "You broke my heart!"

My moment of guilt ended immediately. I was headed for emotional arrest, and self-preservation kicked in. It was like my mind was taken over by a computer program, the one specially designed for when a guy cheats on you.

I sneered. "So it's my fault? It was retribution?"

"No!" He grimaced at me and became quieter. "Of course not. I—"

"What happened?" For some reason, this time I needed details. "Tell me exactly what happened."

"After the funeral in Scotland, we went back to Cambridge for a few days. I saw her at the pub. I was completely shit-faced. And—"

"And what?"

"And we were smashed…things got a bit out of control in the back room at the pub." He looked at me pleadingly. "We didn't have sex. I promise."

"I feel so much better." I'd said it sarcastically, but in reality it was the truth. Yet I still couldn't help asking for the details that I didn't want to hear but had to know. "So did you…touch her?"

He nodded.

I imagined him with his hand up her shirt or, worse, down her pants. My self-esteem took a massive hit, and I wanted to hit him back.

I quickly followed up. "And I'm sure she touched you."

With his eyes closed, he nodded again.

I pounced, hoping he was embarrassed, because I was humiliated. "So she gave you head? Please just say yes or no."

"Yes." He'd whispered it, but his voice became stronger, saying, "That's where it ended. David walked in on us, and Kate ran off."

Hmph. What restraint. I nodded toward his face. "How'd you get the black eye?"

"David hit me."

I rolled my eyes. *I should've stuck with the cousin.*

"He was trying to sober me up." Adam touched his eye. "As soon as he hit me and said your name, I snapped out of it. I was such a bloody mess."

"I bet you were."

"Please believe me, Nicki. Kate and I are over. It was a stupid mistake. It meant nothing to me."

I looked at Adam and held his eyes for a moment. "That may be, but it means something to me. It means something to me."

Adam reached for my hands, but I wrenched them away, tucking them inside my arms, which I crossed over my chest. I felt like I'd been attacked, and I needed the physical protection, even though it would do nothing for my imploding heart. Keeping my hands tucked away also seemed like a good idea just in case they betrayed me and reached out for his.

When he saw that I'd physically rejected him, his face crumpled. "No, Nicki. Please no. You've got to believe me. I love you. I truly never meant to hurt you."

"Well, you did." I closed my eyes, desperately trying to squelch back the tears, but my body heaved with a sob of painful regret. "I should've known."

"Fuck! No!" He looked panicked. "If I could take back that night, I would. I was very close to my grandfather. I was depressed about his death, but mostly I was devastated that you wanted to break up with me. I've hated myself from the moment David walked in."

"What if David hadn't walked in?"

"I don't know…"

"Well, I do!"

"But it *didn't* happen." He touched my arm and said with a begging voice, "I don't want to lose you."

I jumped up from the sofa and cried out, "Oh yeah? Well, I wish I'd never met you! Go away and don't come back."

As soon as it had come out of my mouth, I knew it sounded juvenile, but at that moment, I couldn't stand seeing him. It was torture. Everything good between us had been tainted with pain and humiliation. Bawling, I shook my head in disgust at both him and myself.

His eyes pled with mine. "Nicki, please. I love you. If I didn't…"

"Just go away!" I couldn't handle any more. I darted toward the stairs, calling back as I sobbed, "Please, just leave me alone for once."

I realized it was a little strange to have left him sitting alone in my living room, but I wanted him out of the house. As a signal that he wasn't welcome anymore, I slammed my bedroom door behind me.

I dove onto my bed, crying into my pillow and waiting to hear him leave. It seemed like forever before the front door closed and his car drove away. My eyes flicked open as I grasped my new world.

Adam cheated on me. I love him, and he cheated on me.

But there was no joy to be had anymore. Maybe he'd liked me, maybe even a lot, but whatever we'd had together wasn't enough for him. I'd been left hanging out there alone.

I whispered aloud what had to be true: "He never really loved me. He wouldn't have done it if he really loved me."

All of his explanations and apologies were meaningless to me. I could only focus on his actions. I would've never done it to him. I would've never hooked up with John just because I was sad about Lauren dying and Adam leaving. It didn't seem possible that anyone who even merely liked someone would treat them that way. For the next hour, I sobbed, because the wonderful, loving boyfriend I thought I'd had was gone — poof — as if he'd never existed.

When Mom came home, I wasn't sure what to do. I couldn't go downstairs and fake being okay. I hadn't been to the bathroom, but I was pretty sure that I looked like shit. If I didn't go down, though, she would come up, and since it was almost noon, I couldn't pretend being asleep because she would just wake me up.

I decided to just suck it up and let her see that I'd cried. She was going to know something was up anyway. I hoped I could get away with as little explanation as possible.

Sure enough, she knocked on my door before walking in. "Nicki, are you up?"

"Yeah." I rolled my head to the side so that I could quickly make eye contact, show her I'd been crying, and go back to my pillow.

Seeing my bloodshot eyes and red face, her voice filled with motherly concern. "Nicki, baby, what's wrong?"

"It's nothing."

"Is it about Adam? About him leaving?" She sat on my bed and gently placed her hand on my back. "You haven't been yourself in weeks, but what's happened now?"

"I told you it's nothing."

"It looks to me like it's something. You can tell me, sweetie."

Could I tell her? No. It was humiliating. I wanted the world to hate Adam as much as I did at that moment, but the thought of telling anyone what he'd done was mortifying. I'd been a fool, and I didn't need anyone else reminding me of it. I answered her by shaking my head into my pillow and meekly saying, "I don't want to talk about it."

"I saw his mother at church. She says that he's very upset right now over his grandfather. She didn't think it would affect him this much."

"I don't care why he's sad. I don't care about him at all."

She was quiet for a moment. When I looked at her again, I saw she was mulling it all over.

Before she could ask me if one of her hypotheses was true, I begged, "Mom, please. I want to be alone."

"Have you two broken up?"

Going back to my pillow, I squinted my eyes shut. "I told you I don't want to talk about it."

"Okay." She sighed, defeated by teenage angst. "I understand. Don't stay in here too long, though. It's a beautiful day outside. If you get out, you'll feel better."

That was a maternal crock of shit if I'd ever heard one. I was going to feel awful whether I was inside or outside, whether I was with people or alone, but in order to get her out of my room, I nodded, acknowledging her conventional wisdom.

After she left, I got under the covers and wore myself out crying. I slept for a couple hours, which gave me a brief break, but less than ten seconds after I woke up, it came back to me: *Adam cheated on me. I loved him, but he never really loved me.*

I tried to think back to the countless times he'd said he loved me. It had always felt like it was true—when he'd given me gifts, when we'd had sex, when we'd snuggle in my bed in the afternoon, or just those times when he'd murmur the words as he sneaked a kiss on my cheek at school.

The last thought made me heave with grief. I'd have to face him the next day at school, and I had no idea how I would react when I saw him. Then I remembered I'd see my friends also. Would I ever be able to tell Lisa and Rachel what had happened? My heart ached so deeply at the thought of it that I knew I couldn't do it.

I quickly thought of Mom and Grandma never talking about what hurt them, and I suddenly realized I might have been too judgmental. Maybe there are things that are so agonizing you can't even say them aloud. I felt that way, plus I was humiliated. So then maybe there are also things so shameful you don't want anyone to know.

I decided right then not to tell anyone. No one needed to know what had happened between Adam and me. It wouldn't do anybody any good at all—least of all me.

Eventually that evening, I made my way downstairs. The house smelled of Mom's spaghetti with meatballs. It was my favorite dish. In a simple way, she was trying to make me feel better. I'd gone to the bathroom, so I knew I still looked like crap. There was no way to hide it.

When she saw me, she said softly, "Oh, Nicki, I'm sorry."

Shrugging, I got myself a glass of water. "It's okay."

"By the way you look, I have to disagree."

What was there to say to that? I turned away as I drank my water. After a few gulps, I asked, "Mom, can I stay home from school tomorrow?"

"Nicki…" She said my name with such disapproval that I knew the answer would be no, but I gave it one more try.

"Please, Mom. Just one day. My grades are great this semester. I don't have anything due. I promise to study. I'll even clean the house. Please, don't make me go to school tomorrow."

"Nicki, I don't think staying home from school is going to make you feel any better. You're going to have to see Adam at some point."

"I know…but please not tomorrow. I want some time alone."

She eyed me curiously. "Nicki, what's happened? Has he done something to hurt you?"

My entire being shut down. Even if I'd wanted to tell her about Adam cheating on me, my pathetic heart wouldn't let me. "I told you I don't want to talk about it right now."

That was a lie. I was sure I *never* wanted to talk with Mom about Adam, but I thought it was polite to leave an opening. Lucky for me, it worked.

Mom sighed, "Okay, but soon. It's not good to keep it so bottled up."

I looked at her sideways; I couldn't let it go unnoticed that she had uttered that particular pearl of wisdom.

Instantly catching my smirk, she gave in. "Oh, all right. You can stay home. Just for one day, though. I expect you in school on Tuesday."

That night, I forced myself to be sociable by sitting silently beside her as we watched show after show on TV. I didn't cry, but my mind was rarely off Adam. I was just saving the tears for when I was alone.

Chapter Twenty-Seven

When Mom left the house the next morning, I didn't hear her at all. I'd had such a crappy night's sleep of crying and feeling sorry for myself that out of exhaustion I slept most of the morning. Before lunch, I reviewed some Spanish for my upcoming exam and then vegged out in front of the TV again. Sometime after lunch but before *Oprah*, I kept my word that I would clean the house. As I scrubbed the bathtubs, I worried about the next day. I would have to see Adam for the next several weeks until the end of school. How could I get out of it?

As I dusted the living room, I developed detailed plans on how to avoid him, but when I heard a car unexpectedly pull into the driveway, I froze. I looked at the mantle, where the clock showed the exact time that I usually arrived home from school. I panicked.

Please, God, let it be Rachel or Lisa. Please.

Adam's distinct knock rattled the front door, and I looked down to see I was dressed in my usual housecleaning garb of boxers and a tank top. Smelling underneath my arms, I confirmed my lack of a shower. I glanced at my reflection in the mirror. My hair was on top of my head in a ponytail, which was kind of cute, but my eyes were still puffy from all the crying.

Damn it. I didn't want him to see me cry again.

Peeking through the peephole, I saw Adam standing in his soccer uniform looking hot as ever. I rolled my eyes. If it wasn't a game day—his last game of the season—I'd say he'd done it on purpose. He knew how much I liked him in his jersey and shorts.

With my heart beating double-time, I opened the door just enough so I could peer at him and give him a wary "Hi."

"Hi, Nicki." His voice was warm. "I came round to check on you. You weren't at school. Are you ill?"

I felt sick then. I had never imagined he would come see me after I'd told him to leave me alone. What was I supposed to say about skipping school?

I hated lying because I was so bad at it. I tried a half-ass one. "A little."

Of course, he didn't believe me. "Can we please talk? Please? I don't want things between us to end like this."

A comment like that helped me locate my spine. "Yeah, right. You've been fine with us breaking up all along. You just don't want to be the asshole."

"Yeah, you're absolutely right. I am an arsehole." He said it with complete sincerity and then, with even more conviction, he continued, "But, Jesus Christ, you're wrong that I want to split up. I've never wanted that. Not today…not ever."

Guilt pinched my heart. I was the one who had initiated a breakup, even if I'd later regretted it. I couldn't talk for fear that I might cry. Instead, I simply pursed my lips and shook my head at him, which unexpectedly set him off.

"Goddamn it. I love you. I'm never going to forget you. I—"

My emotions were all over the place, but my intellect was still intact. For such a smart guy, Adam really was a lousy debater. I was my father's daughter, and if he was arguing in court, there was no way my dad would ever leave an opening like that alone, especially if he had his own weaknesses in a case. It was time to go for the jugular. "You're never going to forget about me?" I taunted him.

"No, of course not. I—"

"Well, you already did forget me…when you were with her. You forgot about me then, and you'll do it again." I closed my eyes, because the thought of him with Kate stung too much. When I opened them, he looked mortified, so I hammered the final nail into the coffin. "Just go. Then I can forget about you."

Right after I'd said it, I shut the door on him and ran upstairs. I heard him get in his car and drive away. Landing on my bed, I sat with my head in my hands crying. When I looked up, I spotted his Liverpool scarf hanging off my dresser mirror. *Goddamn it.* After that incident, the last thing I needed were reminders of him around me.

I snatched it off the mirror and threw it in a sweater drawer that I knew I wouldn't open for months. Then I found the leather book he'd made for me and threw it in there, too. Finally, rifling through my jewelry box, I located the necklace he'd given me. As I held it in my hand, I stopped for a moment.

I didn't know what to do with it. His words came back to me: "You have my heart." *Did I once? Did I really have his heart? Even if for just a little while?* For a few minutes, I tenderly touched the pretty heart pendent, thinking about that day on the beach. I'd always heard people say that something felt like a dream — that day back in February felt like a fantasy to me. Yet the necklace was real; it wasn't something I'd made up.

I sighed and placed it back inside the jewelry box. Wiping away the tears trickling down my cheeks, I fell back on my bed, crying yet again.

The nervous knots in my stomach woke me up the following morning. Even though I'd planned it so that I'd stay as far away from Adam as I could, I remained anxious. I started off the school day by arriving at my locker by half-past seven, which was early enough so he'd still be at home.

I took out all of my books and folders and stashed them on a bookshelf in the back of the drama department's practice auditorium. Lots of theater people left books or clothes in there if they were too lazy to go to their locker. I just happened to take up a whole shelf. I still had to run the gauntlet of Rachel and Lisa, but I hoped that I could deflect them just as I had Mom. I'd refused to talk with them about Adam for weeks anyway; my behavior wouldn't be anything new.

I thought everything was going as well as could be expected until the end of lunch. Rachel, Tom, and I ate together just as we always did, and nothing seemed different. At one point, though, Rachel mentioned a party at Lance's on Friday night and said Adam and I should go.

I quickly found a lie, which came out panicky but was reasonable enough to pass for the truth. "I'm going to my dad's this weekend."

"Too bad. It should be fun." Rachel continued on talking about her weekend plans, but I caught Tom's eye.

He looked at me intently. It was then I knew that Adam had told him. I'd never been on bad terms with Tom in my life—and I'd known him since kindergarten—but instantly, I considered him the enemy. I glared at him, frowning a little. I wanted him to know that I wasn't talking about it.

As soon as I left lunch, I started to worry about getting through the last weeks of school. With Tom watching over me, Adam would be present even when he wasn't. Unfortunately, I'd also have to talk to Rachel and Lisa at some point, even if it was just to say we'd broken up for good, and it was inevitable that I'd see Adam every day in class.

I was glued to Lisa's side as we walked into English that day. Somehow I made it to my seat without looking at Adam at all. He didn't say anything to me, and I kept my body angled in my desk so that there was no way I could see him. It was pretty uncomfortable, but I figured I could handle it for one hour a day for the next few weeks.

What I didn't plan for was Lisa. About halfway through the class, she began looking at me curiously, and her stare became more and more annoyed as the hour continued. When the bell rang, she asked in a voice louder than necessary, "Nicki, can you show me where that passage is again?"

Out of the corner of my eye, I saw Adam's body slowly move past us. I fumbled around for my book, foolishly hoping Lisa actually needed help with *The Great Gatsby*.

"What is going on?" She was aghast. "You didn't talk to Adam the whole class. Did you two break up?"

She'd asked her question quietly, but she might as well have yelled it. I shirked back in my seat and looked down. She was my best friend, but the fact was, I didn't want to tell her anything more than I'd told Mom, so I simply nodded.

"What happened? Why didn't you tell—"

"I don't want to talk about it." I jumped out of my seat and added, "Can you do me a favor? Can you tell Rachel?"

"Wait a second. What's happened? I know you two weren't happy, but I thought that was because he was leaving."

Then it clicked for her. She looked at me accusatorily. "Did you tell him you didn't want to go to England? Did *you* break up with *him?*"

"I told you I don't want to talk about it, okay? Can you just leave me alone?" I sounded like a broken record. *How many times am I going to have to say it and to how many people?*

"Nicki, I know this year has been tough on you," she said, "but what did you do? Have you made it worse?"

Of all the questions she could've asked, she asked *that* one?

I spit out my answer. "*I* didn't do anything. Now can you please let Rachel know so I don't have to?"

Leaning back like I was dangerous, Lisa exhaled. "Okay…if that's the way you want it…"

As I walked a totally roundabout way home that I knew Adam would never travel, my hands still shook from my conversation with Lisa. The truth was that I did feel like I'd done something to Adam; in a way, I'd let him down. I'd pushed him away. It didn't justify him letting that bitch Kate suck his dick, but I was a little at fault, too.

Trudging along, I considered my predicament. I had a month left to deal with him at school. I was just going to have to take one day at a time, knowing that it would soon be over. School would be out, Adam would leave, and I could get on with my life—whatever that would be.

As expected, the next couple weeks sucked. Rachel and Lisa were on pins and needles around me, acting like I was going to go mental at any moment. It pissed me off a little bit, but I had to admit they had good reason. I was acting pretty freaky, barely talking to them and avoiding Adam by any means necessary.

I did pretty well at staying away from him, but a few times in English our eyes inadvertently met. He always looked so glum that I quickly looked away. He may have sliced up my heart, but the sight of him unhappy still made me want to brush the hair out of his eyes and give him a hug. It was all very confusing, and I was always glad when that last bell rang, signaling I'd made it through one more day.

The weekends weren't any better, though. Since I'd flat out lied to my friends, I was in self-imposed prison in my house. Being under Mom's twenty-four-hour surveillance was annoying, but it wasn't like I was itching to go anywhere. In fact, going to parties would be terrifying. Adam might be there, and it crossed my mind that he might even have a date or leave with another girl. Just the thought of it made me want to puke, which then invariably brought on a crying jag.

Afterward I would lie there, beating myself up. I was pathetic. I couldn't hate the guy properly, because I was still in love with him, and I couldn't be with him because he was only going to break my heart again.

Chapter Twenty-Eight

As another Monday rolled around, the school day went along uneventfully as usual until after lunch. Tom told Rachel that he'd walk with me to my class because he needed to talk to a teacher. I thought it strange when he'd said it, and I knew it was a complete sham when he tugged me into an empty doorway.

"Nicki, I want to talk with you."

My eyes widened. *Shit. Shit. Shit.* I played nonchalant. "What about?"

"I gotta first tell you that Adam doesn't know I'm doing this. In fact, if he did, he'd probably clock me." He rolled his eyes at the thought and smiled. "But what the hell. Somebody's gotta step in here."

"What do you mean?" He was trying to be nice, but it was still uncomfortable.

"Well, I think I'm the only one who knows the whole story. Am I right about that?"

I studied his face, trying to understand what was going on. *So Adam told him, but he's figured out that Rachel doesn't know anything.* "I guess you talked with Adam." I felt humiliated just saying it aloud.

"I did, but don't worry; I'm not saying anything to Rachel. That's between you and her. But Adam did tell me. You know, I'm his only friend here…now."

He raised his eyebrows at me, and I wanted to slap him upside the head. There was a very good reason that Adam didn't have me as a friend anymore. I looked away and said under my breath, "Whatever."

"C'mon, Nicki. He fucked up. He's the first one to say it. He feels horrible…and rightly so, but—"

"How do you think I feel?"

"You feel like shit, too!" he said, throwing up his hands. "That's the problem. You two still like each other."

"Yeah," I said reluctantly. "But so what?"

"If he was sticking around, I wouldn't put my nose in this, but he's not, so I feel like I gotta say something. You two don't have the time to let things heal on their own, and you're not giving him a chance. That's not like you."

"He's leaving. What difference does it make?"

"I don't know." He shrugged and smiled. "I just want my friends to be friends again."

No matter how annoying he was, it was always hard to be mad at Tom. It was like being mad at a mischievous toddler. I smiled half-heartedly. "Point taken, Tom. Thanks."

I tried not to think about what Tom had said while I was at school because I didn't want to let anything slip around Adam. When I walked into English, our eyes met for a moment, but I looked away before I could communicate anything to him. I wanted to remain strong.

That night was a different matter, though. Lying in bed, I thought back to my conversation with Tom. He was right that if Adam stuck around, we would've had time to repair things. But we had no such time; time was against us.

When I remembered how happy we'd been together—or at least how happy I thought we'd been together—I got unbearably depressed. Curling up on my side, I pulled my legs up to my chest, trying to contain myself before I split in two or three or maybe even four. He'd treated me terribly, but I missed him. Sometimes I got so lonely for him that I'd forget I was supposed to be angry. I missed his smile that had seemed like it was only there for me. I missed the way he'd teased me endlessly, and I even missed his inexplicable obsession with soccer.

Late at night, though, mostly I missed those few times when he'd fallen asleep after we'd had sex. He'd always looked completely content. Silly me had thought his peacefulness had been because he was next to me, because that's the way I'd felt next to him.

The week trudged by just like the ones before. When it got to the weekend, Lisa and Rachel invited me to go to see a movie, but I said no. I didn't want to be trapped with them for hours in case they planned on interrogating me.

On Saturday night, Mom announced, "Seeing as how you're not going out tonight, I expect to see you in church tomorrow."

"Why?"

"It's my birthday, of course. Have you stopped looking at the calendar?"

I rolled my eyes—like I wasn't painfully aware of every single day. My mind went on red alert, though, when I remembered there was an outside chance Adam could be there.

I grasped for an excuse to give Mom, but there was really no way to get out of it. Instead, I said, "Okay," and started heading for the stairs. "I should find something to wear."

Rummaging through my closet, I noticed that my heart rate was going nuts. It didn't make any sense for me to be anxious about seeing Adam. After all, I saw him every day at school, and yet I did everything in my power to avoid him. Seeing him at church shouldn't be anything special, and I didn't even know if I *would* see him there.

As I tore through my clothes, I realized what potentially made to-morrow special; it could be an opportunity to be dressed up in front of him. He really had only seen me dressed up once before, and I wanted to look nice. *But why? Why do I want to look good for a guy I don't want?*

On Sunday morning, I sat in church with Lisa and her family while Mom sang in the choir. We sat in the back, so it wasn't until I walked back from communion that I saw Adam. He sat with his family near the front, and as I turned from the communion railing to walk down the side aisle, I saw Sylvia, who gave me a little wave. It was the first time I'd seen her since they'd gotten back from the funeral. Then I peered to her left, where Adam sat beside her. He gave me such a big smile that it startled me.

I immediately looked down and blinked as I took in what had happened. When I saw the flounce of my dress, I smiled, too. *He must've liked my dress.* I was wearing another thrift shop special, but even Mom liked it. The vintage dress was dark blue chiffon with tiny Swiss dots, full skirt, cinched at the waist with a matching belt, and covered by a sheer blouse. When I paired it with my navy kitten heels, Rachel called it my "slutty June Cleaver dress."

After church, Lisa ran off with her family for brunch, and I was left awkwardly alone, waiting for Mom to get out of her choir robe. I was pretty sure that Adam had left; I didn't see him around.

Wasting time, I went to the bathroom in the parish hall, and after I walked out, I jumped when hearing Adam's voice from out of nowhere.

"Hi, Nicki."

I gaped at him, truly speechless. There he was, leaning up against a wall, looking like he had been lying in wait for me. In navy blue trousers with a light blue shirt and dark tie, he was way too handsome for a seventeen-year-old boy. As soon as I started to check him out, I felt myself blush because I knew he knew I was eyeing him over.

I stumbled over my words. "Oh…hi, Adam."

After I said his name, his whole face lit up. "It's good to see you." Then his voice softened. "You look…beautiful. You always do, but especially today."

I was dying. It was just like the time back in the fall when he'd made me swoon while standing around the church coffee hour. I tried to shake it off. "Oh, it's just…that I'm in a dress. No big deal."

"Well, you look gorgeous."

Before I responded, I stared at his eyes. Their dark color stood out compared to the light blue shirt, and they seemed to twinkle directly at me. It was enough of a spark between us that I nervously looked away. "I gotta go."

"Nicki…" The twinkle was gone when I looked at him again. He was pleading once more. "Don't go. Can we talk?"

I didn't know what to do. I felt every emotion possible — anger, love, agony, joy, you name it — and they were all overwhelming. I shook my head, trying to sort out these feelings so I could pick out the one I should have, but that didn't work. Instead, I decided to flee, which seemed like the safest response.

As I trotted down the hallway, I didn't look back to see what he was doing. I just wanted to get outside for some air. After finding the door to the choir room, I parked myself by it so I could pounce on Mom as soon as she got out.

Trying to collect myself, I heard Sylvia's chirpy voice greet me, "Hi, Nicki!"

I didn't smile at her until I saw she was alone. Then I grinned. "Hey. How are you?"

"Oh, okay. Mum has been making us go to church because of my grandfather, you know."

"I'm sorry about that." A wave of shame hit me again. What if Adam had wanted to talk to me about his grandfather?

"Thanks. Things are fine, really. It's just not very fun right now with school ending and all. Too many assessments before exams." She groaned. "And I'm sick of packing."

Packing. They would be packing, wouldn't they? I tried to be cool about it. "You sound busy. You must be excited to be going back home."

"I am, but I'll miss some things about being here." Her voice got uncharacteristically low. "I'll miss you."

My throat tightened. We weren't close, but she was such a trippy character, and I'd always liked her banter with Adam. I contemplated never seeing her again.

I will not cry. I will not cry. I whispered, "I'll miss you, too."

Grabbing my hand, she said, "Adam would kill me for talking to you about this, but I just have to. I don't know what's happened between you and him. Whatever it is, I'm sure it's his fault because it's usually his fault. But please, Nicki, talk to him. He's been a miserable shithead for weeks, and even more since we were home, since he had that fight with David. He won't tell me what's wrong, but he says you won't visit us or even speak to him now. Can you just talk to him one last time before we go?"

I'd never expected to be lobbied by Sylvia, and I didn't know what to make of it. "I don't know."

"Oh hell, do it for me." She laughed and touched my arm. "Just talk to my git of a brother so that he stops being such an awful arse to be around."

Right as she said it, Mom came out the door and straightaway picked up on our odd conversation.

After she and Sylvia exchanged hellos, Sylvia scooted off, but not before begging one more time, "Please talk to him, Nicki—for me."

Mom turned to me. "What does she want you to talk to Adam about?"

"Nothing."

Later that night, I was flipping channels but not watching anything. I wasn't even paying attention to what I was doing because I was too busy debating myself. Part of me desperately wanted to talk to Adam. I wanted to walk up to him the next day at school, wrap my arms around him, and tell him everything would be okay between us. But there was still a part of me that wanted to walk up to him, kick him in the balls, and tell him I never wanted to see him again. I didn't know which one would have made me happier.

Close to bedtime, Mom sat down in the chair beside me and announced, "Nicki, I want to talk to you about something."

"Uh huh." I was suspicious.

Not liking my response, she took the remote from my hand and hit mute. "It's serious."

"Okay." I'd been right to be worried.

"I've been watching you. You haven't given me much to go on, but it's obvious things between you and Adam ended suddenly and badly."

"Yeah?"

"And from what I can tell, you still love him, and I think he still cares for you. Is that right?"

"Maybe…"

"Well, I just wanted to give you something to think about. When your dad and I divorced, there were *many* things wrong between us. It wasn't his affair that broke up our marriage."

My mouth dropped open. "What are you saying, Mom?"

"Like I said, I'm not sure. I'm only guessing but just thought you should know that you can't judge a person or a relationship by one bad act, no matter how bad it is." She got up from her seat and walked toward the stairs. "Don't stay up too late."

Right then, I vowed never to make another dumb Mom joke. The woman was psychic.

Chapter Twenty-Nine

Mom had told me not to stay up too late, so I went to bed, but then I still couldn't go to sleep. All night long, I ruminated not only on what she'd said but also my conversations with Sylvia and Tom. I never came to a conclusion, but I got so little sleep that evening that I woke up late the next morning.

When I realized I was literally running to school, I asked myself, *Why am I running? Who cares if I'm late?*

I knew the answer: I wanted to see Adam. For the rest of the day, I anxiously prepped myself for talking to him. I decided to do it before English so that we could continue talking after class.

Wanting to have some element of surprise, I went out of my way to find him before English. I knew where his earlier class was, so I happily walked down the hall toward his physics classroom, looking for him, but when I spotted him, I stopped at once.

Adam stood there with Emily Riordan, a gorgeous blond cheerleader with way too many teeth. She giggled as she handed him a piece of paper. He smiled, saying, "Thank you very much. I was looking for that."

"Not a problem, but I could use a favor in return. Maybe we could study together," she practically cooed.

After she said it, Adam glanced aside, and our eyes met. I immediately whipped around and started running down the hall. I hated myself for ever thinking I would talk to him again. *Why did I do it? Why did I expose myself like that?*

As I ran I heard Adam call my name repeatedly, and he caught up to me within seconds. When he grabbed my arm and turned me around, I flinched back. I felt like a scared, frantic animal, but I was shocked when I saw how angry he was.

He blurted out, "That's it. I'm fucking tired of this bullshit. You're going to listen to me."

As he pulled me toward the school doors, I feebly reminded him, "We have class."

"Fuck the fucking class. I want to talk to you."

I was speechless as he led me outside the school, and he didn't stop until we got all the way to the football field. After he let me go, he ran his hand through his hair, like he was trying to calm down and figure out where to start.

Waiting only a few seconds, he asked impatiently, "Did you honestly think I was flirting with that dim bird?"

"I don't know." The words came out a little sad and ashamed.

"Well, I wasn't. She picked up a bit of homework I'd dropped on the floor." He exhaled hard. "I know that I don't deserve you to believe me."

I bit my lip, trying to figure out how I should react. Things were moving so fast, my mind couldn't keep up with my feelings. I wanted to throw my arms around him, but I was pretty sure my better judgment wouldn't approve.

He jumped on my silence by taking both of my hands in his. "Nicki, I'm not asking for you to forgive me. I'll never even be able to forgive myself, and that's not an exaggeration. But, please believe me, I'm truly sorry."

Studying his expression, I was sure that even my most judgmental side would say he was contrite. I wanted to let him know I was willing to put it behind us, but I wasn't sure how to say it. I sounded like I had marbles in my mouth when I finally spoke. "I was walking down the hall, hoping to meet you after your class."

"Really?" A smile spread across his face. "What did you want to say?"

"I don't know." I shrugged and smiled back. "I didn't think that far ahead."

"Well, can we spend some time together before I leave?"

"Why?"

"Why? Why?" He laughed and shook his head. "It looks like I've got to start all over again."

Feeling unsteady but wanting to appear strong, I rolled my eyes. He teased me by rolling his own before he continued, "I want to spend time with you because I like your company above anyone else's…and you're quirky and you make me laugh." His voice became serious. "And because you're the strongest person I know…probably ever will know."

I had to look down; I certainly didn't feel strong with our eyes locked. I felt like a weakling as everything he said turned me into emotional mush.

"Please," he continued. "I'm only going to be here a couple more weeks. Let's be friends."

I looked back up into his eyes and nodded. Softly, he brushed his hand across my cheekbone. It felt so intimate I had to lay some ground rules:

"Things can't be the same…that way, though." Having sex with him again would be a bad idea. There was only so much my heart could handle.

He nodded solemnly; he got it.

I added my other requirement. "And when you leave, it's over. We both move on."

"I understand." He sounded regretful. "I have no right to ask otherwise."

"And let's not talk about *that* again, all right?"

He must have understood what I meant because he wholeheartedly agreed, "Gladly."

Having everything settled with him made me joyful. I squeezed his hands. "Should we go to class now?"

"No fucking way!" Without warning, he began leading me toward the school parking lot. "I'm living on bloody borrowed time with you. I want to make the most of it. Let's go to the beach."

While Adam drove us to Galveston that afternoon, we made small talk in the car about school and what we might be missing in English. I could just see Lisa smirking at our two empty desks. I'd have some explaining to do in the morning.

When we got to the coast, we kicked off our shoes and rolled up our jeans. As we walked down to the water, I tried to keep my arms at my side, but he was intent on holding hands. I'd made the decision I wouldn't have sex with the guy again, which meant that I really shouldn't kiss him either since one thing always led to another with Adam. Yet he'd already been holding my hand when we'd talked back at school, so that bit of PDA seemed like it could continue. Deep down, I didn't mind. I was tickled that he still felt something for me.

I needed to live in reality, though, so I asked, "Sylvia said that you were packing. How's it going?"

Adam gave me a double-take. We'd never before talked about the details of his leaving, only the prospect of it. He raised his eyebrows as if to acknowledge that things truly had changed between us. "It's okay. I'm pretty sure Mum's got me doing most of the work for the whole bloody family."

"Really? Sylvia made it sound like she was doing a lot of it."

"Rubbish. I'm the one lugging the fucking boxes everywhere."

Then he looked at me with suspicion and asked, "When did you talk to Sylvia?"

"Yesterday at church."

"What did she say?"

I wrinkled my nose and stifled a giggle. "That you were being a git. I'm not sure what that is, but it sounded bad."

"*Hmpf.* It's true…I suppose." He squeezed my hand. "I'm happier now."

"I am, too." I quickly looked out onto the water. If Adam and I were going to be friends these remaining days, I'd need to be stronger. Otherwise, I was going to end up right back where I'd been — goofy in love with a guy who was leaving forever.

I changed the subject away from feelings and back to facts. "What are you doing when you get back? Do you start school again or do you have a break?"

"I'm not staying in bloody Cambridge when I get home. I'll be away all through the summer."

A shot of happiness hit me. He would be away from Kate. I had no title to the guy anymore, but I was glad he wouldn't be immediately going back into her arms. I hid my smile and asked, "Where are you going?"

"David and I are traveling up to the family's pile in Scotland. We'll stay there through August doing up that dive."

"David? So things are…okay with you two?"

"Yeah." He shrugged. "He did me an incredible favor."

I looked back at the water for a brief moment. *Favor? Like saving you from that bitch?* "Why did he do it?"

"He was furious with me because he thought I was being a stupid fucking arsehole, which I was." Adam's expression became apologetic again. He worked up a smile and added, "David likes you."

"David, my hero." A low laugh escaped me.

"Well, he's not always Mr. Chivalrous." Something didn't seem to sit well with Adam, because he took his hand away. "He's no saint either. If you really knew him…if you knew how many girls he juggled at any one time, you'd think differently about him."

"It was a joke, Adam."

"Sorry. I…well…he's always…"

Shaking my head, I let him off the hook. "Why don't you tell me about this place up in Scotland? What's it like?"

"It's in the Highlands. It's very remote."

"So is it a castle?"

He hemmed and hawed. "Well, I suppose…technically…really, it's very run-down. The state National Trust for Scotland owns it now. We're sort of tenants, if you understand me."

"Tenants?" I giggled at the thought of renting a castle. "Like you lease the place like an apartment?"

"Sort of. The family still has quarters. The rest of it is open to the public."

The whole idea of my family ever living in a castle seemed so ridiculously impossible. I had to tease him. "And are there serfs tied to this land?"

"Not since the eighteenth century," he said with a smirk. He tugged me to his side and wrapped his arm around me. "Though you're welcome to become one."

Being so close to Adam felt wonderful, and my instinct was to melt into him. I knew that wasn't the healthiest thing to do, though. Instead I gave his waist a friendly squeeze. "So are you like Prince Charles? I've seen pictures of him wearing a kilt when he's in Scotland. Do you do that?"

"Fuck no." He gave me a dismissive look before conceding, "But Dad's been known to."

"Is it true that you don't wear anything underneath them?" *Oops.* It was not the appropriate time to learn the truth about kilts.

He pretended to be shocked. "What? You naughty girl! Do you want to look under my dad's kilt?"

"No!" I smiled and nudged him. "I was just wondering."

"Oh yeah? Well, maybe I should wear one. You could find out that way."

I tried to poke his side for being such a tease, but he began tickling me and pulled me with him onto the sand. I was squirming and giggling and forgetting that I'd not wanted to get that close to him. Before long, he was hovering over me. His face reached mine, and I watched his smiling lips come closer and closer to my mouth. I wanted to kiss him, but my weak heart held me back.

Brushing the hair out of his eyes, I softened what was going to be a blow to his ego. "No, Adam. I can't."

"Please, Nicki." He seemed so earnest. "I love you, sweetheart."

There. He'd said it. I'd spent the last weeks questioning if that could ever have been true, but now he'd said it just as he always had. And by the looks of him, he meant it. So, very tentatively, I said what I also felt. "I love you, too, but I'm…confused…and if I kiss you I'll be more confused than I already am."

Adam reluctantly nodded before he pulled back a bit and sighed. "I understand. It's just that I'm happy being close with you again, and I've missed you so much."

"I've missed you, too, but if I kiss you…one thing will lead to another. And I'll miss you that much more when you leave. I'm sorry."

His voice was solemn. "Nicki, I will *always* miss you."

I looked at Adam objectively for a moment. Could this hormonal teenage boy know his heart that well? Was that possible for anyone our age? Could I say the same for myself?

After what had happened between us over the last few weeks, I doubted it. I wasn't lying when I said I was confused. Yet there was one thing I knew deep, deep in my heart: I would never forget Adam Kincaid.

Overwhelmed by the emotional pressure of it all, I lovingly ran my finger down his nose and attempted a joke. "Just so you know, it's hard for me not to kiss you."

"At least that's mutual." He smiled and rolled over onto his back in what appeared to be frustration.

"Is it going to be a long two weeks?" I laughed.

"Yes, it is." Looking over his shoulder to me, he touched my hair again. "Actually, no. Not long enough. Not long enough at all."

I drew in a sharp breath. "Oh, Adam…"

He smiled, again reversing his demeanor almost entirely. "I'm breaking my own rule. We're supposed to be having fun." Sitting up, he offered his hand. "Let's finish this walk, and I'll take you out for dinner."

For the rest of the week, Adam and I crammed in as many good times as we could during the daylight hours. We both came to school early to hang out together, and at the end of the school day, we were either studying for exams at my house or out for a walk in the gorgeous spring weather. Only two things kept us apart: writing our term papers and sleeping.

Since I'd instituted the no-sex rule, neither one of us brought up the possibility of him hanging out in my room. Keeping our hands to ourselves was challenging enough without being near my bed. Still, I missed being close to him.

Earlier in the week, Rachel and Lisa had cornered me, demanding to know what had happened between us. I felt awful for being so lousy to them the last few weeks. They really meant well, so I'd told them Adam and I were friends again, but I still didn't want to talk about it. They hadn't really liked that answer, but they'd let it slide. When Adam left, I was going to have to be a better friend.

On Friday night, we planned to go to Tom's for another Pictionary tournament. When Adam picked me up, he nodded over to his car, where I saw Sylvia waving to me from the backseat.

"She begged," he apologized. "Mum would've killed me if I said no. I hope you don't mind."

"I like Sylvia. No big deal. It'll be fun." Then I thought to myself, *After all, it's not really a date.*

No one blinked twice that Adam and I were together, although they seemed confused as to why Sylvia was with us. And as the evening wore on, it was clear Adam hated having his little sister tagging along. Sylvia was just as good at the game's drawing and guessing as Adam, which stole some of his spotlight. She'd also interrupt when he and I were figuring out a clue, so he took to rudely turning his back on her so we could talk alone. Eventually, he booted her over to the other team, totally exaggerating by claiming nepotism if she remained on ours. That didn't help his situation, though, because she made sure her new team had clues to stump him.

When it came down to the final round of the night with teams tied, I picked out a clue that was obviously written by Sylvia: *Mies van der Rohe.* The name sounded familiar, but I couldn't remember who it might be — not an author, I was pretty sure — and I was stumped on how to draw it. Somehow, Adam was able to come up with the name when I drew a van, a deer, and a man in a rowboat.

As our team cheered for our win, I asked him, "Is he an artist?"

"Close. An architect." Then he turned to Sylvia and snarled, "And you're a little shite."

She stuck her tongue out at him.

By the end of the night, Adam was barely civil to her. On the way back to my house, Sylvia babbled about her opinions on modern architecture. I told Adam that he didn't have to walk me up, but he insisted. After I told Sylvia goodbye, the way he slammed my car door behind me seemed to warn her to mind her own business.

As we got to the porch, Adam asked, "So you and your mum are coming over tomorrow, right?"

Adam's parents were throwing a party to say farewell to all their friends in Bellaire, and Mom had been invited. She was looking forward to it. Even though she hadn't said anything directly, she was pretty happy that Adam and I were hanging out again. She must've thought it was because of her. I wasn't about to tell her that she was even partially right.

"Sure. It'll be fun, right?"

"Given the amount of bloody work my mum is making me do for it tomorrow, I hope so." Then he smiled. "It'll be fun, if you come."

Looking into his happy eyes, I absorbed the atmosphere around me. It was a warm spring night, and I was standing on a doorstep with a handsome boy after a date. The scene just begged to be played out—I was supposed to kiss the guy.

Instead, I demurred. "I had a good time tonight. Thanks."

Raising his hand to stroke my hair, he said, "We make a good team."

My heart leapt. It was a corny, romantic thing to say, but it was also true. We did make a good team.

Standing on my toes, I reached up and gave him a peck that lingered a little longer than I'd intended—so much for my self-restraint. Afterward, I whispered, "I love you. I'll see you tomorrow."

"I love you, sweetheart," he said as his whole body responded as well; he hugged me flat to his chest like he wanted to snatch me up while he had the chance.

"Adam, Sylvia is watching us."

"She better fucking not be." He grinned. "Just one kiss?"

"Just one." I gave him another slow kiss and made it last even longer this time. But when his tongue began to press against my lips, I pulled away with a snicker.

"Oh, bloody hell." He laughed. "I shouldn't even try. The last thing I need is a stiffy right now. Goodnight, sweetheart."

Chapter Thirty

The following night, the Kincaid house was crowded and loud with laughter. After meeting us at the door, Adam first dropped Mom off with his mother in the kitchen and then took me upstairs to his room, where he was hanging out with Tom and Rachel. They sat on Adam's bed, laughing, but after a fleeting smile and a nod, I didn't look at them again. I was too taken aback by the emptiness of his room. Other than some school books and papers on his drafting table, the room was bare, save for the furniture.

I snapped my head to look at Adam for confirmation of what I was seeing. He put his arm around me and gently stated the obvious. "I'm leaving, Nicki."

I couldn't respond; I was standing in the middle of the old nightmares I'd pushed down for so long. I was in the presence of all the physical signs that Adam was leaving. If I looked around in every room in the house, I'd no doubt see even more—boxes, luggage, plane tickets.

When Tom called to me, I went over to them and started chatting, but I was barely there. I couldn't get over the reality around me. Adam was disappearing from my life.

We ended up hanging out in his room with them for the next hour. I talked a little, but mainly I kept quiet. I noticed Tom checking his watch occasionally. When he winked at Rachel, I knew they were going to head over to his parent-less house for some private time.

After they left, I walked over to Adam's drafting table and touched a stack of his drawings. "What are these?"

"Oh. Just some sketches of the coast. They're not very good."

Of course, they were beautiful. He'd used both charcoal and a black ink pen on them, perfectly evoking the beach on a gray day. Impulsively, I asked, "Can I have one?"

The words came from my mouth, but I couldn't believe I'd said them. Why would I want another thing to remind me of him? Why would I do that to myself? Some part of me did want it, though, because I prompted him, "Please?"

My eyes darted up to his to see why he wasn't answering, and I watched as a wide smile spread across his face. "You really want one?"

"Yeah." I tried to downplay it. "Why not?"

"I never thought you'd want anything from me again."

I melted. My repentant ex-boyfriend had taken my request for one of his drawings as a sign of forgiveness. Maybe it was a sign. Because at that moment, I wanted him to know that things were okay. I grinned and began to inch my head closer to his to kiss him.

Then I heard Sylvia call behind me. "Hey, Nicki! I've been trapped downstairs talking with all the parents. How are you?"

Adam was none too happy at having yet another kiss thwarted by his sister. He looked over my shoulder and snapped, "You can leave."

"But I won't!" she said as she walked in the room. "What are you showing Nicki?"

I smiled and picked up the prettiest drawing. "Adam's given me one of his sketches."

Sylvia gave a quick inspection of the drawing and sneered. "*Hmpf.* It's okay." Then she perked up. "Oooh! Let me you give you one of mine. It will actually be worth something someday."

As she scampered to her room, I turned to thank Adam, but he was snarling. "She's such a pain in the arse!"

"She's funny."

"Funny like a batty, obnoxious old lady. Never mind her." Then he grinned and sounded almost proud as he offered, "I want you to have it. I'll get it framed for you."

Sylvia's voice piped up again. "Oooh! That's a great idea!" She'd returned and held in her hands an abstract watercolor about twice the size of Adam's drawing and opposite in every way. His was stark and real, while hers was colorful and dreamlike. "Do you like it?"

"It's gorgeous. It's very kind of you, but, really, it's too much."

"Not at all. It's a gift, and now I get to find the perfect frame for it."

"Who the fuck said you were coming with me?" said Adam.

"I did. I can't trust you to choose the right frame. You have horrible taste." She smiled at me apologetically. "Except for picking Nicki, of course."

"Of course." I giggled.

Despite Adam's grumblings about her, we spent the rest of the time with Sylvia watching a movie in their den. When it was time to go, Mom found me and escorted me over to Adam's parents to say goodbye. In my most polite voice, I used all of my available good manners to thank Mr. and Mrs. Kincaid and to wish them well, even remembering to call Adam's dad Professor Kincaid rather than just plain old Mister.

He seemed to like that and was even nicer than his usual combination of distinguished and dorky. "Well, Nicki, it's been such a pleasure meeting you. If I don't see you again before we leave, please know you're always welcome to visit us. We would love to have you."

Thankfully, I'd been blessed with Dad's prosecutor poker face, because all I could think was, *Yeah, right…* But he'd always been so nice to me that I knew he wasn't completely insincere. He just didn't want me visiting for so long that I might distract his son from being little Lord Kincaid or whatever the hell his title was.

Mrs. Kincaid didn't let me answer him. Grabbing me in a tight hug, she whispered, "You're such a wonderful girl, Nicki. I'm so happy that we had the opportunity to get to know you. You've been so good for Adam. He's going to miss you. I hope we hear from you very soon."

I could only think her last line was a not-so-veiled plea for me to be in touch with her son. Yet as I stood there with his dad staring at me, I was sure that he and I were in agreement that it wasn't the best thing to do. I looked over at Mom, who seemed perplexed by all of the exchanges; she knew something was odd, but she kept it to herself.

The following afternoon, Adam came over. When I let him in, he saw that my mom wasn't home and grinned with approval. I liked the idea of an afternoon alone with him, too, but I realized I might have gotten his hopes up.

"I should tell you I'm really not sure when she's going to be home."

"Where is she?"

"At the cemetery." It sounded awful, probably because it was.

"Why today?" His smile had vanished.

I shrugged and continued walking toward the living room. For the last month, I couldn't think about Lauren. Dealing simultaneously with all my Adam crap and the anniversary of her death would have been too much.

After I plopped on the sofa, I turned to him. "She wanted to clean up the gravesite. You know, make it pretty. People will be visiting it again soon."

"Nicki…"

I didn't say anything as he sat beside me.

After a moment, he asked softly, "When is the anniversary?"

"A few days after you leave."

"Christ, I'm so sorry." He was somber and sounded like he was thinking aloud. "I knew it was soon, but I thought it was later than that. Maybe if—"

"No. Don't worry about it. I'll be fine."

"But this is shit. I'm leaving at the worst possible time."

He was getting really worked up—far more than I was about it.

I tried to calm him down. "Adam, it's okay. I'm going to be fine. I swear."

"Fuck." He grimaced. "You're going to be by yourself on the actual day? I'm letting you down again."

"No, you're not. Don't say that." I reached over and brushed the hair out of his face, but he was angry at himself. He lowered his head away from me, so I brought his face back up to mine.

"Listen to me. I'm going to have to deal with Lauren's death alone for the rest of my life. You aren't letting me down." Flashes of all the times he'd talked with me about Lauren came to my mind. Straight from my heart, I told him, "You've been here for me for so much.

You've been there when I needed you most. I couldn't have gotten through it without you."

I should've been crying by then, but oddly I wasn't. Adam looked away, so I stretched so I could look him in the eye. Whereas my eyes were dry, Adam's were tearing up. He squinted and shook his head, either to force the tears back in or to keep me away — probably both. I didn't like it. The only thing I could think to do was plant a soft open-mouthed kiss on him.

"I love you, Adam."

He must've preferred kissing to talking, because he responded by cradling me in his arms as he opened up his mouth to me. For the next few minutes, we had the weirdest make-out session. We were kissing and groping and even grinding a little, while salty tears continued to run down his face.

When I felt that he was hard, I laughed to myself. *He's crying—with an erection. Scientific evidence that there's no connection at all between a guy's dick and his brain.*

Our hands were all over each other, but it didn't go anywhere. Adam might've been tired or embarrassed from crying, so just as quickly as things had escalated between us, they wound down. We ended up snuggling under the afghan and then falling asleep.

I woke up an hour later when I heard Mom's car pull into the driveway.

"Adam, we need to get up. My mom's home."

He startled as I spoke, and his eyes flashed open. He blinked a couple of times. "Shit. Yeah. Okay."

We got situated on the sofa so that we weren't horizontal when Mom walked in. She greeted us happily and even pretended she didn't notice that my hair was a mess.

After she left us alone again, Adam was a little awkward until he kissed my cheek. "That was a nice nap."

"It was." I smiled and returned the kiss. "C'mon, I'll walk you out."

The school week passed quickly. Like the week before, Adam and I made as much of the daylight hours that we could together. We didn't talk much about him leaving on Sunday morning. With the normalcy of exams and papers, the fact that he really was leaving for good at the end of the week seemed impossible. Sure there was that feeling of finality with the end of school, but that still felt normal.

It was only at the giant party that Lance hosted on Friday night that everything changed. I should've known what would happen, but I was still in denial. As soon as we got there, Adam started getting hugs and backslaps from people wishing him well and asking what life would be like back in England.

I walked into another room straightaway. It was selfish, but I didn't care. Adam's future without me was not something I wanted to hear about. I justified leaving him by telling myself he didn't want to talk about it in front of me either. There had to be some truth to it.

Sylvia had again tagged along that night, and she followed me right into the empty dining room. "Nicki, I wanted to talk with you now because Adam told me you two are spending tomorrow alone."

That was welcome news to me, making me smile. "So, what's up?"

"Well, he and I talked last night. I suppose I understand where you're coming from about not talking or writing after we leave. It's just sort of harsh."

Oh God. I was being reprimanded by Sylvia. My silence must have tipped her off that I was uncomfortable, as she then tempered what she'd said.

"But it's very mature of you—like you know you two have your whole lives ahead of you. You're young, and you don't know how things will turn out."

Clearly, Adam had conveniently failed to tell Sylvia about his little fling with Kate. That had told me exactly how things *would* turn out, but I wasn't going to bring it up. Although I wasn't going to forget it, I'd forgiven him.

I nodded. "Well, you know…"

"Daddy has said something similar to him, but I know even Daddy wouldn't like to hear that you two don't want to talk at all. Adam is going to be gutted." She grumbled. "And he'll be an utter git again."

"Sorry about that."

"It's okay. He's an arsehole to me most of the time anyway." She then pleaded, "But, Nicki, can't we stay in touch? I want to live in the States when I'm older—in New York. I'd like to have a friend when I'm there."

"New York?" I laughed. "I'll probably never get out of Texas."

"That's okay. You don't have to tell me anything personal that you don't want Adam to know. Just let me know where you are if you move…where you go to university…that kind of thing." She stood a little taller and was smug. "That way, I can invite you to my first exhibition."

Sylvia. What a trip. She was a shy, adorable Goth of a girl with more self-confidence than I'd ever have. How could I not want to see how she turned out?

"Sure, Sylvia. I'd like that."

We talked a little longer about her dreams of New York before Lisa and Rachel found us. Sylvia scooted off to get us beer, which was good because my best friends were looking at me like Mom often did when she was both worried and curious.

"Nicki, why are you in here?" Lisa asked gently. "Is it hard seeing everyone tell him goodbye?"

"Maybe." I shrugged.

Rachel gave me a hug and scowled at Lisa. "Then let's not talk about it. Let's talk about our trip to Austin next weekend!"

"You two are the best. I'm sorry I've been such a bitch."

Rachel didn't skip a beat. "No more than usual."

"We're used to it by now," Lisa said and smiled.

My friends and Sylvia kept me occupied for the next hour, and it wasn't that late when Adam came to see if I wanted to go home. He looked bummed—like it was time to leave because he couldn't handle any more. But he still had to say goodbye to Lisa and Rachel, which turned out to be pretty funny.

Lisa gave him a perfunctory hug, and I heard her give him a backhanded compliment. "Bye, Adam. You turned out to be a much nicer person than I expected."

He stepped back in silence. Her American directness had confounded his British manners. Then Rachel lightened the mood for everyone as he hugged her in turn. "I'll keep up with you through

Tom. Expect a visit from me in a few years. And if I'm not with Tom then, I'll need a date…maybe with that gorgeous cousin of yours. So you should warn him."

Adam laughed nervously, not knowing what to make of Rachel's demand, but I rolled my eyes. I could see it coming. Tom or no Tom, if Rachel was over there and had the opportunity, she was going to pounce on David. Maybe he could cure her fixation on uncircumcised dicks.

After we left, Adam drove Sylvia home first. I got out of the car to give her a hug. "Bye, Sylvia."

"Bye, Nicki." She squeezed the life out of me and whispered, "I'll send you a postcard when we get home."

"Take care of yourself." With a squeeze and a whisper of my own, I added, "And also Adam for me."

Adam and I were silent driving back to my place. The emotions of the night had gotten to him. When we started walking up to my porch, he said three words that perfectly summed up the evening: "That was hard."

"It was."

He smiled at me as he reached for my hands. "I have got to go home and finish packing—plus do a few things for my mum. I want to spend the whole day with you tomorrow, though, if you'll let me."

"Just the day?" Considering we'd only kissed since our make-out session on the couch on Sunday, I was being a pretty big tease, but he took the bait right away.

"Well, the night, too, if you'll have me."

I reached up to kiss his smiling face. "Until tomorrow, then."

As I turned to unlock the door, I heard him call over my shoulder, "I'll get here early—before nine. And wear your swimming costume."

"Why?"

"Because it's supposed to be over a hundred degrees tomorrow. We're going swimming."

Chapter Thirty-One

Because of all my nervousness over Adam's last day, I got no sleep that night before. The anxiety turned to panic in the morning, though, when I surveyed my swimsuit collection. There wasn't a one-piece to be found. Rachel had told me once that even though I had "no tits," as she put it, I should show off my ass to make up for it.

The day had come when I rued her advice. I put on my favorite itty-bitty polka-dot bikini and almost cried at the sight. I looked like something out of a bad horror flick. In my mirror stood a fair-skinned, teenage girl in a tiny black bikini with hideous purple and brown slashes all over her torso. Adam may have seen every inch of my body, but in broad daylight compared to normal girls, I'd scare him. I threw on one of Dad's old v-neck t-shirts and a pair of shorts and then crammed some underwear and a change of clothes into my bag. The t-shirt wasn't just a cover-up; it was staying on me if I went in the water.

As promised, Adam arrived before nine, and we started our day off with a quick trip to the frame shop to pick up his and Sylvia's pictures. They were even cooler in their frames. I gushed thank you after thank you to Adam, but he would hear none of it, only saying, "It truly is my pleasure."

We picked up some sandwiches before heading out to the beach — the same spot he'd taken me on Valentine's Day. I gave him a knowing look. "We've been here before."

"We have."

Even though it was a hot day, no one was around. It was after lunchtime, so we ate our sandwiches sitting on a thin blanket he'd brought. He also pulled out a camera, and he'd surreptitiously take pictures of me when I wasn't looking. When I protested, he explained, "But I haven't got any photos of you by yourself. Only my sketches."

I squirmed but relented. "Okay, but just one more."

"Good." He took the shot quickly. "I just want something to remember you by."

Our eyes met, and I went weak-kneed.

After neither of us spoke for a few seconds, he tossed the camera aside and jumped up. "Let's go for a swim."

Kicking off his running shoes, he tugged his T-shirt over his head like only guys do. There he was in all his sculpted glory, only covered by a pair of swim trunks. I had to avert my eyes or he'd know I was ogling him.

I unlaced my shoes and shimmied off my shorts, but I kept the T-shirt on. Adam didn't notice until we got to the water.

He tugged at it. "Why are you still wearing this?"

As I crossed my arms over my stomach, I hoped he'd realize I was uncomfortable. "I don't have a one-piece. My scars look pretty bad in a swimsuit."

Adam frowned and shook his head dismissively before he moved my arms to the side and pulled the shirt over my head. My arms immediately went back across my belly.

"See? I told you," I said.

"Any tosser who can't see past a few silly marks isn't worth your time." His voice was rough. "I hope you know that."

I didn't know what to say, but he saved me from a reply as he turned and dove into the waves. When he emerged, he shook his head out like he was ridding himself of both water and something he didn't want to think about. Eventually, he called over to me, "It's great."

I jumped in, too, and for a while, we horsed around, laughing and swimming. It was a lot of fun, but I was also very aware that it was the first time in over a month we'd been so physically close. It was almost entirely skin on skin. We both played along, though, pretending like it was no big deal. Or as Grandma Johnson always put it, pretending like there wasn't an elephant behind the butter in the fridge.

When I thought we were getting a little too close for public, I went to the blanket to warm up in the sun, and Adam soon followed me, saying, "You know, you look really fucking sexy lying there."

"I doubt that."

"Shouldn't I be the one who decides these things?"

"Oh yeah?"

"I think you're gorgeous." He sat next to me. "I won't let you put yourself down."

With his wet hair and glistening skin, I thought he was gorgeous, too. All thoughts of denying myself any intimacy with him disappeared. The mind was strong, but my body was weak.

I pulled his face to mine and gave him a long, slow kiss. He groaned into my mouth, but after a few minutes he pulled away. Looking into my eyes, he asked, "Are you sure about this?"

Blinking a few times, I asked myself the same question: *Do I want to have sex with him?*

I answered both of us as I leaned in for another kiss. "Yes."

After a few minutes of heated snogging on the blanket, Adam suggested we go to his car that was parked a ways away. I was too sex-starved to reject him, and a car was more private than a public beach.

It was early enough that no one was around, so two horny and determined teenagers climbed into the backseat. With a quick kiss out of the way, his mouth ventured down my body as he pulled my swimsuit aside. Whether he went down on me because of guilt or a desire to speed things along, I don't know, but it felt damn good. I came in minutes, and afterward one thought came to mind: *This is something I'm going to miss.*

It seemed polite to return the favor, and ever the guy, Adam's face lit up when he saw he was about to get a blowjob. I undid the string on his swim trunks and pulled them down, exposing his hardening penis.

Of course, I had one other goal in mind — to give a better blowjob than that bitch Kate. I had no measure to judge it by, except that Adam was groaning and moaning the whole time. His balls tightened, and I expected him to come in my mouth any second.

Instead, he pulled out, grunting, "Fuck. So good, but I want to come inside you."

I looked up into his sex-crossed eyes and smiled. "I want you to, also."

Hearing that, his eyes really crossed. I shimmied off my bikini bottoms and looked out at the now-filling parking lot. Taking a risk, I lowered myself onto him. His mouth gaped as we felt each other, and he groaned, "God, Nicki, I've really fucking missed this."

He was so deep inside of me, and it had been a while, so I felt especially full with him. I was also relishing the connection. "I've missed it, too." We started to move together, which felt amazing. He was thrusting and cursing up a storm, and we came within minutes.

After the quickie in the car, we went back to the beach and stayed there the whole afternoon. When it got late, we changed and drove to my favorite Chinese restaurant for dinner and talked about places we wanted to travel. At the end of the meal, some butterflies twitched in my stomach when I saw the fortune cookies. It was stupid because they were mass-produced, stale cookies with random pieces of paper in them, but I still always wondered what they might say.

He offered them up for me to choose, and I picked the one nearest me and read it aloud.

"'Good luck will come later in your life.'" I frowned. "Great. Is life going to suck until I'm old?"

"It doesn't say that. It just says that you've got something to look forward to later."

"Very nice spin."

"I'm right. And it's silent on what your life will be like until then. It could just as well be good rather than bad."

"Whatever. What's yours?"

"Mine says, 'You have good intuition.' Huh. What do you make of that?"

It could have been interpreted so many ways, but Adam was pretty good at reading things around him. I nodded. "It could be true."

Staring at me, he looked like he was going to say something but then decided against it. Instead, he shrugged it off and paid the bill.

"So what else do you have planned?" I asked.

"Let's go for a walk along the bayou."

We spent the rest of the evening strolling along or sitting in the grass, talking and stealing kisses. As the hour drew toward ten, he stroked my hair and announced, "I'd like to spend the night with you."

I nodded solemnly. It was slowly sinking in that despite the fun we'd been having, time was marching on. He would be gone the next day.

"We're leaving at seven in the morning. I could go home now and be back at your place by midnight."

"How am I going to get you in?" Somehow the fact that my mom would kill me if she found him seemed a secondary concern.

"I'll climb onto the porch and through your window."

"Okay." I laughed and then timidly asked, "And in the morning? When do you need to be home?"

"Six fifty-nine. I really don't care if I've showered and shaved, and I certainly don't fucking care if I get in trouble."

At that point, I didn't care if I got in trouble either. "My mom doesn't get up until eight on Sundays."

"Then let's do it!" He grinned.

When I got home with the framed pictures in hand, Mom quietly asked me, "Was the goodbye hard?"

I'd forgotten that she'd think Adam and I would've said our final farewell by now. Lucky for me, I didn't have to resort to my bad acting when I croaked out the truth in a tight voice. "I don't want to talk about it. I'm tired. I'm going to bed." The idea that he was coming to see me for the last time in only a few hours hit me in the gut just as hard as if we *had* already parted ways.

Thankfully, Mom accepted that was all she was going to get out of me, and she let me be for the rest of the night.

As promised, Adam arrived at my window shortly before midnight. After stifling our giggles from his Spiderman behavior, we spent the first hour cuddling, making out, and then very quietly having sex.

This time, it was emotionally intense, not like the raunchy, playful sex we'd had in his car. Instead, it was missionary with our eyes locked and his weight heavy on me. Nothing was said, but we were both taken by it.

We eventually got to talking again. For the first time, he asked me a million questions about what my life was going to be like, both in the immediate future and further on. I didn't have a lot of answers, except that I doubted I'd ever be far from my parents. With Lauren gone, I'd always want to be close to my family.

I concluded with my fortune. "Remember, my good luck is coming later in life."

He didn't laugh. It took him a moment to ask, "Nicki, will we ever speak to each other again?"

"I…don't know." After the day we'd just shared, it seemed impossible to say no altogether, despite all of my adamant protests. Yet there were facts that couldn't be denied. "I guess never say never, but it's kind of unlikely. Our lives are going to be very different. I mean, we really do live a world apart. An ocean apart, anyway."

After that, his silence was deafening. So much so that I felt like I had to make an offer, but it was so improbable, I was pretty comfortable saying it. "Maybe. Maybe, if we were living in the same city."

"As you said, that's probably not going to happen."

"Probably not."

"But what if…what if I was thirty-five and still single? Could I contact you then?"

What he described seemed unimaginable. I couldn't really comprehend what it would be like to be thirty-five. And the idea that he would *ever* be single was ridiculous. But I played along. I tried to think about what it would be like if he called me when I was that old. Of course, if I was still single or even just casually dating someone, I'd be elated.

What if I was married, though? Lying in bed with him at that moment, with his arms around me, it seemed impossible that I'd find anyone who would at all measure up to him — someone who I'd love equally. But what if I was older and lonely? Or what if I wanted kids? Would I settle? I was a practical person; I knew I'd happily take what I could get. But would it then wreck my world to have Adam Kincaid burst into it? Without a doubt, I knew it would.

Yet, I said yes. "In the highly unlikely event that was the case, I'd say sure."

"Really?"

"You've got to admit, it's probably not going to happen."

He happily kissed my nose. "Maybe, maybe not."

We spent the rest of the night intermittently sleeping and kissing. When it was near six, we had one more round of slow, quiet sex.

It was so dark in my room that I couldn't quite figure out the noises he was making, but when they continued afterward, it sounded like he was sniffling a bit. I kissed his cheek and tasted tears.

Once again, my boy was crying, and I wasn't. It was inexplicable. Maybe after all the tears I'd cried in the last year, I didn't have any left.

We silently cuddled for the next half-hour. Then, without a word, he got up and started putting on his clothes. I only stared at him because there was nothing to say. When he snapped his watch back on, it was the sign he had to go.

Still naked, I finally got up and kissed him. He was still pretty broken up but managed to say, "I'm not saying goodbye. I love you too much to say that."

Nodding, I kissed him once more. "And I love you."

He didn't look at me again as he climbed out the window. The whole scene was so surreal; I went to the open window and watched him jump down, making almost no noise. He started walking quickly, but then stopped near the driveway. Placing his hands to both his eyes, he crouched down. He was bawling.

Without another thought, I yelled out my window, "Adam!"

Before he could see me, I grabbed my bathrobe and sped out of my room and out of the house.

As I ran toward him, he squinted and said, "Nicki?"

Throwing my arms around him, I whispered in his ear, "I'll always love you, Adam. Remember that."

We embraced for a few seconds before he pulled away and grinned through his tears. "I will."

After a final quick kiss, he walked toward his car, which he always parked down the block. He didn't look back. I turned to the house in dread, knowing that I might've woken up my mom when I'd yelled Adam's name. I was probably going to catch hell for him spending the night, but I didn't care. I smiled. Like everything about Adam, it had been worth it.

Epilogue

Adam Kincaid

Washington, DC

January 2009

lied, and I felt the remorse as soon as I ended the call with my boss in London. I hadn't said anything contradictory to the truth, but the amount of information I'd withheld was tantamount to a lie. I considered my breach of ethics and panicked for a moment, but I soon justified my actions.

After all, I *was* interested in a different assignment, and I'd disclosed all the facts to management. The emotions that accompanied those facts weren't facts themselves and, thus, not necessarily material. I felt safe in my denial, though it was utter crap. I even believed my own bullshit for a few weeks. I was certain I could do my job with a clear conscience, but then I walked into the White House press briefing room, where my lies hit me again.

"I heard you might be here," said an exaggerated baritone voice.

I looked to my right to see Dan Roark, ABC News White House correspondent and all-around American arsehole. He eyed me suspiciously.

"I missed reporting." I shrugged. "And these are interesting times."

"Hmm." Dan raised his eyebrows. As he walked to his prized seat front and center in the room, he said, "*Very* interesting times to bring Adam Kincaid out of his ivory tower."

Wanker, I thought. I began determinedly scrolling through the messages on my phone to regain my composure. When that didn't work, I checked the Premier League results, but Dan's remark haunted me. *He's right. Really, why am I doing this? Does she wonder as well?*

If Dan had heard I'd taken a temporary assignment to cover the new administration, would she also have? We were now working in the same field in the same city—albeit improbably. She should know where I was working simply by gossip, if not the trade press. She would know I'd be standing here today—just like the rest of the White House press corps. *Does she care that I'm here?*

As the noise in the room diminished, I looked at the podium. Standing in front of the iconic blue and white oval sign with an illustration of the most famous white house in the world was Matthew Foster, press secretary for President James Logan.

Still high from the inaugural honeymoon, Matthew smiled as he cleared his throat before greeting the room. "Good morning to you all. Welcome to our first official press briefing. I'm sure we'll soon get sick of seeing one another every day."

Laughter at the joke reverberated through the room, but my attention was focused on finding her. A minor player in American media, the BBC shared its seat with *The Baltimore Sun,* far back in the steerage of the room. When the *Sun* reporter arrived, I nodded for her to take the seat today. No doubt she thought I was a chivalrous Englishman, but really I wanted to stand for a better view. Unfortunately, my height wasn't helping me. As I searched for her, I began to doubt myself. *Do I no longer recognize her?*

My frustration ended when Matthew spoke again. "Before we get started, I want you to meet our team. First, I'd like to introduce you to our deputy press secretary, Nicole Johnson. If you were on the campaign trail with us, you know Nicole well." Then he motioned toward a small crowd of men behind him, saying, "Nicole, get out from behind Jeff so you can say hello."

She emerged from the collection of men's suits, smiling and with a small wave of her hand. Taking to the podium with confidence, she addressed the audience, and her soft Texas twang warmed the room.

"Hello, everyone. Being new in town, it's nice to see some familiar faces from the campaign. And I'm looking forward to getting to know those of you I haven't met yet."

My eyes never left her as she moved to stand not far from Matthew's side, and I didn't exhale until Matthew spoke. Forgetting all of my professional responsibilities, I stopped listening to Matthew. My focus was on Nicki because she was the same—just the same.

Physically, she was as beautiful as I remembered her. Fifteen years later, she only looked different to me because I'd never seen her in a suit before—but why would I have? We'd been in secondary school together. She wore her dark hair up at the back, and I knew that look on her; occasionally, she'd worn her hair in a ponytail. Her figure was just as enticing, petite as she was and accentuated by a jacket belted at the waist. But it was those dark eyes that I couldn't stop staring at.

My colleagues battered Matthew with questions, and he blathered on about the economy, health care, energy, climate change, the Middle East—all the news of the day. But I took in none of it. I noticed Nicki's small hands, which she clasped in front of her skirt. It came to me that I knew that woman the way no one else in the room did. I knew how her hands felt when you walked hand in hand with her and when you held both of them in your own. Moreover, I knew how those hands felt on my body—when they tickled the back of my neck or stroked my chest. Or held my dick.

I knew her. I looked around the room and saw all the men who wanted to know her—Dan Roark being one of them. Obviously checking her out, Dan ogled her lean legs. Did he see her scar, I wondered?

Her scars. I knew her scars. I'd never forget them. Scars from the accident covered her body. I still could picture many of them, and my mouth remembered kissing the brownish purplish lines, wishing I could make all of her pain disappear. I wondered what they might look like now. Were they just faded ghost lines criss-crossing her torso? Maybe the dark memories had faded as well.

I kept a steady gaze on Nicki's face. Her skin was bright as ever, and the small indentation between her eyes was most likely only noticeable to me. When we had been together, it would appear when she was serious or concerned or sad. But fifteen years of life had fissured her otherwise flawless skin; like a river creating a canyon, sorrow had eroded a tiny crevice where none should be. At once, I felt sick to my stomach because I'd had a part in the cutting of that line. I'd caused anguish that had torn at both our hearts. *But why does hers have to be visible?*

In the back of my mind, my reporter's sixth sense kicked in, telling me now was the time to ask my question. I raised my finger to Matthew, who I already knew.

"Adam," Matthew said with a nod.

"As a candidate last autumn, the President made lukewarm comments toward the relationship between the United Kingdom and America. Is the Logan Administration going to mark a new era in the two countries' special relationship?"

Dutiful to my job, I scribbled some notes as Matthew answered my question, saying the "special relationship" was as strong as ever and comments during a campaign had to be taken with a grain of salt. As I wrote, I thought Nicki had to have seen me; she had to have at least had a glimpse of me.

With my question and answer over, I allowed myself to look at Nicki again, who now had that Jeff character at her side. They were talking quietly as the press conference continued.

Why isn't she looking at me? Is it on purpose? Or does she simply not care?

For the rest of the hour, I stewed on all of my questions about her and vowed I'd get an answer before I left the room. *After all, you didn't nab this bloody assignment just because of the work. Admit it. The work was secondary.*

When the briefing finally ended, I casually but quickly made my way to the front, occasionally greeting a friend but never stopping for conversation. Matthew was backslapping the inner circle of America's Fourth Estate, whilst Nicki answered a few reporters' follow-up questions.

Soon, Matthew started to head for the door. He caught my eye. "Welcome, Adam. I hear you're going to be with us for a while."

"Yes, thank you. I'm looking forward to it."

As soon as I replied, Nicki turned to face me. We stood only a few feet apart as our eyes met. Instantly, I felt like I was being pulled toward her, but soon I knew something was wrong. My heart caved as I realized there was no reciprocity. She only gave me a blank stare. *Doesn't she feel anything for me?*

"Nick—"

I only wanted to say hello—or anything that might give me some insight into her—but I was interrupted by Matthew as he said, "Nicole, we need to move on."

She turned on her heel and followed him without looking at me again. I swallowed hard as I watched her leave. I was devastated.

And then everything changed.

Nicki stopped for the briefest moment and peered over her shoulder, wrenching my heart again with another indifferent stare. But this time, her mouth twitched ever so slightly, just like it always had when she was anxious. A shy smile crossed her face, and without a word, she turned back around and quickly exited the room.

Is she happy to see me?

I couldn't tell, but I didn't care. Nicki still felt something, and that alone was enough.

Acknowledgments

As the first novel I ever wrote years ago, this book has been a long time coming. It's fitting that I begin these acknowledgments by thanking two dear women whom I've known since first grade, Laura Comstock and Mary Clausen Hooker. Along with my old law school friend, Julia Gannaway, they read the first draft and gave me the encouragement to keep going. God love them for stomaching the writing of someone who had no idea what she was doing.

Thank you also to the ladies from my beloved fanfiction community who helped the story in its next phase: Catherine Waring, Corey Ward, Jada D'Lee, and a few others. Your generosity and talents are enormous.

Finally, the book today is the product of the great work of Omnific Publishing—Elizabeth Harper, Enn Bocci, and most importantly, my editor Colleen Wagner, who seemed to know Adam even better than me. Thank you so much.

About the Author

Even before she graduated from law school, Mary knew she wasn't cut out to be a real lawyer. Drawn to politics, she's spent her career as an organizer, lobbyist, and non-profit executive. Nothing piques her interest more than a good political scandal or romance, and when she stumbled upon writing, she put the two together. A born Midwesterner, naturalized Texan, and transient resident of Washington, D.C., Mary now lives in Northern California with her two daughters and real lawyer husband.